MW00353136

Wild Mint Tea

A Farm Fresh Romance

Book 2

Valerie Comer

GreenWords Media

Copyright © 2014 Valerie Comer
All rights reserved.
ISBN: 0993831362
ISBN-13: 978-0993831362

No part of this publication may be reproduced or transmitted for commercial purposes, except for brief quotations in printed or electronic reviews, without written permission of the author.

This is a work of fiction set in a redrawn northern Idaho. Any resemblance to real events or to actual persons, living or dead, is coincidental.

Cover Art © 2014 Hanna Sandvig, www.bookcoverbakery.com.

First edition, Choose Now Publishing, 2014
Second edition, GreenWords Media, 2014

Printed in the United States of America

Endorsements

"Wild Mint Tea is very much my kind of story! The writing is breezy and fun, and the characters have just the right amount of spice. Speaking of spice, this romantic tale is loaded with yummy food images that will leave you craving a tasty organic meal. Highly recommended!"
~ Janice Thompson, author of the *Weddings by Bella* series

"With humor and poignancy, Valerie Comer draws readers into her characters' lives, and in no time, they feel like old friends. Heartwarming and encouraging, Wild Mint Tea will refresh your spirit!"
~ Loree Lough, author of more than 100 award-winning books, including reader favorites like *Raising Connor* and *Devoted to Drew*

Dedication

For Hanna
Foodie Extraordinaire

Books by Valerie Comer

Farm Fresh Romance Novels
Raspberries and Vinegar
Wild Mint Tea
Sweetened with Honey (November 2014)

Christmas Romance Novella Duo
Snowflake Tiara (September 2014)

Fantasy Novel
Majai's Fury

Acknowledgements

Thanks to so many who have helped bring *Wild Mint Tea* through its journey to publication.

Love and thanks to my husband, Jim. You are always my best supporter and cheerleader.

Thank you to my kids, Hanna and Craig, and Joel and Jen, for your love of fresh, seasonal food, and for teaching my little granddaughters to appreciate it, too.

I appreciate Julie, Carol, and Christina, who took precious writing time of their own to critique and comment on this story while it was in process. Thanks to Nancee, Janet, Linda, Susan, Heidi, and Paula for entering the contest to create Noel's recipe for Taco Stew. Each recipe had the potential to come out on top. Congratulations to Linda Sprinkle for the winning entry! I also appreciate Hanna, Jen, Julie, Bonnie, Jean, Jenn, and Tracy for judging the contest and making a difficult decision possible.

Nicole, you took your "life goal" of getting your critique partner published to a whole new level. Thank you for everything. Angela, your friendship means so much to me. I'm delighted God brought you into my life.

To the many fans who read, enjoyed, and reviewed *Raspberries and Vinegar*. Thanks for bonding with Jo, Zach, and the gang from Green Acres, and being eager to get your hands on this second volume in the Farm Fresh Romance series.

And to Jesus: thank You for imagination, for grace, and for calling my name. For (God) says, "In the time of my favor I heard you, and in the day of salvation I helped you." I tell you, now is the time of God's favor; now is the day of salvation. (2 Corinthians 6:2 NIV)

Chapter 1 ---

"Do I have anything stuck in my teeth?" Claire Halford twisted in the VW's passenger seat and bared her teeth at her friend.

Sierra Riehl grimaced and plugged her nose. "The worst offender is kale, and we haven't had it all week. Are you telling me you haven't brushed that long?" She fluttered her fingers in front of her face.

To wave away Claire's bad breath? "Of course I brushed." But in all the unaccustomed staring in the mirror that morning, had she truly examined her teeth? She'd taken a dollop of mousse to her short hair and dug makeup nearing its expiration date from the back of her drawer. Once she wouldn't have left the house without either, but the rototiller didn't care.

She'd even allowed Sierra to slather her nails with polish, but only to cover up the fact she hadn't been able to scrub all the garden dirt from underneath them.

Claire stared at the small-town hotel at the end of the parking lot. Poor thing had seen better days, probably before she'd been born. Somewhere in there a decrepit old dude had set up a temporary office to hire a chef. Well, maybe he was only middle-aged. Forestry contractors couldn't be too ancient and still hike the nearby mountains every day. Could they?

She puffed out her breath and smoothed her gray slacks. Even for an interview she couldn't do a skirt and heels.

"Look, you're totally going to rock this. Relax. How bad can it be? You're applying to cook for a reforestation crew. This is not some swanky restaurant on the pier."

"But I need this job. There isn't another 5-star a block down the waterfront to try next." Though Michel's invitation to operate his newest Seattle restaurant was a temptation. No, it wasn't. Working with him had been inspiring and challenging. Living on Puget Sound had been great, but not as a place to put down roots. Not like Green Acres, at least if she could pay her portion of the mortgage.

"Don't worry. We'll manage without it."

Claire stiffened and checked her watch. Five minutes to show time. "Easy for you to say."

Sierra just spent three weeks in Mexico with her parents and siblings, for crying out loud. Must be nice to have enough money in the bank to lounge around in the sun, even though Claire had no desire to go anywhere on vacation. This was home. And home was enough.

"Seriously. It's a nice idea, but cooking for thirty people day in and day out for three months will take a lot of time and energy, and we've just started getting word out that Green Acres is a destination worth coming to."

"Are you trying to talk me out of it? Because it's not working." Sierra's family might be able to afford expensive vacations, but that didn't mean Claire could take advantage of her. She'd pay her own way, even if it meant working long days cooking for a demanding work crew.

"No, of course not." Sierra's eyes belied her quick words. "But it isn't the only game in town. We can pour our resources directly into the farm instead."

"By resources, you mean cash. And I don't have any."

"Earth to Claire. Not only money. You've done a great job on the Green Acres website. It looks totally pro. Any day now we'll start seeing results from it, at least once we get that search engine optimization stuff working in our favor."

Claire shoved the car door open with probably more effort than required and climbed out. "Thanks. I appreciate your vote of confidence." And she did. But what did Sierra know about scraping to make ends meet?

Her friend leaned across the center console to meet Claire's gaze. "Don't worry about it, girl. God's got it."

Claire sucked in a breath. "I know. It's just hard to remember." She tucked her folder and purse under her arm and flicked a wave back at Sierra.

She marched forward into The Landing Pad, Galena Landing's premiere—well, only—hotel. Could a town be any more off the beaten track, even in northern Idaho? Which meant a tree-planting crew was her best bet at raking in some cash this year.

The front desk attendant sent her to a suite of rooms down the corridor. A hand-scrawled sign stuck to an open door. *Enterprising Reforestation.*

Deep breath. Please, God. You know I need this job.

Claire pasted on a bright smile and breezed into the room. "Hi, I'm Claire Halford. I have an interview at ten."

A petite woman with a boyish haircut glanced up from her iPad. "Noel will be right with you."

As if on cue, a side door opened and a plump middle-aged woman came out. "Thank you so much, Mr. Kenzie," wafted back over her shoulder. She nodded at the receptionist and took Claire in with narrowed eyes as she swished past.

"Noel will see you now, Ms. Halford."

"Thank you." Claire offered the woman a smile, wishing she could wipe her sweaty hands. Was Sierra serious when she said it might leave stains on her pants? Best not to risk it. She paced to the now-open door, entered the temporary office, and stilled.

What had she expected to see? Not a guy of about thirty with a hint of stubble and slightly messy brown hair longer than hers. He looked up, and his brown eyes widened.

He had no right to be this cute.

"I'm Noel Kenzie." He rose and reached across the folding table to shake her hand, giving her a good view of a tan t-shirt stretched across a muscular chest and covering the top of a pair of faded blue jeans. A lethal combination.

Better keep some distance from this one. "Hello, Mr. Kenzie. I'm Claire Halford here about the contract for feeding your tree-planting crew." Marks on her pants, nothing. If only she weren't leaving stained creases on the folder she clutched.

He took his time looking her over.

Could he tell this wasn't her style? She didn't do ruffles, but Sierra had insisted.

"Just call me Noel."

Through her lashes she could see he watched her, a speculative gleam in his eye. That gleam better be about the good food she could feed his employees.

He sat and motioned her to the straight chair across from him.

Claire complied, laying her proposal on the edge of the table.

Noel picked up the papers and glanced through the top few. "It looks like you downloaded all the pertinent information regarding crew size and dietary needs, Claire. Tell me what you can offer that's within our budget."

"Yes. The crew runs about thirty people, with five vegetarians and two celiacs." Hopefully he wasn't one of the vegetarians, but what did it matter? "The menu details are on the next pages."

Noel's eyebrows arched as he scanned the sheets. "This doesn't look very exotic."

He wanted haute cuisine? For tree planters? Claire's shoulder muscles tightened. "More like good, healthy meals made from local ingredients wherever possible."

Noel shuffled the papers to glance over a new one. "I don't mind telling you my crew is expecting a bit more flair." He frowned, still reading. "Your resumé said you'd trained in Paris and worked with a French chef in Seattle for several years?"

"I did." That had been enough traveling to do her a lifetime.

He laid the papers down and folded strong, tanned hands over them. "I'm not seeing that influence in your menu, and I must admit those credentials are what led to this interview."

"I don't have easy access to those ingredients here." She met his gaze.

Noel shook his head. "Food service trucks come to northern Idaho. Where do you think the local restaurants get their stuff? I thought you'd be aware of that."

Claire forced her jaw to unclench, at least enough to answer civilly. "I'm aware, Mr. Kenzie." Too bad if he didn't want to be called that. She needed the distance. "I've worked as the night chef at The Sizzling Skillet for the past year and have placed many of the orders. It's really not the same as getting fresh ingredients at Pike's Place Market."

"Then, why…?" He raised his palms and tilted his head to the side. His wavy locks slid over one eye, and he didn't bother brushing them out.

Claire's fingers itched to reach across the table and do it for him.

Focus. Not on the guy, but on the contract. The contract she was about to lose before she had a real shot at it, if she wasn't careful. And then she'd never see Noel Kenzie again. That would be a good thing. Except she needed the money.

Claire squared her shoulders and looked him in the eye—the one not hidden. "Your crew puts in long hours of hard physical labor. They need the best possible fuel their chef can provide." She tapped the papers in front of him. "This menu represents a tasty, well-balanced diet to maximize their metabolism."

He pursed his lips. "Thanks for coming in. I'll consider it, and if I have any questions, I'll let you know. Your contact info is in here?" He riffled through the stack.

His body language said he wasn't going to hire her. "Yes, my cell number is on the cover page."

He found the right sheet and slid it on top of the others. "All right, then. Unless there's something more you wanted to add?"

Like she'd sell out to the food service industry? Not hardly. "I'm a good chef, Mr. Kenzie. My entrees got starred reviews in the Seattle newspaper, and I pride myself on finding the best, freshest food I can to work with. You and your crew will be delighted with the menu."

A glimmer of humor peeked out of his eyes and twitched at the edges of his mouth as he stood. "I'll keep that in mind as I make my decision over the next few days." His gaze swept her body. "Don't worry, Claire. I'll be calling you. Either way."

Yeah, right. She clenched her teeth into the best smile she could. "Thank you, Mr. Kenzie." She gave him a stiff nod as she rose.

Men. Couldn't he keep his personal life out of his business interviews? All she wanted from him was a chance to prove she could earn a decent living here in the boondocks. Not in the city. Seattle wasn't the dream she and Jo and Sierra had been building toward for years.

If Claire couldn't work for Enterprising Reforestation, she'd find some other way to pay her share of the farm. There'd be one. She just had to find it.

oOo

Noel raked his hands through his hair. No doubt the whole mess stood on end by now, but even those zillion antennae sticking straight up weren't bringing in the signal he needed to make his choice.

Not that there was one. Polly Solomon's proposal offered everything his crew was used to eating, right on budget. The vegetarian items were heavy on tofu, but whatever. They fit the parameters.

No, the problem lay with stinkin' cute Claire Halford. Her dark red top with angled ruffles emphasized curves in all the right places. Her face was pretty, too. So earnest.

Only once had she almost smiled, and that hint of animation was going to haunt him. Almost enough to invite her back, so he could feast his eyes on her when she relaxed. But while Noel wasn't opposed to a few months worth of flirting, he couldn't let it get in the way of his crew's culinary needs.

He flipped through her proposal again, her intense brown eyes seeming to beg him for the chance.

Noel frowned and turned the papers over then headed into the adjoining room. "Any other interviews lined up today?" he asked his foreman.

Jess swiped off her iPad and glanced up. "The guy from Wynnton couldn't make it today. We rescheduled for tomorrow."

Then he wasn't all that dependable. Noel was stuck choosing between Polly and Claire. He sure knew which woman he'd rather look at over meals, but that was no way to decide.

"Neither applicant suitable?" Concern lined Jess's voice. Or maybe only curiosity.

Noel grimaced. "No clear winner." He crossed to look out

the window into the hotel parking lot. Beyond the pot-hole-ridden concrete marched a band of trees. Long, narrow Galena Lake lay beyond, glistening in the morning light with tree-covered hills watching over it from the eastern shore.

A guy hardly needed food with a view like that. He couldn't see any of the clearcuts from town. Clearcuts he'd come to replant with new trees, new life for the future.

"Oh, come on. That Claire Halford doesn't look like a loser."

"Give it up, Jess. She's too serious. It doesn't look like she's cracked a real smile in years." It would be fun to see if he could get laughter out of her. She wouldn't be one of those girls who flirted and giggled all the time. Her laugh would be quiet but genuine, more like a chuckle. What would it take to make that erupt?

Jess's sharp elbow to his ribs brought him back into the hotel room. "A sense of humor isn't required in a chef, you know. Maybe she's a great cook."

He glanced down at the spunky gal who'd been his foreman the past four seasons. "Not required, perhaps, but it helps. You know how Simon keeps the crew entertained with his one-liners." Too bad his regular chef needed time off for a family emergency.

"There's only one Simon."

Did he imagine her wistfulness?

Jess quirked her eyebrows at him. "Polly has a sense of humor, I'm sure, though I hadn't picked up on it."

"Whatever."

Jess poked her chin toward the door. "If we're done here, let's check out that farm on Thompson Road."

"Yeah, Elmer's place. It would be handy to set up the rigs and tents right at the base of the access road."

"I looked up Claire Halford's address. She lives down that way. Mighty handy for her getting to work on time."

16

He shot Jess an irritated glare to cover the flicker of interest she'd evoked. "That's not a good enough reason. I don't know that she can pull it off. She doesn't have experience with this type of work."

"Only one way to get it. It's not like she's new to the cooking world."

Noel narrowed his gaze. "Whose side are you on, anyway?"

"Yours." She grinned. "She got your attention, didn't she? You could use a stabilizing influence in your life."

Noel choked back a snort. "Grab your bike, girl. Elmer's is only about five miles out of town. Maybe some wind in your face will scourge those thoughts right out of your head."

And maybe out of his.

Chapter 2 --

"So you don't think you got the job?" asked Jo. Although signed on as one of the three original owners of Green Acres, she'd married the guy-next-door the previous summer. That didn't stop her from frequenting the new straw bale house she'd helped to build. Or having an opinion on everything.

Claire grimaced. "Probably not. I'm not mainstream enough."

Sierra folded manicured fingers together and tilted her head to one side. "It was a long shot, anyway. Let's get back to our primary focus, getting the farm recognized as an event destination. That's where the real money will lie."

As if Claire didn't know. It'd be nice to have time—and cash—to sink into the dream.

"Did you talk to Zach about that search engine optimization stuff?" Jo took a sip from her mug of mint tea then set it back on the long plank table. Her dog, Domino, collapsed at her feet. He obviously figured on a long visit.

Claire nodded. "Our site is starting to rise in the search engines for people seeking eco-friendly workshops and organic farm experiences in Idaho." All the way from page one billion to page 48, last she checked.

"We need something more." Sierra leaned her elbows on

the table. "We need...weddings."

Claire choked on her tea. "Of course we do." Just not hers. "Are you volunteering? Who's the lucky guy?"

"Yeah, Sierra, is there something you forgot to tell us?"

Sierra rolled her eyes. "Um, no. You two will be the first to hear about it."

"Seriously, though." Jo twirled her cup on the table. "Weddings? I thought we were going to focus on farm-based workshops. Greenhouses and gardening and being sustainable."

"We're not set up for it this summer." Sierra surged out of her chair and paced over to the long window that overlooked the deck. "Those are going to take more coordination. We need to practice on smaller stuff."

Claire gave her head a shake. "A wedding is smaller stuff?"

"Well, yes." Sierra pointed out at the pole barn across the yard. "That thing can probably seat a hundred or more. We'd have one big day, and then it would be over. We'd figure out what we learned and apply it to the next event."

Her tea was cold. Claire went into the kitchen and pulled the quilted cozy off the teapot. "Anyone else want a refill?"

Jo lifted her mug and Claire carried the pot over. She needed coffee, but Jo had gone off the stuff so they all drank herbal tea when she came over.

"Come on, Jo. You got married last summer right here. Wouldn't it have been great to have an event coordinator to handle the details?" Sierra waggled her finger between herself and Claire.

Claire raised her eyebrows. So now she was an event coordinator?

Jo chuckled. "You mean besides my mom?" Jo and Zach's wedding had been put together in under two months, but Jo's mom and step dad had plenty of money to smooth such a quick turnaround. The wedding had suited Jo, who'd never been much for doing things like everyone else did anyway.

Sierra laughed. "Yes, besides her. I really think we could pull off amazing weddings."

What would Noel Kenzie look like in a tux? First he'd have to comb his hair. Maybe even trim it. Nah, he looked good with it long.

"What do you think, Claire?" Sierra's voice pulled her back to the sun-drenched dining room.

The catering part sounded awesome. Claire nodded. "I don't see why we couldn't add that to our list of options."

"We'd have to set up a mock wedding for photos." Sierra tapped her finger against her chin. "Maybe Jo and Zach can get their wedding duds on for a photo shoot."

Jo rolled her eyes. "You must be crazy. That dress was so uncomfortable."

Claire leaned forward. "It's not like any of the rest of us have wedding dresses lying around, Jo. And you're so tiny no one else would fit in yours." She'd ordered a wedding dress once and lost her deposit when she canceled. Would she want the same style today, or had her tastes changed? Not a sheath like Jo's, but nothing too frilly, either. Wasn't likely she'd ever be engaged again, though. Not after Graham.

"Yeah, yeah. I'll have to ask Zach. When do you want to do this?"

"The sooner the better. Tomorrow's Saturday, and no one has to work the day job."

Claire raised her hand. "I do have to work the *night* job. I don't think we can pull it together in one day anyway."

"But—" Sierra grasped the back of her chair and leaned over the table. "We can't wait too long. Couples are planning summer weddings now."

Reality started to sink in. "Most of them started last year for this summer's weddings. Besides, it takes time to make it look real. If all you want is photos of a happy couple, Jo already has a bunch, but if you want it to look like a real wedding, we need decorations and food." She met Sierra's gaze. "A cake, even."

"Okay, so it will take a couple of weeks."

And Claire had thought Jo was tough when she sank her teeth into something? Jo had nothing on Sierra at the moment.

"I'm not sure it's a good idea to create a fake wedding, that's all. It'll be expensive to put together just for photos." It wasn't like Claire had any cash to spare. "What we need is a real event to cater."

Sierra slumped back into her seat. The three of them looked at each other.

Finally Jo broke the silence. "Anyone know someone getting married? Celebrating an anniversary? A retirement? A graduation?"

"A grad cake doesn't look much like a wedding cake." Claire hated to say it, but it was true.

"I suppose." Sierra's purple fingernails, shorter than she used to keep them, tapped on the wooden farmhouse table. Her face brightened. "We could check around town for an event to handle, but we can also offer one wedding at half price for advertising purposes. Then we can get all the photos we need for the website."

"Are you telling me I can leave my dress wrapped in tissue?" Jo laughed. "It's up in my in-laws' attic with a bunch of other stuff, waiting for the cabin to be ready so we can move in. I don't even remember half of our gifts."

"China and crystal, if I remember correctly." Claire grinned at Jo. "Might be a stretch for a log cabin, but they'd look awesome on a wedding buffet, if you're willing."

"Focus, people." Sierra knocked on the table. "Let's divide up the research and try to have all our info in place as soon as possible. I'll look for an event to cater. Claire, we could use an itemized menu for—say, one hundred guests. Jo, how about flowers and decor?"

"Right. Stick me with flowers. You know that's not my forte."

"What would you rather research?"

Jo narrowed her gaze. "I think I'll find an event, and you can handle decorating."

Claire shook her head. "I think all of us should look for an event, and we should split up the decorating duties."

"We need a theme," said Sierra.

"First we need an event," Claire answered firmly. "We might find an event with a ready-made theme, so there's no point in getting carried away ahead of time."

She looked from one friend to the other. "Hey, I've got an idea. Why don't we pray about it?"

Jo took a deep breath. "Now there's an idea."

o0o

"Hello, Polly? This is Noel Kenzie, just calling to let you know we're awarding you the contract to cook for the Enterprising Reforestation crew." There was nothing about the middle-aged woman that would keep Noel awake at night. Not the way Claire Halford continued to haunt his dreams.

"Why thank you, dear boy. When is the start date again?"

"First of April, ma'am. The crew will be ready for breakfast at four thirty. We'll take the packed lunches and snacks along, and be back onsite for dinner by six thirty."

"That will be fine. Just fine."

Too bad she didn't infuse him with more enthusiasm. Noel had no doubt Polly was an adequate cook. Her references had checked out fine. Just fine.

He ran his fingers through his hair. Oh, man. This was probably a mistake. But the guy from Wynnton's papers had been incomplete, to say nothing of late. So the only alternative was Claire. No matter what Jess said, Noel couldn't afford the distraction. Claire didn't look the flirting kind, and Noel knew he wasn't the staying kind. Best to simply avoid her and hope her face drifted from his mind.

"Mr. Kenzie?"

Oh, right. Polly. "Pardon me? I missed what you were saying."

"I asked if you'd hire my son. The boy needs a job. I'm sure he could plant trees."

Like hiring Polly meant he had to take on her entire family? Fat chance. Noel gritted his teeth and turned away from the window. "Sorry, ma'am. My crew is full. We handle all our hiring through the company headquarters over in Missoula." Otherwise known as his mom's basement.

"Oh." Polly's voice turned a bit frosty. "All right, then."

Jess strolled into the room.

Hmm, he could slide more of this off on her. "I'll be in touch with you in about two weeks. If you've got any questions meanwhile, you can call my foreman." He rattled off Jess's cell and ended the call. The fewer number of times he needed to talk to Polly, the better.

Jess kicked his shin.

"Ouch. What was that for?"

"Nice try, boss. Bet if you'd hired Claire you wouldn't have told her to call me." She batted her eyelashes at him. "No, I get the people you don't want to deal with yourself."

He grinned. "That's what you get for being second in command."

Jess lounged against the window. "Have you called Dreamboat yet and told her you picked the other woman?" She held up her hands. "And before you get any ideas, the answer is no. No, I will not call her and do your dirty work for you.

Sticking me with Polly is bad enough."

Noel could feel the smile fading from his face.

Jess poked her chin in the direction of his phone. "Call her."

He cast her a helpless look.

"Give it up. Do it."

Had he really made the right decision? This was nuts. He never second-guessed himself. It was part of his charm. Snap decisions, no regrets. Love 'em and leave 'em. He shook his head.

Jess shifted further from him and crossed her arms. "I'm not doing it, boss."

Noel focused on his foreman. "Wasn't asking you to. I'll call her. Later."

"That's not fair to either of you. You're going to be on edge until you get it over with."

He could tell Jess to leave the room, but she'd never let him forget it. Best to prove to her—and himself—this was nothing but a business call. "Fine, then." He took a deep breath and tapped the number beside Claire's name.

Jess snorted. "You had that coded in already?"

Yeah, just in case. In case of *what* wasn't a question he could answer. He turned away slightly.

"Claire speaking. "

This really was a mistake. He glowered at Jess, who raised her eyebrows. No, he was stuck with the decision he'd already made. "Noel Kenzie speaking. From Enterprising Reforestation."

Jess's eyes twinkled.

Think what she might, Noel had no way to know whether Claire remembered him as clearly as he remembered her. He couldn't assume she'd spent the last two nights staring at the ceiling, thinking about their brief meeting.

"Hi, Mr. Kenzie."

Awkward silence. Time to man up. "I'm calling to let you know that you didn't get the contract to supply meals for our crews."

"Did you say…did *not*?"

He steeled himself, imagining her holding onto something for support. How much had she wanted—needed—this position? "Yes. Someone else entered the winning package."

"Oh. Well, then…" A funny little laugh drove straight to Noel's belly, weakening him. "I guess it's on to plan B."

"I need you to know you presented a quality proposal, Claire. It wasn't an easy decision." Because offering her those words was going to help? He hated himself.

"My roommates said it would probably take too much time away from our plans to make the farm a destination resort." She laughed again.

Her laugh didn't sound like he'd imagined. Too forced.

"If you know of anyone needing a wedding planned, feel free to send them my way."

Now why did his gut feel like it'd just been punched? He pictured Claire all dolled up in some fancy white gown, silvery stars dotting her thick brown hair and a bouquet of…what would suit her best? Noel was at his best with wildflowers, not fancy floral arrangements. "Uh, yeah. I'll do that."

"Thanks for calling, Mr. Kenzie."

"Noel," he replied automatically. Did it matter, if he wasn't going to talk to her again? He couldn't bear that. "Maybe I'll see you around."

That sharp intake of breath at the other end of the line couldn't possibly be his imagination. He clutched his cell phone.

"Maybe. Goodbye."

The silence this time was of a connection gone dead. He turned slowly to face his foreman. "Know anyone who's getting married?"

The smirk on Jess's face faded into confusion. "Pardon?"

"Claire wants to cater a wedding." No wonder Jess looked confused. He felt the same way.

"Didn't your sister get engaged the other day?"

Noel cracked his palm against his forehead. "Right."

oOo

Claire clicked off her cell and turned slowly to face Sierra. "You didn't get it, huh?"

"No." Claire shook her head. "I realize all the reasons for it being a time sink and all, but it would have been good money." That wasn't all of it, though. Not at all. She'd been fantasizing setting a plate of roast beef and Yorkshire pudding in front of Noel then maybe a plate of rhubarb cream pie. Seeing his face light up as he enjoyed the meal and told her it was the best ever.

That *she* was the best ever.

"Money isn't everything."

"Easy for you to say. You've never lived in short supply."

"Don't be silly, Claire. If you're worried we'll kick you off the island because of finances, we won't. You know that. The farm is doing fine. Our business plan allowed for a few years before we began to see a profit. It'll all work out."

Claire shook her head and swiped the back of her hand across her eyes. A little damp. "I know. I just...worry."

"Don't." Sierra pulled her into a hug. "We've got options. We've got time."

"Yes. I know. It's not that."

"Then what is it?"

Like she was going to tell Sierra that she had a sudden urge to be loved? Even watching Jo and Zach get all moon-eyed over each other last spring and summer hadn't filled Claire with

26

longing. Not like ten minutes in Noel Kenzie's office had the other day.

"Never mind."

Chapter 3 --

Claire rubbed the sleep out of her eyes and peered at the computer monitor again. The email forwarded from the website's contact form was still there.

> *Dear Green Acres,*
> *Your farm looks like an awesome setting for a wedding, but your site doesn't say if you offer this as one of your events. My fiancé and I live in Missoula and are planning a small late July wedding. Would it be possible to talk about the option of using your location?*
> *Amber*

A wedding! And Claire didn't even need to hunt one down or make special offers. Her fingers hovered over the keys, ready to write Amber back and say "Yes" with a thousand exclamation points behind it. But seriously, she should talk to the team.

The grin would not stop spreading on her face. Planning someone else's extravaganza should take the edge off these new feelings of desiring romance in her own life. She'd get vicarious pleasure from seeing Amber's dreams come true.

Sierra was right. They could do the wedding while she kept

her job at The Sizzling Skillet. No cutting ties prematurely, though she might need to beg off a few shifts as Amber's big day neared.

Claire pushed away from the computer. She tightened the sash on her bathrobe while padding into the kitchen. After flipping the switch on the coffeepot, she stretched her arms high above her head and did a little twirl. She loved this beautiful room with ovens and a commercial range built into the thick rock wall that helped stabilize the temperature. This summer they should be able to glaze the south wall of the sunroom on the other side, but even without additional trapped heat as a bonus, she and Sierra had been very comfortable over the winter.

It'd been weird not having Jo living with them after all their plans, but Jo hadn't been looking for love. It had found her anyway. At least Zach was a local guy, unlike Noel.

Why couldn't Claire get the man out of her head? This was ridiculous. At twenty-seven, she should be out of the stage where she daydreamed about every cute guy she met, especially one with no ties to a place. Even Graham exuded some kind of stability back when they dated in Seattle. He was a dentist in a thriving practice, making enough money to provide security. He'd owned a sweet little house before he'd met Claire.

A shudder slid through her. It had burned to the ground one summer night mere weeks before the wedding from some wiring problem. All she could do was thank God neither of them had been there.

Claire thought they'd rebuild together, but Graham had come up with the brilliant idea of heading overseas with Dentists Without Borders. Yeah, kids in third world countries needed dental care. She understood. But they didn't need it from Graham. Not with her tagging along, never in the same place for more than a few weeks.

Maybe things would've been different if she'd met Graham at a different stage of her life. If she hadn't been so needy. She'd probably loved his house—and the stability it exuded—more than she loved him.

Now she was the homeowner, along with her pals. She wasn't moving ever again, which left no place for a transient like Noel Kenzie.

"Lost in thought?"

Claire jolted and focused on Sierra. "Yeah, apparently. I didn't hear you come in."

Sierra poured two mugs of coffee and passed one to Claire. "What are you doing up so early?"

"Couldn't sleep. Oh, hey! Go look at the computer screen. I think we've bagged us a live one."

"A live one what?" Sierra turned to the library end of the great room.

"Wedding."

"Suh-weet." She pulled out the wheeled chair, bumped the mouse to cancel the screensaver, and scanned the short message. "Wow! We can totally manage that, can't we?"

Claire poured cream into her coffee and cradled the mug as she leaned on the peninsula counter. "I don't see why not. I'm not sure how she found us, though. We haven't changed the website yet to include weddings."

Sierra shrugged. "Doesn't matter. She's here. Did you email her back?"

"No, not yet. I just saw it a minute ago and figured it wouldn't hurt to have a coffee and talk it over first."

"Didn't we agree two days ago that we'd do it?" Sierra spun the chair around to face Claire.

"Well, yes." But did it have to be at six-thirty in the morning?

"Then what's to discuss?"

"You mean, besides terms and stuff?"

Sierra waved a hand in dismissal. "First we need to find out what this Amber person wants. We've got the basic event pricing on the website, so it won't be that difficult to add in her extras."

Claire nodded slowly.

"So just email her back already, saying it's a tentative yes, if we can agree on the details." Sierra turned back to the computer. "Unless you just want me to do it while I'm here."

"No, that's all right. I'll get it in a minute." She raised her mug. "Just need enough caffeine to write coherently."

"Okay." Sierra grabbed her own coffee and stood. "Four months isn't a long time to plan a wedding."

Claire laughed. "Half an hour more won't make that big a difference." Though anyone's life could change in the blink of an eye.

oOo

Noel backed his holiday trailer under a maple tree on Elmer's farm. In just a few days his crew would start arriving, bringing campers, fifth wheels, or tents to sleep in for the duration of the tree-planting season. Jess would be up Wednesday with her truck and camper.

He liked having a few days to settle in before a new contract, even though he lived in the little trailer more months of the year than anywhere else. A few weeks at Mom's in Missoula, a few months in Mexico or Dominican Republic or Belize. It was a good life, even if Mom did say it was time he settled down. Didn't make any difference telling her men twice his age led the same lifestyle. That this life was what he wanted.

"But they don't live with their mothers in the off-season, do they?" she'd asked.

"Hey, I thought you liked having me around." Besides, he needed a fixed address to conduct business.

She tapped her manicured fingernails against the polished table. "I'd like it better if you bought the house next door, got married, and gave me some grandchildren."

Noel glanced around his little trailer. Maybe Amber would have kids soon. Shawn's office was only a couple of miles from Mom's place, so maybe *they* could buy the house next door.

Funny. Amber didn't see it that way. She figured it was time for him to grow up, too.

They didn't seem to understand he loved his work. Loved being in the woods for much of the summer. Loved watching the sun come up over a tumbling stream or mountain lake. Loved putting the forest back together after a logging crew had ripped through.

Enterprising Reforestation brought in decent money, plenty enough to pay his crew well and still play in the tropics for a few months while the northern states froze in winter's icy grip. He even had a nest egg socked away. No clue what he was saving for, but someday he'd need a little extra, and it would be there.

Noel pulled his harmonica out of an overhead cupboard and stretched out on his bed. He closed his eyes, letting his hands and mouth decide what music to play. A little jazz, a little blues. An old gospel song surprised him a few minutes later.

He'd forgotten he knew *This World is Not My Home*. Noel sat up in the bed and put his soul into playing it. His kind of song, that one. He was just passing through, all right. Moving along where the work and play took him, season after season.

Not that he had treasure laid up in heaven like the hymn said. Something else Mom nagged him about. Well, there'd be plenty of time to worry about stuff like that when he was older. For all his mother's complaints about his chosen life, he was a long way yet from the end of his days. Why not live a little in the meanwhile?

His cell jangled, clashing with the harmonica's descant. With a sigh, he set the instrument aside and glanced at the call display. "Hey, Amber."

"Hey, yourself. Where are you at right now?"

"Just got into Galena Landing a couple hours ago. How about you?"

"At Mom's. Thanks for putting me on to that event website. I've been emailing with a woman there by the name of Claire and it looks like it may all work out."

"Cool." That relieved his conscience a wee bit. After dashing one of Claire's other dreams, it was kind of fun helping one come true.

"How far is Green Acres from where you're living?"

Noel narrowed his eyes. "Less than half a mile. Why?"

"Because I'm coming up on the weekend to meet with the event coordinator at the farm, and I thought maybe I could stay with you."

He sat bolt upright on his bed. "Uh, no. I'm in the trailer. There isn't privacy for two of us in here."

"Oh."

Man, he hated when her voice drooped like that. "I can ask Jess if you can stay with her."

"No, thank you."

He could argue with Amber and remind her of all Jess's great attributes, but it wouldn't likely matter. Amber hadn't been able to figure out his and Jess's relationship in the first five minutes of learning about it, so she'd given up. It wasn't that complicated, really. Half the time Noel forgot Jess was a woman. They simply worked well together.

"Uh, well, let me know when you arrive, and we'll get together. Maybe I'll have you over for a meal while you're here." He might not be a chef, but he knew his way around his little kitchen just fine.

Amber sighed. "Sure, that would be great."

"Look, you can stay in my trailer if you want. I'll bunk in with one of the guys." Whoa. Where was this offer coming from? "Camp's pretty noisy at five in the morning, though."

"It's fine. Really. I'll make other arrangements."

What did she want him to say? She was the one who'd turned into a prissy woman after being an almost-fun kid years ago. No way was Noel going to change to suit his sister.

She said goodbye and hung up.

Hard to believe the little girl in pigtails had grown up and was getting married. Shawn had seemed like a nice enough guy, before Noel found out he was a rep for a pharmaceutical company. Noel couldn't imagine that kind of a job.

If he had to quit planting trees, what would he really want to do? He stretched back out onto his bed and let the harmonica play itself. Maybe a fishing or hunting guide? He could get a little lodge at the edge of the mountains, like Green Acres, and run pack trains into the backcountry.

That wasn't a bad idea, actually.

oOo

Claire double-checked her reflection in the mirror. This was worse than a job interview. Everything depended not only on her, but also on tidiness and whether Amber could see the promise of the farm's beauty in July. End of March? Not so much.

Strange as it seemed, Amber elected to drive over alone from Missoula for this brainstorming visit. If all went well, she'd bring her mother and fiancé on a subsequent trip.

Claire set a vase filled with snowdrops and crocuses on the concrete bathroom counter. A matching posy sat in the guest room where Amber would stay. If they were going to have guests often, they'd need cabins, but that took money, too. Everything did.

"A car just turned in the driveway," called Sierra.

Claire stared at herself in the mirror then nodded sharply. She headed for the great room where Sierra and Jo stood waiting. They watched through the window as a silver Mazda pulled in beside their old VW.

"This is it," whispered Jo.

Sierra pulled them together. "Lord, we ask that our home might be a blessing to Amber and that You would guide our time together."

Claire nodded at the crux of the matter. "Amen."

A young woman with long black hair stepped out of the car and started toward the deck.

Claire wiped her hands on her gray slacks and glanced at her friends. Then she stepped forward and swept the French door open. "Hi, you must be Amber. I'm Claire. We spoke on the phone?"

"Yes, that's me." Amber glanced around the covered deck, with its porch rockers and swing. "Nice place you have here."

"Thanks. Come on in and meet my roommates, and we can get to know one another." Claire held the door wide.

After introductions, they all sat in the great room. Suddenly the old leather love seats looked a little shabby. Well, they couldn't deal with everything at once.

Amber craned to take in the space. "The website said this house is made of straw?"

"It is," Jo answered. "We built it last summer."

"Claire and I moved in just before Christmas," Sierra put in. "By then Jo was married and living next door."

"It's beautiful here. So friendly and warm. What a great homey atmosphere."

They were going to be best friends. Claire could see that

already. Anyone who appreciated Green Acres entered the inner circle. "We love it."

"We haven't done a wedding here before," said Sierra. "Except for Jo's, but that wasn't planned with coordinating services for other brides in mind. Why don't you tell us a bit about your hopes and dreams? How many guests? Any particular theme?" She opened a notebook and poised a pen over the page.

Good for Sierra being so organized. Claire would've tried to remember all of it until later. Except the menu, of course. Her forte.

"It's to be a very small wedding." Amber clasped her hands together on her lap. "Forty guests or so. My mother was an only child, and there's only my brother and me. No other relatives in the west at all. Shawn's family is a little larger, but not much." She looked down, twisting the diamond that glinted as the sun's rays hit it through the window. "We both have a few close friends, but we want an intimate gathering."

Sierra leaned closer to Amber. "My cousin got married on the beach in Mexico, and hardly any of their friends or relatives could go. But their church had a reception for them a couple of weeks later, so folks could wish them well."

Amber nodded. "Yes, we talked about doing something like that. My mom thinks it's a great idea. Me, I don't want to get married in Missoula. It's a nice enough city, but I want a change of scenery." She flashed a smile at Claire. "Mexico is out of the question, budget-wise. I'm a secretary, and Shawn works for a pharmaceutical company."

"Besides, the wedding is only one day," said Jo. "The marriage is for the rest of your life. It doesn't pay to bankrupt yourselves for one day."

Whose side was Jo on anyway? Claire didn't want to break the young couple's bank account, but they weren't doing this as a charity, either.

"We're going there for our honeymoon, actually." Amber put her hand over her mouth, eyes wide. "I'm not supposed to tell anyone."

"It's okay." Claire stifled a grin. "Everything said here is confidential. Mexico sounds great. We won't tell a soul." She'd personally didn't want to travel anywhere she'd need a passport. Any chance she could have her own honeymoon right here at Green Acres? She shot a glance at her roommates. Okay, bad idea.

Focus, Claire. It's Amber's wedding, not yours.

"My brother goes south nearly every winter, so he's arranged a beachside cottage for Shawn and I."

"Nice brother." Claire smiled at Amber. Her own brothers were next best things to bums, living in a cheap apartment, earning money delivering pizzas. Possibly other ways, too, which Claire preferred not to know.

Amber's eyes crinkled when she smiled at Claire. "Sometimes he's great. I'm sure thankful he told me about you."

"Me?" Claire put her hand to her chest. "You mean about Green Acres."

"No, I meant you."

Claire stared, and Amber's gaze faltered. "He said you asked him if he knew anyone getting married. That you wanted to do some events here."

Jo leaned closer. "You didn't find us through an online search, then?"

Amber shook her head.

Claire's brain raced in circles, latching onto nothing. "Who's your brother?"

"Noel. Noel Kenzie."

Heat flooded Claire's face. He'd taken her that seriously,

even when she wasn't good enough to cook for his crew? But he was trying to do her a good turn. She supposed.

"Noel Kenzie?" Sierra turned to Claire. "Who's that?"

"The guy from Enterprising Reforestation who didn't hire me."

Sierra's mouth formed a round 'o' before she turned toward Amber. "What exactly did your brother say to you?"

"Just what I said." The young woman bit her lip. "That I should contact Claire at Green Acres if I wanted help with my wedding." She met Claire's gaze. "That it was a beautiful spot. He said I'd be in good hands."

Chapter 4  --

Noel pulled his truck into the Green Acres driveway. Why did Amber ask him to pick her up here? She had a car and could easily swing by Elmer's place and pick *him* up.

This was a bad idea.

He didn't really want to see Claire, but he'd done this to himself. Why had he bothered passing her message on to Amber? Easy. To help his sister. He squelched the niggling thought he'd been looking for an excuse to see Claire again. He'd had the chance. If he'd hired her, he'd have seen her for hours a day for months.

Maybe his subconscious wasn't on speaking terms with his brain. Like that would be a first.

A group of women sat on the deck attached to a stucco house. Amber waved at Noel, but made no effort to get out of the Adirondack chair.

Noel's eyes found Claire then shifted to the other gals. He was so out of his element. Yeah, Jess was his foreman and females made up nearly half his crew, but that was different. These weren't tree planters, and this deck was their turf, not his.

Amber waved again, beckoning this time.

Noel stifled a groan. She was supposed to be ready to head

out. No way could he stay sitting in the truck. It would be plain rude. Bah. He yanked the door lever and swung his legs out of the vehicle, hoping he'd combed his hair, then strode up the grassy path to the steps.

If he'd been wearing a hat, he'd have tipped it. "Good afternoon, ladies." His gaze swept the lot of them, hesitating on Claire, who sat on a porch swing with one of the others. Then he crossed to the chair Amber sat in and touched her shoulder. "Hey, sis."

Amber jumped up and gave him a hug. "I'd like you to meet my new friends, Noel. This is Sierra."

Noel nodded at the curvy blonde. "Pleased to meet you."

"And this is Jo. She and her husband live next door."

A woman no taller than Jess got to her feet and shook his hand. "Next door for now, anyway. Then it will be the other next door." She pointed toward the mountain. "We're building a log cabin."

"Nice." Nothing better than having trees encircle him.

"And you've met Claire."

"Yes, I have." His gaze met Claire's for a long moment. "Good to see you again."

"Likewise." She averted her eyes.

Sierra hopped off the other end of the swing. "Let me grab a pitcher of iced tea." She waved at the vacant spot. "Have a seat, Noel. I'll bring out another chair from inside when I come back."

And sit beside Claire? These gals couldn't possibly know how uncomfortable the thought made him. His hand twitched the neck of his t-shirt. He needed more air.

Noel made a show of plopping down next to Claire and giving the swing a little scoot with his foot, setting it moving. He winked at her. Her mouth twitched as she shifted slightly away. Interesting. He turned to Amber. "Thought you wanted to go into town."

She leaned her head against the chair's tall back. "I do, but it can wait a bit. I wanted you to meet the team and have a look around the farm."

Too bad she hadn't said so on the phone. He could have put off coming until later. He shrugged. "It doesn't matter to me what kind of wedding you want. No opinions here."

Claire moved further from him. Maybe he shouldn't have said that, though it was the truth.

Sierra came out of the house with a tray of tall glasses.

"Don't be silly." Amber reached for a glass. "You're walking me down the aisle, brother-of-mine."

Noel jerked and the swing twisted sharply, throwing Claire against his shoulder. Too bad she pulled away immediately. "Uh, no. The wedding is in July? I'll be a long way from here by then. I may not even be able to make it back."

Time and activity on the deck stood still.

His sister's face fell.

Noel spread his hands. "What? You know I only have a three-month contract here. I'll be somewhere on Montana's east slopes by the end of July. Depending on the weather, I may not be able to get away."

"But—" She bit her lip.

Man, he hated that. A whole deck full of women, and not a one of them would understand the way he lived. Where was Jess when he needed an ally?

"Y-you weren't planning to come to my wedding at all?"

The total stillness around him provided everyone's opinions. He'd blown it. This trying to care about his sister thing was a new sensation. Did it matter what all these strangers thought of him?

Maybe Claire.

Now where did that come from?

Noel reached over and took Amber's hands in his. "Look, sis, I'll try. I just don't know where I'll be or what the situation might be. You know what my summers are like. If you need an absolute commitment out of me, set a winter date."

"Then you're in the tropics." She tugged her hands free.

"Well, I could work around it." He studied her face, searching for clues. "Want to reconsider?"

Amber glared at him. "No. Shawn and I have chosen the date, and you—" She leaned forward and stabbed him in the chest with a forefinger. "You better be here, buddy. That's all I can say."

No pushover, his sister. He guessed that was reasonable. They did share genetics, after all. He mustered a grin. "I'll do the best I can."

"With a tux."

"A what?"

"You heard her," Sierra put in. "The bride's the boss."

"But it's outside. On a farm. Who wears tuxes to events like that?"

Claire chuckled. "You do, apparently."

He twisted to look at her, glad of the excuse to rest his eyes on her for a moment. Today she wore jeans and a plaid shirt tucked in behind a wide belt. She could've been in her grandfather's overalls and she'd still look cute. "Seriously? She's not making this up just to spite me?"

Claire met his gaze. "Not at all. She wants a formal wedding, even on the farm."

He turned to Amber. "But that's—" He was gonna lose, no matter what. "Never mind."

Jo chuckled. "Good job, Noel."

"Did you make the guys do the tuxedo thing at your wedding, too?"

She grimaced. "My mother did, but that's beside the point. I challenged her on all the stuff that mattered to me."

Fighting for the guys in her life hadn't counted, apparently. Yep, his instinct was right. In this situation, being a guy meant he lost. Unless… "What if Shawn doesn't want to wear a tux? Then I don't have to, right?"

Amber burst out laughing. "Nice try, Noel. Shawn already has his picked out." She turned to the girls. "He wears a suit and tie to work every day. He wanted to make sure things were special for the wedding. His tux has tails."

Figured. Noel had met the guy enough times he should've known Shawn wouldn't be an ally. Thankfully Amber was Noel's only sister. He could live through this, if he had to. Once.

If he could get away that weekend.

He glanced at Claire and caught her peeking at him through her eyelashes. She turned her face, chin jutting out, as a slight blush spread up her cheeks.

Maybe he'd rather be here than planting trees. Maybe.

oOo

If she ever married, Claire's brothers would put up a bigger stink than Noel about dressing up. Amber was lucky her brother cared even this much about her. Claire wasn't sure she'd even invite hers to her wedding. But if she did marry some day, it'd have to be some guy like Noel who didn't want a formal affair. Casual would be fine with her.

She took a sip of her iced mint tea, wishing it would cool off her heated cheeks.

"Is there anything else, then?" Noel asked Amber. "Or are you ready to head to town?"

Jo shifted in her seat. "If you're from Missoula, I'm not sure what you expect to find in Galena Landing. It's a typical small town, though Lakeside Park is pretty."

"You gals have been so good to me, I just didn't want to impose upon you all the time. I thought Noel and I could get a meal and give you some space."

Sierra waved a languid hand. "Oh, not to worry. We'd love to have you both stay for dinner. Wouldn't we, Claire?"

Claire shot a venomous glare at her so-called friend. What choice did she have? Her mind scrambled over her menu for tonight. "Sure, that would be fine. I hope you can stay." She'd put frogs in Sierra's bed later. Or something.

In an effort to sound like she meant it, she met Noel's gaze. Maybe she did mean it. Maybe this would prove to him that she was an awesome cook and he should have hired her.

Maybe today would be a first and she'd burn dinner.

A slow smile crossed Noel's face. "Really? That'd be great. I can take Amber to town for lunch tomorrow, and she can see everything."

Jo laughed. "In twenty minutes or less."

Claire checked her watch. Definitely too early to excuse herself for cooking. Which meant Noel Kenzie would sit on this swing beside her for far too long. She leaned forward. "Amber, what would you like for a reception menu? I know we talked about a formal garden theme for the ceremony, but how do you see that translating into food? Are you looking for a sit-down dinner or hors d'oeuvres?"

Amber's eyes begged Noel for an opinion.

Claire turned away to hide her grin. The guy was so not going to want to get roped into this discussion.

Jo winked at Claire, glanced at Noel and back then raised her eyebrows.

Claire scowled. Her former roommate had been on a mission to find men for Claire and Sierra ever since her own marriage last summer.

Jo smirked as she leaned forward. "Most of your guests will be staying in RVs or at the Landing Pad, so it seems like a real meal might be the best option. Everyone is going to need to eat at some point anyway."

"But it wouldn't have to be a hot meal," Sierra put in. "We could do salads and sandwiches, even so."

Amber's face lit up. "Oh, fancy ones? Like cucumber sandwiches, with the crusts cut off?"

Claire winced. Next the girl would want pasty white bread.

"Sure we can." Sierra nodded enthusiastically. "Cucumbers should be in season by then."

A frown crossed Amber's face. "In season?"

Oh, the education. "As in, ready to pick from our garden or in the neighborhood." They'd probably have to plant extra if they hoped to do several weddings this season, and not just cucumbers would be in demand.

"I see." But Amber's furrowed brow belied her words.

"Radishes are also wonderful, for those who like a little extra zing in their sandwiches." Claire raised her chin and met Noel's gaze. "We'll have plenty of those all season long as well."

He grinned. "Sounds good. You can even leave the crusts on mine."

That was more like it.

"Strawberry shortcake?" asked Amber.

Claire shook her head. "Strawberry season is well passed by then."

"I don't understand. Is it that your grocery store doesn't carry them? Because I can bring some from Missoula if you like. I've never known our supermarket to be out."

Tact, Claire, tact. "I'd prefer to see what we could do with cherries, which are on at that time of year. It's part of our philosophy at Green Acres to enjoy food that's in season right here, whenever possible."

Amber looked from one to the other, a frown puckering her forehead.

Claire's brain scrambled for a diversion. "Tell you what. The girls and I will create a list of options for July, and you can choose from that."

Noel slouched down in the swing and crossed his arms, a grin twitching the dimple on his cheek.

"But I've wanted strawberries at my wedding my whole life."

Claire shot a glance around at the girls, but neither of them looked like they were about to be of any help. Great. She got to be the bad guy. "I'll see what I can come up with." She could probably find a recipe that called for frozen berries. Or would it really be so bad to buy just a few baskets at Super One Foods to make a bride happy?

Noel quirked an eyebrow at Claire.

If it made the bride's brother happy, too, wasn't that a bonus?

Amber straightened in the Adirondack chair. "Really?"

Claire swallowed a sigh. "Yes, really."

"Oh, thank you!" Amber leapt to her feet and twirled around, hands in the air. Then she bent and gave Claire an enthusiastic squish.

Whoa. Somebody was demonstrative. Claire patted the girl's back, gently easing her away. "We'll create a menu all of us can be excited about. Just you wait and see."

"Oh, I'm so happy! I can't wait for Shawn to come and meet all of you. And Mom, too, of course." Her eyes shone as she grabbed Noel's hands and bounced them up and down.

He tugged free and leaned closer to Claire. "Sometimes she's even worse."

"Aw, she's adorable."

His eyebrows did that quirky thing again. "You think?" He

turned to look at his sister as though he hadn't seen her before, tilting his head to one side.

Claire's insides turned a little mushy, watching his face, dark tousled hair obscuring all but his jaw. He was quite adorable himself.

Jo's foot nudged Claire's knee. "Oops, sorry."

Yeah, right. Claire glanced over and Jo shot her a knowing grin. Sierra seemed to be in her own world, watching ice swirl in her glass.

Claire scowled at Jo, but the responding grin grew.

Sierra stood. "Why don't Jo and I give you two a tour of the property? We already showed Amber the pole barn where the ceremony can take place, but there are good spots you may want to see that are suitable for photos." Sierra looked from Noel to Amber. "Are you handling the photographer or are we?"

Amber cast a helpless look around.

No wonder she wanted to have wedding planners at her beck and call. So she could demand strawberries and tuxes and leave the choices she deemed uninteresting to someone else.

"It's not a decision that needs to be made today." Sierra turned to Noel. "Ready for a tour?"

"Sure." He glanced down at Claire. She scrambled upright as he leaned closer. "Thanks," he murmured. "She's a good kid."

Yeah, she seemed to be. It wasn't Amber's fault she wasn't aware of seasonal food. Education. That was the key. Claire would get right on that after making a killer dinner.

Chapter 5

Noel glanced around the airy light-filled room. He'd never seen anything like it.

"Isn't it great?" Amber bounced on the balls of her feet beside him. "They built this house out of straw bales and plastered it."

Noel turned toward Claire, only to discover she'd disappeared into the kitchen that bumped off the center section of the great room. He took a few steps closer. "This is really cool. I'd heard of this type of construction but never seen it before. Was it hard to find a general contractor willing to do it?"

She glanced at him over the sink counter that divided the spaces, her brows furrowing, while Amber passed her, apparently heading for her bedroom.

Sierra came up beside him. "We did much of it ourselves."

Noel still focused on Claire. "Really? You three?"

Claire stood over a sizzling frying pan, a small grin playing at her mouth. "Jo wasn't much help. She broke her arm part way through."

He looked from Claire to Sierra and back again with new respect. "You mean you two did it all?" That couldn't be right.

"We acted as general contractors, anyway. And did what we could ourselves."

Noel shifted to see the rest of the way into the kitchen. The sight of a rock wall lined with stoves and ovens greeted him. He backed up a step and looked through the living room window. That rock wall must be three feet thick.

"Thermal mass," Sierra said. "Once we get the sunroom on the other side glazed this fall, it will work even better."

Claire came around the corner. "To answer your original question, Sierra's dad and brother helped us with the timber framing and getting the bales in place. We ordered the trusses, and a bunch of men from our church came by and installed them."

"So you subbed out the utilities and roofing?"

Sierra raised her eyebrows. "I did the electrical."

Okay, this was crazy. She couldn't have done that much physical labor in her life by the looks of her nails.

His disbelief must've showed because she stared him down. "I took the classes at Home Depot. It's not that hard. The tricky part was hooking up the solar panels." She leaned closer. "Trust me, we had the inspector go through everything. No one around here wants a house to burn down."

"Not that this place would burn easily." Claire looked around, satisfaction evident. "Still, with all those trees right there on the hillside, we wanted to make sure."

Noel took an involuntary step in her direction before noticing the tall stools on the dining room side of the sink cabinet. Apparently folks were welcome to be near the kitchen, just not in it. He took a seat and watched Claire as she moved around the stove, her plaid shirt tucked into jeans, showing off a trim figure. Not so trim he could put his hands around her waist and have them meet, but he'd like to try.

Sierra took the other stool. "Smells awesome, Claire. What's for dinner? Need a hand?"

"Chicken cordon bleu." She didn't turn around. "Baked

potatoes are nearly ready to come out, if you want to scoop and mash them."

Noel's gut rumbled.

"Mmm, double baked? You haven't done that in a while." Sierra slid off the stool and rounded the end of the counter. She grabbed a set of tongs, opened the wall oven, and removed what must've been a dozen potatoes.

A glimpse of something deep orange caught Noel's eye before the oven closed. "Butternut squash?"

Claire glanced over her shoulder at him, their eyes catching for an instant. "Yep. One of the few we have left from last summer's garden." She turned back to the meat roll-ups sizzling in a cast iron frying pan and flipped them over.

She'd offered to cook for him every day for three months, and he'd turned her down. Dumb decision. Something tantalizing hung in the air, unrelated to the pretty girl doing the cooking. This straw house wrapped him in hominess.

"Jo and Zach coming for dinner?" Sierra asked as Amber reentered from the hallway.

Claire nodded. "They're working on the cabin this evening. Anyone who wants to lend a hand is more than welcome."

Though she wasn't looking at him, she might as well be. Who else could she be referring to? Likely all the women were already doing so if they could. With the exception of Amber, of course.

Noel looked at his sister's soft hands with their long painted fingernails. Sierra's hands worked across the counter from him. They looked rougher, the purple nails much shorter than Amber's. He glanced across the room and couldn't see any color on Claire's. Hadn't they been pink the day she'd given him her bid? That had been weeks ago, though. Maybe she'd considered it a special occasion.

His insides warmed. It had been a special occasion for him,

at least, and he'd made the wrong choice after it. He was too much of a businessman to entertain the thought of overthrowing his decision for more than a second, telling Polly her services would no longer be needed.

At least he'd be able to come over here some evenings off and get to know Claire a bit better, though probably a dumb idea since he'd be drifting on at the end of the season. There really wasn't a permanent place for a woman in his life.

He watched her easy grace as she did her cooking thing.

If there'd ever been a time to consider changing his lifestyle, this might be it.

oOo

Claire looked around the spread on the plank table with satisfaction. The meal had turned out perfectly, and she'd placed Noel and Zach around the corner from each other at the far end. Away from her.

Noel's gaze seemed magnetically attached to hers. Every time there was a lull in the conversation—rare, with this bunch—or if she spoke, his eyes found hers.

She kept her gaze down and her mouth shut as much as possible. Except to eat, of course. She wasn't used to this much attention. Even Graham, whom she'd known for nearly a year before they'd become engaged, hadn't seemed this obsessed with her.

Everyone else couldn't help but notice. Jo already had, and Sierra wouldn't be far behind. The ribbing and teasing later would be merciless.

What could she do? He hadn't said anything. She couldn't just up and tell him to leave her alone. What if she imagined his attention? Head kept low, she glanced up between her lashes into Noel's admiring gaze. Definitely not her imagination. Zach said something and laughed, and Noel looked away, giving a rejoinder.

Claire missed the words. The entire ebb and flow of conversation around the table buzzed in her ears. Maybe it had been a mistake putting the men together. What if they actually hit it off and became friends?

Zach complained—good-naturedly, of course—of all the female companionship his marriage to Jo had produced. With his newly widowed best friend having hopped a flight to Romania to work in an orphanage for a year or two, Zach suffered from an overdose of estrogen.

Looked like he lapped up the guy talk. If Claire wasn't mistaken, Noel agreed to come by the cabin and have a look tonight. Jo entered the men's conversation with a bright laugh.

Across from her, Sierra and Amber debated the merits of roses versus gardenias in a wedding bouquet.

Mistake. One gigantic mistake.

Claire hated being left out but, even more, she hated being the center of attention. She'd keep as quiet as possible until time to get dessert out of the freezer.

Why had she gone all out with this dinner, right down to rhubarb mint sorbet? It was like some part of her wanted to impress Noel, remind him what he'd lost when he picked someone else to feed his crew.

Or just impress him.

She shook her head in an effort to dislodge the thoughts.

"You okay?" Sierra placed a hand on Claire's arm.

Conversation stilled as everyone turned to look at her. Claire surged to her feet as a flush crept up her face. "I'll go get dessert. Be right back."

Even the kitchen wasn't far enough, still in full view of everyone seated at the table. She fled across into the hallway then ducked into the bathroom to splash cold water on her face.

Drat the man. If he affected her this thoroughly, it was a very good thing she didn't work for him.

oOo

Noel whistled at the sight of the unfinished cabin nestled in the woods.

"You like it?" Zach grinned and patted the log wall. "Windows and doors are supposed to arrive next week, so we're hoping to have the roof on by then. Metal, like the main house, because of fire danger."

Noel had never built a house nor participated in the act. And even though he lived in a twenty-two-foot holiday trailer seven months of the year, this cabin looked small. Cute, definitely, but also tiny. "Looks pretty good," he ventured, taking a few steps so he could see around the corner. No, his first impression had been correct. The sight line wasn't much longer the other way.

Zach went through the empty doorway, his Border collie at his heels. Noel followed him onto the smooth floor.

"It's going to be like the main house." Zach scratched Domino's ears. "Etched concrete."

Noel nodded. The hazy impression he'd had of the straw bale house's floor was some kind of tile. Could've been concrete, for how close he'd looked.

No, he'd been too busy watching Claire. Something had sure gotten into her over dinner. Even her friends had noticed. When Zach had offered a tour of the cabin he and Jo were building, Noel jumped at the chance to get a little air, a little distance.

But now he noticed her absence. He shoved his hands deep in his jacket pockets to ward off the late March chill. He hadn't noticed a woman in years, not the way he'd become aware of

Claire. He met and worked with women all the time. Jess and half his crew, for instance. But there hadn't been anyone he wanted to touch, to hold. Anyone he simply wanted to look at.

Or possibly kiss.

Oh, right, Kenzie. Don't do anything stupid now. Nothing would be much dumber than putting a move on a classy gal like Claire, then shimmying out of her life three months later.

He could stay.

Zach flashed his headlamp around the dim interior of the cabin, mumbling to himself.

If Zach could pull one of those girls out of the loop and marry her, why couldn't Noel? Well, Zach was likely the stay-at-home type anyway. A veterinarian, he'd said over dinner.

Man, Noel's brain galloped way out of control for a woman he'd met all of twice. He forced himself to focus on the small space around him. Why would the couple build if they couldn't afford anything bigger than this?

"You know, Claire is practically a sister of mine." Zach rubbed the dog's ears.

Noel, startled, stared at Zach. "Uh…"

Zach narrowed his eyes. "Hey, I could be wrong. Happens all the time, but seems to me you're a little taken with her." He held up a hand to forestall any comment Noel might make. "She doesn't trust easily, and her roots here on the farm are very deep. Just so you know."

Was that a warning or something else? Noel twisted the words around in his head for a few seconds. "She seems a nice enough girl. What's her story?" Best to avoid the man's gaze, so he crouched down and patted the dog. Mom had never let him have a pet. Turned out to be a good thing, after all. The trailer was way too small for a dog this size.

"That might be best coming from her. I'm simply letting you know she's not a flirt. Not saying she can't or won't have a little fun now and then, but she's very serious and dedicated to Green Acres." Zach waved a hand, possibly encompassing the whole farm.

Noel's chin came up. "You accusing me of toying with her?" Because he'd known better than that from the get go.

"Didn't say that, man. Not even going there. You just do your job as the brother of the bride, and let Claire do hers."

Noel straightened. "You're warning me." How did the guy get off on this, anyway? He didn't own Claire or have designs on her. Anyone seeing Zach with his wife beside him at dinner would never suspect him to be anything but very much in love and loyal to a fault.

Zach flipped off his headlamp and shoved his hands in his pockets. "No, not a warning." He sighed. "I don't have the right to, at the very least. But I'm not sure Claire will tell you."

"If she's interested in me—and I'm not saying she is, or that it's mutual, mind you—then why don't you trust her to make her own choices? She's no kid."

Zach shoved past him, out the rectangular hole that served as a door, and into the full dusk of the evening outside. "Forget I said anything."

"It's not that easy." Noel and the dog followed him. "I think I have a right to know why you're protecting her. Is it me, or would you do the same to any guy coming around the place?" He could only hope that sounded vague enough Zach couldn't quote him as being hung up on Claire.

Zach strode down the path, leaving Noel behind. Not that Noel was afraid to be in the woods after dark, nor afraid of getting lost. The forest was more his home than anyplace else—his trailer, his mom's house, or the beach in Mexico. "Zach!"

The other man slowed, then turned, his jaw working. "What?"

"You didn't answer me, man."

"Look, her dad hauled her family all over the lower forty-eight while she was growing up. Her brothers are bums. Her— never mind."

What other man had been in her life that Zach had been about to mention? "I have no intention of hurting her, if that's what you're worried about. She's a cute girl. I could use a friend while I'm in the neighborhood. What's wrong with asking her out a few times?" Whoa. How did his mouth get so far ahead of his brain, anyway?

Zach's eyes searched his for a long moment. "It's a free country." He strode away, Domino loping at his side.

Chapter 6 --

"Full house!" sang out The Sizzling Skillet's hostess.

Claire wiped her white sleeve across her forehead and scraped a stir-fry onto an ironstone plate. "Order thirty-two up." She slid the line of clipped orders and glanced over the next several.

Once she'd thrived in this type of environment, wanting nothing more than to own a busy restaurant with her own name above the door in sparkling lights. But that had been then and this was now. Yes, it would make a difference if she were the boss. She'd set her own menu instead of making the same old recipes that had been used in countless diners for half a century.

A crash reverberated through the kitchen. Claire barely dared to glance up with all the meals she had going.

"Stupid clumsy kid," shouted the prep cook. "Sweep it up."

"What happened?" Claire called out, whisking a sauce so it wouldn't scorch.

"Dropped an entire stack of clean plates."

Claire cringed. Better to drop dirty ones. The place had been so busy they'd all been having trouble keeping up, and the new dishwasher kid was no exception.

Of course, better to drop no dishes at all.

"That does it. I quit."

Don called the poor kid every name under the sun.

"Cut it out, Don." Claire moved the sauce off the heat. "It's not like he meant to. Come over here for a minute when you're done sweeping, Tony. I could use a hand."

"We could use some more clean plates." Don shoved past her and thrust the broom into the lad's hands. "He'll burn the food."

"Can you sweep that up quick, Tony?" Claire looked at the gangly teen. Barely more than a kid, he probably thought working a shift or two a week would buy all the video games he could want. "Then please come talk to me before you leave."

The teen shot her a surprised look, most likely at the "please." Or maybe that she took his quitting seriously. Well, she would if she had to, but with any luck and a little respect, she'd get him to stick out the shift and even come back next weekend for another one.

Tony's lips drew into a tight line as he awkwardly handled the broom and dustpan.

More mamas should teach their kids how to sweep. It was all Claire could do not to go over there and do it for him. She might've if she didn't have every burner going and half the griddle full.

She could drop everything and return to Seattle. Michel actually wanted her ideas, unlike Nevin, who seemed threatened whenever one of her few acceptable additions took off. He'd cut her Eggplant Parmigiana out of the menu only last month, after it built good reviews from the town.

"Yes'm." Tony stood at her elbow, glowering down at her.

She pointed a spatula at the far corner of the griddle then pressed the utensil into his hand. "Mind stirring that pile?"

"Me? I said I quit."

"Yes, you. That pile of veggies. Quickly, before they burn." Gambling a client's dinner on winning the boy back? She'd probably lose.

He huffed a big sigh and shoved the vegetables around a bit.

"Like this." Claire scrambled the next pile over, making sure the pieces browned evenly.

Just the smell of all these conflicting foods made her queasy.

Tony awkwardly tried to follow suit. "Why am I doing this? I don't wanna be here."

"Now you're in charge of both those mounds. Keep them moving, okay?" She began plating up the order. "Are you usually a quitter, Tony?"

He startled. "Me? No."

"Then why start now? Toss the veggies beside the couscous here, please."

She heard his sharp intake of breath, but she was too busy filling the plates with the rest of the entree to pay attention.

A waitress set a heavily loaded tray of dirty dishes on the counter. "Need clean glasses and coffee cups!"

Tony shrank down beside Claire as though he could conceal himself behind her. He might be skinny enough to do it horizontally but, at a head taller, he couldn't hide.

"Thirty-four up," called Claire, setting the plates they'd just loaded onto the shelf and pulling the heat lamp down.

"Claire? Can I go now?"

She glanced over her cooking surfaces. Nothing was going to burn in the next few seconds. "Do you want a negative mark on your conscience, Tony? Or do you just want to put your head down and do your job to the best of your ability?"

Tony's chin jutted in Don's direction. "He doesn't need to yell at me all the time."

"He probably doesn't, but if you'll notice, he yells at everybody. Even Nevin when he's in here. It's how he copes with pressure."

"That's stupid."

"Yeah, it is." Claire began plating an order of meatloaf, mashed potatoes, and gravy. "But quitting is also a stupid way of coping."

Tony's shoulders slumped a little.

"Why don't you go run a load or two of dishes through? Keep that machine humming until they're all done. Might be midnight before we're cleaned and caught up." Horrid thought. "Then think through your decision when you're not under the stress of the moment."

The boy sighed. "I guess."

She met his gaze. "Thanks, Tony. I really appreciate it." She poured a ladle of gravy on the mashed potatoes and added less-than-perfect vegetables to the side. "Order thirty-three up."

"I wish I could cook like you. That'd be way more fun than running the dishwasher."

Claire allowed a small smile to play around her lips. "I washed plates all through high school, Tony. It's the apprenticeship system restaurants work under. Do a good job and when the time comes, you'll be ready to move up."

"Really?" A lilt of hope lifted his voice.

"Yep, really." Maybe this was why she was here. Not just for her, but for kids like Tony.

o0o

Elmer's farm had turned into a campground over the weekend with a bunch of tents, a few truck campers, and several bigger rigs. Noel had arranged for four biffy-in-a-jiffy outhouses on site. A series of solar shower bags, fed by Elmer's garden hose, hovered above a hand-wash station. The cook trailer had been angled in beside the tarped-over mess area with its picnic tables. He might need to replace the canvas by next year.

But though he was ready for the season to start at the crack of dawn tomorrow morning—he wasn't. He'd been doing this, what, ten years? He'd started tree-planting summers in college and spent a few seasons fighting fires. He'd dug tens of thousands of holes and plopped tens of thousands of seedlings into them over the years. He still put in long hours next to his crew most days.

He was getting too old for this. He stared at the ceiling of his trailer, listening to his crew's laughter around the distant campfire as old friends reunited. A bit of booze probably passed from one to another. Jess was out there. She wouldn't let it get out of hand.

Good money, and he loved being in the backwoods. Besides, it paid for long vacations in the tropics. Somehow it didn't seem enough any more, when a few weeks ago he was certain he'd still be doing this at fifty.

What happened? What changed things for him? Nothing had gone wrong. It was shaping up to be a lucrative year, maybe one of his best yet. So what was the problem?

Claire. It wasn't just her, but Amber. Yeah, his little sister had her annoying moments but she'd done a lot of growing up since Shawn had come on the scene a couple of years ago. Those two were crazy in love, kind of like Zach and Jo over at Green Acres. Amber was convinced beyond a shadow of a doubt that she and Shawn were destined to be together forever. That God had brought them into each other's lives.

God wasn't that involved in Noel's life. Course maybe he wasn't asking, either. Mostly he figured the Big Guy would still be around when Noel was ready to settle down and take life seriously. Which wasn't now.

He wasn't cut out for the kind of love and trust Amber had. He hadn't seen much good role modeling in his life. In that way he and Claire were a lot alike from what Zach had said. Noel's own father had drifted off when Noel was just a little kid, leaving only a few wispy bittersweet memories behind. He'd been in touch a few times, more often in recent years, but they had no relationship.

With Noel's penchant for wandering, maybe he already had too much of his father in him. A woman would be destined to let him go after a while. His kids would suffer, if he were lucky—or unlucky?—enough to have any.

No, there wasn't any room for a woman like Claire in his life. She deserved better than him. She didn't need a drifter.

If only she'd stop drifting through his mind, then, and let him get to sleep.

oOo

"Makes for a lot more traffic past our place, doesn't it?" Sierra stared out the living room window as several cargo vans drove past.

Claire flopped onto a love seat. "Doesn't take much for it to be more, living at the end of the road as we do."

"Or so we thought. We should head up that logging road sometime and see where Noel's crew is planting trees."

The smile slid off Claire's face. "Why?"

Sierra turned back into the room. "Why not? I've never seen an operation like that. Have you?"

"Nope. I'm not that interested." She'd be more curious if it weren't so high up there.

"Aw, come on. And here I thought you kind of fell under that guy's charm the other day."

"He's the brother of our first bride. That's all." She held Sierra's gaze for a long moment. "Which reminds me, have you checked out what quantity we can buy through Nature's Pantry on some of the bulk orders?"

A shadow crossed Sierra's face. "I talked to Doreen. She figures we should go through the regular route as she doesn't really have the connections we need."

Claire hated to admit defeat and open her own account with the food service companies. Not to mention word might get back to Nevin before she was ready to tell him herself what Saturday nights she'd need off this summer. He'd probably blow a fuse.

She couldn't wait to be rid of him by whatever method it took.

Short of murder.

Barely.

She heaved a sigh. "Yeah, I know. I'd much rather deal with a health food store than one of these big companies who refuse to understand the words *organic* or *sustainable*."

"Amber wants those little chicken breast roll-ups."

"We can't buy thirty birds and only use the breasts."

Sierra dropped into the other love seat across from Claire. "Sure we can, if we get a couple of cases of breasts from the food service guys."

Claire straightened. "That goes agai—"

"Oh, I know. I'm just saying there is a way. We could also buy thirty birds, use the breasts for the wedding, and eat drums and thighs ourselves all winter."

"Yuck."

The grimace on Sierra's face was mirrored on her own. "Something else to consider..." Sierra let her words peter out.

"Hmm?"

"There will be other weddings. What if those brides want chicken breasts too?"

Claire stared at her friend while the gears in her brain spun wildly, barely contacting each other. "B-but..."

"If we're thinking bigger, we need to think bigger. Lots

bigger."

"I don't understand. What do you mean?"

"We need menus that use the whole bird, which is just an example, of course. Same problem with beef, pork, you name it."

They'd managed easily as a group of roommates. Whatever odd cuts of meat came with the halves or wholes they'd bought from local farmers—they used them all up before ordering again. Even if it meant someone had to get creative with pork hocks or beef brisket.

"So you're saying if Amber wants chicken breast roll-ups, she also gets some kind of chicken salad that uses the dark meat."

"Yeah, like that."

Claire nodded, pondering. "We kind of jumped into this without thinking everything through."

"Kind of. But we're quick learners." Sierra winked.

Claire took a deep breath. Was she? Didn't seem like it some days. She'd thought she learned her lesson with Graham Maxwell. The lesson was simple—men do not equal security. In fact, they're the antithesis of security.

And here she was, three years later with another man wedged in her brain. Graham was long gone. Fine. She'd missed him at first, missed the idea of the refuge he seemed to have offered. But it hadn't been real, and she'd become very glad since they'd parted ways. Rumor had it he'd married a nurse last year, and she wished them all the best.

Really. Someone else could be at his globetrotting side. Someone suited for it. Thankfully that someone was not her.

If she were destined to be attracted to some guy again—she would *not* call it falling in love—reason said it should be a solid, stable guy who lived right here in Galena Landing. Not some transient worker who wasn't committed enough to his family to promise to attend his own sister's wedding.

She could do without Noel in her life or in her head, thank-you-very-much. Too bad she'd told herself a hundred times a day this week, and it wasn't making a dent.

"Earth to Claire."

She blinked, focusing on Sierra, who stood in front of the computer desk farther down the great room. "Yes?"

Sierra shot her a look. "We got us another one, looks like."

Claire gave her head a shake. "Another one what?"

"Another inquiry. This one's for September."

"A wedding?" Claire surged to her feet and headed for the computer. She dropped into the chair, Sierra leaning over her shoulder, and read through the message sent by their website's contact form. "At least there's more seasonal food to choose from in September."

"That's true."

Claire glanced up. "Is it really this easy? Are we in business?" She couldn't wait to tell Nevin she was quitting. Of course, it would take more than two weddings a year to equal her current income, but still. Maybe it wasn't just a pipe dream. Maybe it could be a reality.

"Isobel says she's from Wynnton, so that's cool. It's not too far for everyone to drive."

Guilt smote Claire. Were they crazy? Destination weddings meant airline seats and cars and all the rest, but people would get married anyway. Transportation costs and carbon footprint weren't good enough reasons to leave the wedding catering to someone else.

Sierra nudged Claire's shoulder. "Looks like we're in business."

How many happy brides could she stand to be around? At least she couldn't possibly fall for all their brothers. One was enough.

Chapter 7

It'd been a cold, drizzly Friday morning. Noel had taken the day off planting to attend to paperwork, the bane of his existence. When the rain stopped and the sun poked through, sending a glow through the gloom, he pulled out his camera-equipment-laden backpack for a trek through the wet woods on the hillside just past Green Acres.

Noel adjusted his camera on the tripod ever so slightly to frame a macro shot. Moss drooping off an aspen begged for a series of them. He'd been having a lot of fun with this weird lighting for nearly an hour now and itched to see some of the photos on his laptop back at Elmer's.

He set the timer to snap the shot. Even the touch of his finger might blur the image. He held his breath until it clicked, then stepped closer to shift the camera to catch more of the bark.

A slight rustling in the wet leaves behind him caught him off guard. He nearly knocked the camera off the tripod as he whirled to see.

Claire, her eyes wide, stood poised for flight, looking about as shocked as he was to see her. She peered out from beneath the sheltering hood of a tan raincoat. Her jeans had been tucked into vibrant pink rubber boots.

He laughed at the sight of the boots. They were just too much.

A multitude of emotions whisked across her face in rapid succession. "Hi. I didn't mean to startle you. I mean, I didn't even know you were here. I just needed some time out of the house breathing clean air before going to work tonight."

"No apologies necessary." And indeed, they weren't. She was a rest for eyes that had intently peered at moss and bark and leaves for far too long. She'd be a respite no matter what. "I hope I'm not bothering you here. I thought I was off Green Acres land?"

No question. He'd seen the property marker. But she might need the benefit of the doubt.

Claire nodded. "Technically, you're right." She pointed to an eight-foot tall deer fence, partially masked behind wild vines, farther up the hill. "We do hold the water rights to the spring that's protecting."

He'd noticed but been too focused on macro shots to give it any thought. Now he stared at the fence for a moment. Anything to rip his gaze from this pretty girl with short brown hair peeking from her hood. She'd been mighty gorgeous the day she'd come to apply for the job, but so much more approachable in her everyday clothes. He unscrewed the camera from the stand and held it up to atone for his trespassing, though of course he wasn't. Trespassing. Or even atoning.

How could one woman addle his brains this badly?

Claire moved closer, her pink boots squishing through the wet, partially decomposed leaves on the forest floor and through a patch of wild mint.

The sweet scent drifted upward.

Her eyes brightened as she dropped to her knees. "Another patch," she breathed, crushing a few leaves between her fingers and looking around her as though calculating the number of tea cups this might fill.

The aroma intensified.

She might be intoxicated by the mint, but Noel focused on Claire. He needed to remember this moment forever. The look of delight on her face, the carpet of mint bushes, the ridiculous pink boots.

He raised his camera, but not slowly enough.

Claire's face turned toward him. Her eyes narrowed and she bounced back to her feet.

Moment gone. Lost forever. Noel took a deep breath. "Want to see some of the shots I've made today?"

She nodded eagerly, tipping the hood back. She ran her fingers through her hair, flicking each brown strand where it belonged as she stepped closer.

Unlike his, which normally stuck up in whatever directions they wanted to go. Noel slid the button to view and shifted so they both could see the little screen. The scent of mint clung to her like an earthy perfume.

Focus on the camera, man.

His gaze caught a squirrel peeking out from behind a tree. "Hold still," he whispered, sinking slowly to his knees to get a better angle. "Come on, little fella. Come out just a wee bit more." He drew the camera toward his face in slow motion as the creature darted out then back again.

No time for sighting the shot. Noel held down the shutter button and listened to the barely audible clicks as the camera aimed in the general direction of the little mammal. Hopefully he lined up enough to zoom in on the laptop later and crop the image. If not, well, so be it. There'd be other chances.

The squirrel rustled around in the leaves for at least half a minute. By then Noel had the camera to his eye and made a few adjustments to its settings. Then, with a final whisk of its tail, the squirrel disappeared up the tree.

"That was awesome," breathed Claire. "Were you able to catch him, you think? We don't see many squirrels here."

For those few seconds he'd nearly forgotten she was there. Back on his feet, Noel leaned closer to Claire as he switched the camera into viewing mode. He arrowed back through the dozens of images he'd captured. A couple might be worth cropping, if his hand had been steady enough.

"Beautiful." Claire, brown eyes shining, looked up at him.

"Yes, you are." He dropped the camera to dangle on its strap and swung it out of the way. He slid his finger down her cheek.

Her jaw tightened and a guarded look crossed her eyes. She didn't retreat, though.

Noel figured he was doing okay. Definitely some kind of spark existed between them. Dimly in the back of his mind he recalled Zach's warning, but he dismissed it. The future could take care of itself. For now, he was in the presence of a beautiful woman who was not completely immune to his charms.

"Claire…"

This time she did step back. "No, Noel."

His brain scrambled for something else to say than what he'd intended, whatever that had been. "May I take some photos of you?" Something to remember her by, but he didn't want to say that.

Her eyebrows pulled together. "Pictures? Of me?"

He nodded. "Maybe you could use them for your portfolio. You know, on your website."

Claire shook her head. "I'm not dressed up for it. My hair's a mess."

Noel tucked an errant lock back into place, letting his hand linger. "Casual is great, and your hair is fine. Please let me."

She closed her eyes for a second and seemed to tremble

under his touch. He let his fingers trace her jaw when all he wanted to do was cup her face in both his hands and kiss her senseless. That wasn't going to work. "Please."

"Uh, why?" she whispered. "Why would you want to take my picture?"

"If you could see yourself as I see you, you'd understand. You're so beautiful."

Hesitation tripped across her features before she bit her lip. "I think...I think it's probably best not, Noel." She took a step back, out of easy reach, and pulled the hood up over her hair. "Besides, I need to get going. I'm due at work in an hour."

Noel's hand dropped to his side. "I'm glad you found time for a walk." Glad he had, too. His eyes captured hers for a long moment. He held his breath, and tried to read what he saw.

Then she shook her head, turned, and hiked away, pink boots squelching through the minty leaves.

oOo

Claire pulled into the driveway at quarter past eleven that night, after a late cleanup at The Sizzling Skillet. Miracle of miracles, Tony hadn't made good on his threat from last week to quit. Any time there'd been a lull she'd called him over to observe, while Don mumbled and whined in the background. Whatever.

It took her tired eyes a moment to recognize the silver Mazda beside the deck. Right. Amber returned for the weekend, bringing her mother to meet with the wedding planners. Hopefully everyone was asleep. Tomorrow would be soon enough.

Claire mounted the steps and opened the door, grateful to be out of the mouse-infested trailer she, Jo, and Sierra had lived in when they first arrived at Green Acres. Thankfully someone had hauled it away. This spacious house and farm were worth everything they'd gone through. It was worth putting up with Don and Nevin and customers who wanted their steaks done to

a crispy death and turned up their noses at exotic vegetables—
meaning anything more interesting than boiled peas, which they
usually left on their plates anyway.

A lamp glowed in the living room on its lowest setting, just
enough light to see by as she kicked off her shoes.

"Hi, Claire."

Her purse hit the floor as she whirled around.

Amber rose from the loveseat.

Claire pressed a hand over her heart. "Oh, you scared me."
She padded into the kitchen and poured a glass of water.

"Sorry. I didn't mean to." Amber slid onto a stool at the
peninsula. "How was work tonight?"

Claire closed her eyes to gather strength for a moment
before turning to face her guest. Her client. Noel's sister. She
shoved the last thought aside and mustered up a smile. "Long.
How was your drive from Missoula?"

Amber chuckled. "Also long." She propped her elbows on
the counter. "I was hoping to catch you for a few minutes
without my mother around."

Alrighty then. This wasn't going to be a quick, "Hello,
goodnight." "She's gone to bed already?"

"Yeah. She was pretty tired."

Claire poured water into the kettle. "Want a cup of tea?"

"Sure, that would be nice."

At this time of night, she wasn't giving the girl the option of
anything caffeinated. Mint would hit the spot. Soothing after a
stressful evening at work. Claire set the kettle on the burner and
brought her glass of water around the counter. She climbed up
on the stool next to Amber. "So, what's up?" Mom trouble?
Fiancé trouble? And why couldn't it keep until morning?

"At first my mom seemed to really like Shawn, but now that
we're engaged and planning a wedding, she seems nervous. I
don't know how to set her mind at rest."

And Claire was supposed to help how? She'd never been the mother of the bride or the bride herself. She'd come mighty close once, but she'd seen the light in time. Thankfully. Didn't mean marriage was evil, just that she'd been with the wrong guy. She turned to Amber. "Tell me why you think Shawn is the right person for you."

Amber's eyes shone in the low light. "Oh, that's an easy one. I made a list. "

Claire set her glass down on the counter with a thunk. "A list?"

"Yeah. Do you think that's weird?"

Definitely. But the wrong answer. "Not necessarily. What kind of list?"

Amber dug into the hip pocket of her jeans and pulled out a folded up piece of paper. She smoothed out the creases and laid it in front of Claire.

Too dark. Claire reached up and flipped on the counter's task light. Amber's list had been printed off a computer, obviously some time ago.

Loves God with all his heart.
Has a sense of humor.
Has a job.

So far so good. Graham had all those things, too. But a good marriage needed more. Apparently Amber knew that, too, as the list went on.

Is active in church.
Volunteers.

Ouch. That one could be overdone. Maybe Amber was safe though. Was there such a thing as pharmaceutical reps beyond borders? Claire doubted it.

Wants to have kids.
Doesn't have a temper.
Respects his mother.
Is polite.
Is fun.

The kettle boiled before Claire read through the second side of Amber's list. Any guy who met all this girl's criteria was practically a saint. "Is Shawn really this perfect?" Claire asked as she poured hot water over dried herbs. Because that would be seriously hard to believe.

"Almost. He did miss a couple of them."

"Oh?"

"Yeah, where it says a dozen roses for our six-month dating anniversary? He didn't do that."

Thank goodness.

Amber chuckled. "But I let him get away with it. Daisies and mums make a gorgeous bouquet, too."

"You're serious." Claire poured two mugs of mint tea and set one in front of Amber. "Cream? Honey?"

Amber shook her head. "Really, though, Shawn is awesome. I can't believe I'm this lucky."

Had Claire ever felt that way about Graham? Really truly believed she was blessed to have him in her life? Or had it been more of a friendship with some common goals thrown in? Someone she liked and respected, rather than loved?

More to the point, had Graham's touch ever sent her blood racing like Noel's finger on her cheek this afternoon? If so, she couldn't quite remember.

The rustling of Amber's paper pulled Claire back to the Green Acres kitchen. The other girl glanced over her checklist and looked up. "What's important to you, Claire? In a guy, I mean. A potential marriage partner."

Claire touched Amber's much-used paper. "Well, I've never made an actual list like you have."

"But you must have thought about it." Her eyes, so like her brother's, darkened. "Unless you're not planning on ever getting married, but I can't imagine that. You're so pretty and so talented."

As though only ugly people expected to stay single? Claire hoped that didn't require an answer. Amber didn't likely mean it that way. "Thanks." Seemed an appropriate reply for the last part, anyway. "I've thought about it. I was even engaged once."

"You were? What happened?"

Claire took a sip of her tea. "Turns out our goals in life weren't the same, after all." She poked a finger at the top line on Amber's sheet. "He did love God with all his heart. But that one—" she pointed at *volunteers* "—was more important than I was."

Amber rubbed her finger over the word. "What kind of volunteering?"

"Dentists Without Borders. All over the world."

"Wow!" Amber's eyes shone. "So many countries to see, so many people to help."

Claire gritted her teeth. "You might have been better suited for him than I was. All I wanted was this." She waved her hand. "A small plot of land, big enough to grow my own food and live gently on the Earth. I respect what Graham is doing, I honestly do. But I wasn't the right person to stand beside him in his work. We couldn't be together and both fulfill who God made us to be."

"So you broke up with him? That's really noble."

"More likely selfish. I didn't want to change for him or anybody." She met Amber's gaze. "I've done some growing up since then."

Compassion filled Amber's eyes. "Do you regret not marrying him?"

Claire shook her head. "Not at all. I'm still a homebody. I still have no desire to travel the world. We really weren't suited to each other—didn't love each other the way a married couple needs to."

"I'm sorry."

"Don't be. I did not cry buckets when we parted ways. I missed him, and hated letting all my friends know we canceled the wedding, but it was better this way." Much better.

"I just can't imagine."

Claire touched Amber's shoulder. "And you don't need to try. If you're certain Shawn is the guy God wants for you, if you're in love and ready to tackle the world together, you don't need to be sorry for something that happened to me several years ago."

"Did it make you say you'd never get married?"

"For a while." Claire stared into her cup. "Not anymore. But I'm content to stay single, too, if that's what God has for me, because I'm not leaving this farm. I'm going to die right here, an old lady."

"Nah." Amber grabbed a piece of scrap paper off a pile on the end of the counter. "You'll get married. What you need is a list. Not exactly like mine, of course, but one made just for you. Now, what's the most important thing?" She looked at Claire expectantly, pen poised.

She wasn't going there with this young woman, the sister of the guy who wouldn't get out of her head. She slid the blank paper from under Amber's hand and set it back on the stack. "A good night's sleep is about the top of my list."

Chapter 8

Noel folded himself into the backseat of his sister's car. "Thanks for picking me up."

Amber glanced at him via the rearview mirror. "Didn't want Mom to have to climb up into your truck."

Accepting a ride was a small price to pay for not having to go by Green Acres. Noel didn't want the next time he saw Claire to happen in front of his mother and sister. They didn't need to notice his awkwardness around their wedding planner.

Noel patted his mother's shoulder. "What do you think of Amber's plans?"

Mom turned slightly in her seat. "I'm not sure. It's hard to imagine that drab farm looking inviting for a wedding in just a few months." She held up her hand. "I know that foliage and flowers will make a large difference, but it doesn't seem the structures have much to work with."

Amber glanced over. "Mother—"

"It's your wedding, dear. I won't tell you what to do."

That'd be a first, but she meant well.

Amber drove across the bridge into Galena Landing. "They're giving me a good deal, being as Shawn's and my wedding is their first one."

Noel bit back the obvious comment that Zach and Jo had married there. It wasn't the same when the bride actually lived on the premises.

Mom's manicured fingers rested on Amber's forearm. "That's my concern. It's not only their first wedding, but yours. I mean, you won't be getting married again, I hope, so this…place…will be the center of all your memories."

Amber spun the steering wheel to turn into The Sizzling Skillet's parking lot, dislodging Mom's hand.

Not here. Not if he was trying to avoid Claire, and he was. Of course, she'd be back in the kitchen and wouldn't know whom she cooked for. Still…he tapped Amber on the shoulder. "There's a diner just a couple of blocks down."

She glanced at him, eyebrows arching. "But this is supposed to have the best food. All the girls say so, especially if Claire's working."

He could make a fuss, but then his cover would be blown. "Oh, in that case, no problem." He managed to get out of the vehicle fast enough to open his mother's car door.

"Thank you, son."

The car beeped as Amber locked the doors. "Mom, that's the thing. My memories won't be centered around the setting, but on Shawn. This will just be a backdrop."

"Don't be ridiculous, Amber Margaret."

So that's the argument his sister was using. Noel managed to keep a grin from appearing with great difficulty. He held the heavy wooden door to the restaurant open. Mom swept through in her silk pantsuit, head held high, with Amber right behind her, wearing fashionable jeans and a checkered top.

"Chin up," he whispered.

Amber flashed him a grin and rolled her eyes.

The hostess paused, a stack of menus in hand. "Do you have reservations?"

"Uh, no. Do we need one?" Noel scanned the rustic interior with its wagon wheel light fixtures and slab tables surrounded by patrons.

"It's always a good idea on weekends." She looked around the space. "Give me about fifteen minutes and I can fit you in."

"No problem." He'd been expecting something more like an hour after her question.

"You may have a seat in the lounge if you like."

"We'll wait right here." Mom's eyes narrowed.

The hostess shrugged and turned away. "Suit yourself."

Blocking the doorway for fifteen minutes—or more—didn't sound that great. Noel turned to his women-folk. "Sure you don't want to go to the diner?"

"I'm good with waiting." Amber glanced around, tucking long strands of dark hair behind her ear. "Look, there's an empty bench."

Noel took his mother's elbow and propelled her to the alcove hidden off the entry, where she took a seat with Amber beside her. Looked a bit crowded for three, so Noel leaned against the window frame.

"Tell me, son." Mom flicked an imaginary speck off her cream slacks. "When are you going to settle down and get married yourself?"

Here they went again. "Not any time soon, Mom."

"You're thirty."

Did she think he hadn't noticed?

She eyed him. "Amber is only twenty-four, and she's getting married."

Amber leaned back out of Mom's line of sight and smirked at him.

Thanks, sis. "Believe it or not, Mom, I'm well aware of all those things."

She spread her hands on her lap, palms up, and looked at

him with raised eyebrows.

And she wondered why he stayed as far away from Missoula as possible. He could barely manage a week or two over Christmas. He'd never hear the end of it if he didn't head home then, even though he spent most days boarding at the Snowbowl.

"Mom, could we talk about something else? Like Amber and Shawn's wedding, perhaps?" Not that wedding-speak was his favorite, but that's what she'd come to Galena Landing for, right? It should be the perfect distraction.

"I just want you to be happy, son."

"Who told you I wasn't?" He didn't dare glance at Amber. "I'm doing what I love."

"You're not getting together with that employee, are you? What's her name? Jennifer?"

"That would be Jess." He closed his eyes for a second. "And the answer is no."

"That's good. I don't think she's quite proper."

Hearing that would break Jess's heart for sure. Noel turned to his sister. "How did plans go today, Amber? Did you and Mom get anything finalized?"

"I think so. Sierra and Claire have some great ideas."

"Like what?" Better to talk about Amber's wedding than his lack of one.

"Oh, just—"

"Kenzie, party of three?"

Noel turned to the hostess. "We're ready." He offered a hand to his mother, but she was already on her feet. He motioned her behind Amber and trailed through the restaurant at their heels.

The hostess took their drink orders, set down menus, and whisked away.

Noel opened the vinyl-covered list. Pretty ordinary small-town food for the most part: burgers, roast beef, pulled pork.

Nothing stood out. He closed the menu.

The waitress appeared. "Ready to order?"

"I'm having the Chicken Caesar." Amber snapped her menu shut and passed it across the table.

Mom nodded. "That sounds good."

"And you?" The girl turned to Noel, pen poised over her small pad.

"What's the special?"

"Claire's cooking tonight, so the special is a roasted vegetable ragout."

Noel cocked his head. Vegetarian didn't usually call to his palette, but with Claire at the range, why not? He nodded. "I'll give it a try."

Amber beamed at the waitress. "Could you let Claire know this order is for the Kenzie family?"

The waitress sent a puzzled glance at Amber then made a note. "Sure." Off she went.

"Why bother her? Just let her do her job."

"She'd want to know." Amber turned her coffee cup in circles. "Don't you think?"

"There are several nice young ladies at that house, Noel. Have you noticed?"

Uh, yes. But he wasn't going there.

"Now one of them is married, Amber tells me. The really short girl. But there are still two others."

Only one mattered, though. No way would he let his mother get a whiff of his interest. "Yes, they seem nice enough."

Amber leaned her elbows on the table, eyes twinkling. "Claire and I had a great heart-to-heart last night when she got home from work."

Noel jerked back, stifling his reaction. Too late.

"Gotcha!" Amber smirked.

"What's this?" Mom looked from one to the other. "Did I miss something?"

Thanks bunches, little sister.

oOo

Last time Claire went for a walk in the woods she'd found Noel. She wasn't ready to run into him again. Not that he'd be in the same place, but the crew took Sunday off, so he could be anywhere. She should be safe enough on Green Acres property, though.

It'd been pretty obvious yesterday evening which item Noel ordered. He didn't seem like a Chicken Caesar kind of guy. But still, brave enough to take a chance on a non-menu vegetarian item? Impressive. Why couldn't she get him out of her head? He'd kept her awake half the night and distracted her thoughts all through church this morning, made worse when his sister sat beside her.

He hadn't been there, and that should tell her something. If he didn't share her beliefs, it was a bad idea to care about him.

Never mind. It was a bad idea anyhow.

Claire stood at the foot of the golden willow near Jo and Zach's cabin. They'd called this a day off building, so no one was around. Which meant the tree house was vacant. She straightened her little pack and climbed up the rope ladder to the first platform. In moments she'd shed the pack and leaned back, eyes shut, against the great tree's trunk.

How had she become so obsessed with Noel Kenzie? Nothing about him matched any inventory she might make. In fact, instead of a list like Amber's, Claire could make one about all the ways Noel didn't fit. But that was dumb, like it acknowledged his power over her.

Something like that could exorcise Noel from her head.

What had been in his eyes when he'd reached out and touched her cheek, not once but twice? Men didn't do that to random people they barely knew. He'd been so gentle. Yeah, pushy in a way, but when she'd called a halt, he'd respected it, though it was obvious he didn't want to.

What did he see in her? Nobody but Graham had ever tried to look into her soul that way, and Graham hadn't meant it.

She fingered her Bible open, searching for the spot in Isaiah where she'd stopped reading yesterday. Ah, chapter 55. She stared at verse 8. "For my thoughts are not your thoughts, nor are your ways my ways."

She'd been trying so hard to align herself with God's ways, His thoughts, His will. When she and Graham broke up, Sierra had asked if Claire was certain God wasn't calling her to missionary work with Graham.

"No," she'd said. "I'm positive God wants me building a farm somewhere, teaching people to meet their physical needs."

"But you thought He called you and Graham to marry."

Claire shook her head. "Only when Graham shared my dream. But God gave him a new dream, a different dream, and they're not compatible. So we're not."

And she'd been fine with her choice nearly every day since Graham had hopped a flight to Uganda. Those questions and all those crisscrossing emotions hadn't come up in three long years.

Now here she was, finally accomplishing her goal, and a distraction presented itself again. Was God saying her part in the farm was done? Or was He testing Claire's devotion to His will?

How could she know? "What am I missing, Lord?"

Funny thing about God. He didn't seem into speaking out loud. Claire read the passage a couple of more times and sighed. She couldn't focus. Couldn't shake Noel out of her brain.

Fine, then. She pulled a notebook and pen out of her pack. She'd seen Amber's list. What was important to *her*?

#1. He has to want to follow God with all his heart.

Graham had that one covered, but he wasn't in the running anymore. As for Noel, she didn't know, but he hadn't really said. If he'd been in church, that would've given her a clue.

She placed a question mark beside it.

#2. Devoted to sustainable living.

The guy planted trees. That was sustainable, right? Kind of?

#3. Roots.

She'd vowed never to move off Green Acres until they dragged her off to Galena Hills Care Facility in her old age. She'd thought Graham was bad, wanting to bring dentistry around the world. Noel didn't even have a home address other than his mother's house. Very large X beside this one.

Cute, funny, and polite. Noel pulled Amber's chair out for dinner the other day. Those things definitely counted. He was adventuresome in his culinary expectations—personally, if not for his crew. His eyes twinkled when they met hers, like they shared a private joke. His hair was always a little unkempt—it could use a cut—but clean.

He valued nature. All those photos he'd taken of moss, and leaves, and bark. She'd seen the subjects anew through a little rectangle that forced her eye to block out all the surroundings.

He'd looked at her—and seen beauty.

Claire touched her jaw where his hand had rested two days before. Even Graham had never called her beautiful. Not with such intensity in his voice. His gaze. And Graham was gone. She needed to stop comparing men to him, though she hadn't done so these past three years. Just now. Just with Noel, a guy she barely knew. Somehow she'd become infatuated with him.

Likely it was her roommate's fault. Sierra had the idea to host and cater special occasions. If Claire didn't have to help plan Amber's wedding—and now Isobel's—these thoughts would not be so close to the forefront of her mind.

God's ways were higher than her ways. But how did she know which of these belonged to Him?

Chapter 9 --

Weeks went by and the garden began to grow. The second bride, Isobel, brought her fiancé to Green Acres to meet the team.

"It's hard to imagine what this place will look like in September, babe," Greg said, looking around.

Vegetable harvest would be in full production, but that's not what the guy meant. "We'll have our first heavy frost sometime in the month, but the days are usually pleasant."

"What if it rains?" Isobel put in.

"That's not impossible. We do have a backup plan." Claire gestured to the pole barn. "Rain won't be much of a problem unless it's also windy. We've put lattice up around the end there and seeded some vining flowers just last week."

"Oh?" Isobel perked up. "Like what?"

"A variety," Sierra said. "Morning glories, sweet peas, and those purple perennials." She looked at Claire. "I can never remember their name."

"Clematis."

"Right."

Isobel frowned. "I don't think those will all go with my wedding colors."

"They'll simply provide a pastel backdrop interlaced with the white lattice." Sierra patted the stripping. "They'll go with any summery outdoor wedding."

Perhaps Sierra had been wise to veto the scarlet runner beans after all.

"If you say so…"

The gal seemed unconvinced, but color was more Sierra's thing than Claire's. Unless it had to do with making a plate attractive, then Claire was all over it. "So what palette are you thinking, Isobel?"

"Black and white and a kind of dark gray-blue. Unless we choose the chocolate and rust."

And that was supposed to be an improvement? "I think you'll find the lattice flowers to be a fine background for the ceremony photos, Isobel. Your colors are vivid and stark. They'll really pop off the white and pastels."

Sierra shot Claire a grateful glance as Isobel narrowed her eyes and tilted her head, considering. "I see what you mean."

Were they going to have to plant color-coordinated flowerbeds around the property? "If your wedding is black and gray, here's the white flowerbed to contrast. Have rusts? Here is the marigold bed." Hmm. That sounded like a ton of extra work no one had time for, and there certainly was no budget for a full time landscaper for a year or two. Possibly ten.

What had they started?

"Can you recommend a cheap photographer?" Greg asked. "My best man's brother-in-law takes pretty decent photos, but we're not sure if that's who we want to go with. Everything about a wedding costs so much."

"I'm sure you get what you pay for in a photographer." There was a slight edge to Sierra's voice. "And in a few years, photos—and love—are all you have left."

If they had that. Either way, Claire would hazard a guess Noel could shoot an amazing wedding. His eye—well, she'd never seen bark and moss that way before. He'd be long gone by September, but surely there was someone in town with talent. "I can check if a photographer from Galena Landing might be available for the day and let you know what you're up against price-wise."

What were the odds they'd be able to get a photographer on staff, along with a landscaper? Next they'd be asking for...

"What do you plan for music here?"

Yeah, that. Claire and the girls thought people would bring their own staff and only use Green Acres as the setting. Apparently they were expected to provide full service.

"We can put together some possibilities and email you," Sierra said smoothly. "Are you into traditional or something else?"

"More contemporary, I think." Isobel scrunched her face, shaking her head. "I'm not sure this is going to work, to be honest."

"Why, babe?" Greg squeezed Isobel's hand. "I thought you wanted an outdoor wedding."

This fickle bride probably changed her mind every ten minutes.

"Well, I do, but..."

Did Claire really want to deal with this gal for months? On the other hand, did she want to stay working for Nevin? She couldn't blame Tony for trying to quit. The boy threatened it at least once a weekend.

Still... "We need a firm commitment by the middle of May, or we can't promise to hold the date open."

Sierra sent a silent stunned stare but recovered quickly. "I'm sure we can work something out."

Claire smiled as sweetly as she could muster. "I'm sure we can, too. And obviously we haven't had a chance to address all the concerns yet. You've given Sierra and me some important questions to discuss. We'll get back to you once we've had a board meeting." By board meeting she meant around the dining room plank table with Jo. "I think we should be able to email you the details of what we can and cannot do by the end of April, don't you think, Sierra?"

Sierra nodded enthusiastically. "Sure, that will give you a couple of weeks to compare us with other venues before we need a final answer."

Greg turned to Isobel with his forehead furrowed. "We're considering other venues?"

"Maybe." Isobel glanced from Claire to Sierra and back again through her eyelashes. Fake ones, for sure, at that length. "But I really want it to work out here. It's far enough from home that Uncle Stanley probably won't come, and that can only be a good thing."

"Uncle Stanley? Is he the one who—"

"Yes."

Curiosity caught Claire for a moment. Uncle Stanley what? But it didn't matter if she didn't know. With any luck the man wouldn't show up at the wedding, which might or might not take place here anyway. Isobel's family could keep its secrets.

"Are we done here today then, babe?" Greg swung Isobel's hand. "If we head out now, I can still catch the game with the guys."

Wasn't he a sweetheart? Claire's throat constricted. Did they have any responsibility to provide marriage counseling for their clients? 'Cause this pair could sure use it.

Like she was one to talk, having walked away from a perfectly nice man who wanted to use his talents for God, and was now infatuated with a much less appropriate guy.

"That's fine." Sierra shook Greg's free hand. "We'll be in touch soon, and if you have any additional questions or concerns, don't hesitate to call or email."

The couple said their goodbyes and headed to their car.

"I'm not sure…" Isobel whispered to Greg.

Sierra waved until the car turned out of the driveway before turning to Claire, hands on her hips and a frown in place. "Well? Do you want to host events here or don't you?"

Claire scowled back. "Look at them! They're two little kids who can't make up their minds about anything. They see only a party, not commitment for life."

"That's not our job. They pay us to create the wedding of their dreams—"

"Whatever that is. She has no clue."

Sierra raised her eyebrows. "Is. Not. Our. Job."

Who'd appointed Sierra the boss? Claire spun on her heel and stalked toward the house. The sun-filled straw bale house with the deck she loved. The place she needed to keep making payments on or go back to Seattle.

"We'll call a meeting," she shot over her shoulder. "With Jo. Then we'll see what's viable and what isn't."

oOo

The grub line under the tarp was mostly silent. Polly was a decent enough cook, if uninspiring.

Noel hung back to the end of the line. He'd come down the mountain earlier than most of the crew to catch up on some paperwork. They needed food more than he did.

Jess paused beside him. "Hey, boss."

"Hey, yourself. How'd it go today?"

She shrugged. "Got into a steep spot this afternoon and some of the guys were whining. They dealt with it and moved on."

Noel grinned. "That's what we do."

Jess craned her neck to see the food bins where Polly and her son dished up dinner. "What're we having?"

"Spaghetti and meatballs, looks like."

"Again?"

He shrugged. "Seems so. She's veered off the menu plan she provided, that's for sure."

"Not fair." A scowl marred Jess's face. "These guys need good carbs, not just inexpensive ones. You better talk to her."

"Yeah, the thought had crossed my mind."

"Bet Dreamboat wouldn't have cheaped out."

Noel whipped his head up and met Jess's gaze. "Since when do you second-guess my hiring choices?"

She poked him in the chest. "Since you seem too wrapped up in your dream world to make smart choices, boss."

That took him aback. "My dream world?"

"Or lack of one." Jess smirked. "Been thinking of her much?"

Deep in his jeans' pocket, Noel's cell vibrated. "Not sure what you mean." He pulled the phone out.

"Oh, nice try, boss. Never seen you so smitten."

Her voice faded as Noel focused on the call display. Claire? She was calling *him*? Blood thundered in his ears as he imagined what might have caused this aberration. "Excuse me," he said to Jess, turning away and sliding on his cell. "Hello?"

"Hi, Noel? This is Claire."

As though he didn't know. "Hi. How are things?" She wasn't calling about Amber's wedding, was she? What could have gone wrong?

"Um, pretty good. Have you seen our website?"

"Why, has it gone missing?" The silence stretched for a couple of seconds. "Sorry, I couldn't help myself. What about it?"

She chuckled...a little late. "It's just that I'm decent at CSS, but a lousy photographer. And our site looks kind of lame."

"Uh huh." He could see where this was going, but she'd

have to work for it.

"We just had a board meeting and decided we needed some good quality photographs. I thought of you."

"I'm honored." And he was, but that didn't mean he should get involved. What was with him? Half the time he was convinced she'd come around if only he pushed a little and at other times, he held back. Here she was, asking him. Why wasn't he jumping?

"You did such a beautiful job of those you showed me the other day."

The day he'd have kissed Claire, given the slightest encouragement. Noel glanced at the grub line. Nearly his turn, or go hungry. Jess had collected her plate and was chowing down with a table of their rookies.

Claire's voice turned crisper. "Anyway, we're willing to pay you, of course. But I'm hoping you might have some good ideas of what photos would make the farm its most attractive."

"Any one with you in it." The words flew out of his mouth before he could hold them back. Should've bitten his tongue.

He could imagine the red creeping up her face. Still, it was the truth. "Claire? Maybe we can talk over coffee. Can I pick you up after dinner?"

The pasta looked even less appetizing than it had ten minutes ago, but he couldn't very well tell her hiring Polly had been a mistake.

"Or you could come over here and talk with the whole group."

Not while she wanted something from him. "That's the next step. First, just you and me."

She gave a nervous chuckle. "Sounds like you're threatening me."

"Nah." He lowered his voice. "Just want to spend a bit of time with you. You have nothing to fear." Sadly, that was probably true. But he might—like falling in love for the first time ever. She was right. A group was best. He opened his mouth to say so.

"Instead of going to town for coffee, why don't we walk the property and I can show you around?"

A miniature war took place in Noel's head. "That's a good idea." He'd ask her for that coffee another time. "What time's good? I'm free in about half an hour." Or in two minutes. Did he have to eat what Polly prepared?

o0o

"I disagree." Sierra drummed her fingernails on the table. "We need more than an improved website."

"I didn't say that was *all* we needed." Claire bit back a sigh. "It's a good start, though. Making it more attractive and also more clear about what services we include and what we don't."

"Music?" Jo frowned. "I can't carry a tune in a bucket and can't play an instrument."

Claire leaned forward. "Honestly, I think it's okay if we don't provide everything. I think this wedding business is getting out of hand."

"I don't know what your problem is." Sierra swung to face Claire. "We're here to make some money and bring this farm into the black, right? That was your worry."

Jo shook her head. "We do need to find some ideas for the farm to pay its own way. But weddings may not be the best choice."

"What we need are some events that require less coordination," Claire said. "Like retirement parties maybe."

"I think we're missing something important," Jo cut in. "What's our mandate?"

Trust Jo to harp on that.

"Staying on top of our mortgage payments?" suggested Claire.

"Teaching people about sustainable methods to live." Jo held up her hand. "I'm not against running some weddings or other events, but I think we need to focus on the long-term stuff. And that's hands-on training for young farmers."

"A work program," Claire stated. "Where they pay us for the privilege of learning from us."

Sierra frowned. "That will take much more time to get off the ground. I thought we'd agreed to try other things in the interim."

Claire's mind raced with possibilities. "But Jo's right. We need to start out as we mean to go on."

"We can't cancel these weddings."

"Not planning to."

A 3/4-ton pickup rumbled into the yard, and Noel swung out.

Claire scrambled to her feet. "I've got to go." The girls didn't need to notice how uncomfortable Noel made her. "If I'm not back before dark, send the troops after me."

Sierra chuckled. "Don't get lost out in the pasture."

Claire grabbed a hoodie off its hook. If Sierra really knew, she'd be more concerned about Claire getting lost in Noel's eyes. But she could handle this. She had to. For the good of Green Acres.

Not because she wanted to.

Chapter 10 --

"The farm is greening up nicely since I first saw it," Noel commented as they climbed through the rail fence. "How much land do you have here?"

"Forty acres. It used to belong to Zach's grandmother. She's in the old folks' home in town, where Jo works." Claire spread her hands to the sky. "We love it here."

"I can see why." And he could. He thrived on tree-covered hillsides like the one along the length of Green Acres. His crew planted the plot behind the same mountain.

"It's almost the end of the Earth." Claire leaned back against the rails. "Except for Canada."

What a shot that would make with her silhouetted against the evening sky. Would she get angry? She couldn't—not when she'd particularly asked him to take photos. Noel took a few steps back, focused his camera, and snapped off several shots. She didn't seem to notice, she was so wrapped up in staring into the distance.

He squatted and plucked a stem of grass. "There are places closer to the end of the world. Terra del Fuego, for instance."

Claire's eyebrows pulled together. "Where?"

"An island off the tip of South America, part of Patagonia. It's their answer to the Canadian Shield, only with mountains.

Not much grows that far south but it's awesomely beautiful. It's one of my favorite places on the planet."

She looked at him like he'd grown another set of ears.

She didn't want to see the world? But there were so many cool places. "One of the most fun things I've done is hiked the Pacaya Volcano in Guatemala. Nothing beats the rush of watching lava flow right beside you. One of my buddies melted the bottoms of his sneakers."

The animation drained from Claire's face.

"Oh, we weren't in any real danger. Someday I'd like to go to Hawaii. I'd skip most of the touristy stuff, but man, I'd like to climb Kilauea. They say you can lean right over the edge and see into a deep vat of boiling lava. Wouldn't that be spectacular?"

Claire shuddered and her eyes glazed over for a moment. Then she shook herself. "I'm sure it's very nice."

Didn't sound like she believed it, though.

She pushed away from the fence and pointed at the dark furrows, currently bare of vegetation. "Zach plowed this small field under last fall and will be planting wheat here soon."

Guess she didn't want to talk about travel or volcanoes for some reason. Whatever. He could switch with the best of them. "Is there a good market for wheat?"

There she went with that perplexed expression again. The question didn't seem that hard to Noel. He waited.

"We aren't selling it."

His turn to be confused. "Then why grow it?"

"To make into flour and eat the results ourselves?"

Now there was a concept. "Isn't it a lot of extra work? Can't you just buy flour?" Galena Landing had a supermarket. It carried flour. He knew that for a fact.

"Sure we could, but that goes against everything we're trying to do with Green Acres."

Noel scratched his head. "Which is to host weddings?" However that related to homegrown wheat.

"No, no. That's just a means of paying the bills. Our goal is to live sustainably. That means growing as much of our own food as we can and making the least possible impact on the environment. It's why the house is made of straw bales and why we have solar panels on the roof."

Oh, great. She'd kind of hinted at that food-growing thing during their interview last month. Somehow he hadn't quite picked up on how deep her obsession ran. Wasn't that the right word? Noel pointed at the neat rows. "Looks like that was done by a tractor to me. That's impactful, isn't it? I keep hearing panicked-out rumors of peak oil."

"We're buying a pair of horses as soon as possible." Claire's chin came up a little and she looked him in the eye. "They'll be my job. I'll learn to manage the team."

If he let her words sink in, he'd be far less tempted to pursue this woman than if he just looked at her. Today her lean body was hidden under a baggy San Juan Islands hoodie. Those preposterous pink boots held in the hems of her jeans. And her face—rapidly changing emotions flitted across it as she watched him from her dark brown eyes. What was she thinking?

Belatedly he remembered he hadn't answered her. "Horses?"

Claire nodded. "Norwegian Fjords. The pair we want are still too young and untrained, but we're hoping they'll be ready by next spring."

She was absolutely serious.

"I, uh, like horses, too. Did some riding last time I was in Australia. Ever seen The Man from Snowy River?"

She let out a long breath. "Old movie. Yeah, I've seen it, but it's not precisely what I'm talking about."

"Little House on the Prairie?" If he kept guessing, he'd

either make her laugh or get it correct. Sooner or later.

Claire shook her head.

Bugged him he couldn't read her mind.

"Anyway, that's what we're doing with this field." She pointed toward the next fence, closer to the mountain. "We're cutting hay in that one for a cash crop. In August we'll till it and replant with spring wheat. It makes the best bread flour ever. Then Zach will plant pasture grass in this one when the crop comes off."

Noel scratched his head. "Sounds busy and complicated. I guess I don't get why you're doing all this. Not really."

She shot him a look. "You mentioned peak oil a few minutes ago. That's one reason."

"Oh, come on. You believe in that stuff?" As soon as the words were out of his mouth, he regretted them.

Claire's lips set in a straight line. "Sure do," she ground out. "Someday we'll have pulled all the oil out of this rock ball and then what will people do?"

He'd never given it much thought. "It won't be in my lifetime."

Her eyebrows shot up. "You don't know that. It's a finite amount, whatever it is. And even if it lasts our lifetime—which I doubt—do you want to send your kids and grandkids into such an uncertain future?"

"I don't have any kids." Maybe the wrong answer, by the fire in her eyes. "Yet. I haven't met the right woman." *Until now.* Crazy thought.

Claire stared at him for a moment, lips pressed tightly together, then turned away.

It seemed like a cloud covered the sun and triggered a chill.

"This will never work," she mumbled.

"Claire?" He jumped in front of her and touched her arm. "You asked me to take photos. We don't need to agree on everything for me to do that."

"Fine." Her eyes sparked. Maybe that cloud harbored a thunderstorm, lightning included. "The back property line is the barbed-wire fence down at the end. Widthwise, it goes from that fence—" she pointed toward the Nemesek farmhouse "—to a little way up the hillside. Just past Jo and Zach's cabin in roughly a straight line back to the road." She pulled her arm away. "I don't think you can get lost."

"Claire, wait."

She narrowed her gaze. "Why?"

He'd regret this big time. "Because I can't stand it when you're mad at me." Which seemed all the time, except when discussing Amber's wedding in a group setting.

"I'm not sure what you're talking about."

Right. He was supposed to believe that? He softened his voice. "Claire, I know you don't believe we have much in common, but I think we do. And, well, I'm really attracted to you."

She shook her head. "Nice try. All we have in common is your sister."

"You love nature." Noel waved his hand across the field. "You see the beauty in my photography."

"Let me make one thing perfectly clear. I love nature. That's true. But I love the nature that is right here. Not in Australia. Not in South America. Not in some…volcano somewhere. I'm sure it's very pretty other places, but I'm not interested in going. If I never leave this valley again as long as I live, I'll die content." She spun on her heel and stalked off down the fence line. "If you have photos to show me later, let me know," she tossed over her shoulder. "If not, that's fine, too."

o0o

The nerve of the man. Claire ducked through the fence and strode across the field, not daring to look back. He thought—he seemed to think—never mind. The whole idea was preposterous. A guy that got a kick out of wandering around lava and fire was not a guy she wanted to know. She shuddered. Anything but fire.

It didn't stop her hands from wanting to touch the light stubble on his cheeks and trace his dimple. It didn't stop her body from trembling in his presence. And it didn't stop her mouth from yearning to be kissed by Noel Kenzie.

Problem was, he'd be willing to do it. Love 'em and leave 'em was probably his motto. She certainly wasn't going anywhere with him. Even if he asked, which of course he hadn't, and now he wouldn't.

A teensy part of her died inside. Had she been too hasty? Too blunt? No.

"For my thoughts are not your thoughts, neither are your ways my ways, declares the Lord. As the heavens are higher than the earth, so are my ways higher than yours."

Yeah, well, Claire's thoughts had been given by God. He didn't change His mind. What was the verse? "Jesus Christ is the same yesterday, today, and forever." That was more like it. Besides, didn't the New Testament trump the old every single time?

"Where's Noel?"

Claire blinked and saw Jo, practically in the middle of her path. She'd nearly run her best friend over. "Back there somewhere." She waved a hand without turning.

Seemed Jo hid a smirk.

Claire scowled. "Why? What's the matter?"

Jo's chin jutted toward the rail fence. "You must've had a fight or something."

She couldn't help but look. Noel was only about ten paces

back, his camera raised. She heard the click. "I'm going to kill him."

"Why, did you forget to smile?"

Claire turned her back on Noel again. "You are *so* not funny."

"Actually, I think it's hilarious."

No comment, because if she made one, Noel was now close enough to overhear.

"Good evening, Noel. You finding lots of material for photos?"

Claire closed her eyes and took a deep breath. Why, God? Why did Jo have to meddle? Claire didn't do that to Jo last year. Well, maybe a couple of times, but not like this.

Click.

Taking pictures of her back? Or of what? Claire huffed out her breath and turned.

Click.

She could hate a guy like this. Seriously. She stared Noel down until he lowered the camera slightly. What was going on inside his head? He was practically stalking her.

"Uh oh," breathed Jo.

Claire grasped her friend's arm and propelled her away from Noel. "That's enough out of you," she whispered fiercely.

"Me? Or him?"

That didn't even deserve an answer. "Both of you."

"Claire?" Noel called.

She bit her lip hard and turned around. There better be no shutter action or someone would pay. "What?"

He glanced at Jo then back to her. "Can we talk for a minute?"

Isn't that what they had been doing before he'd become a total jerk?

"Hey, I can take a hint." Jo patted Claire's arm and leaned closer. "Fill me in later." She waved at Noel and disappeared up the path to the log cabin.

How did Claire get stuck talking to him again? She planted her hands on her hips. "What?"

"Look, I'm sorry. I wasn't trying to offend you."

Normally it was a lot harder to upset her. Noel seemed to have a special knack for it. "I'm not sure what you want me to say." She wasn't changing for him, that's for sure. And he had his own way of living. At his age—must be close to thirty—she couldn't expect him to be the one to give up everything. Why didn't he just graciously bow out of her life and let her carry on?

Oh, right. She'd invited him over.

He moved so close she could smell tree sap on his clothes. The honest scent of a hardworking man. He reached out and touched her cheek.

Claire shifted enough to break contact.

It didn't make any difference, as his hand followed her. "Can we call a truce?"

A delightful shiver ran the length of her body. A truce had nothing to do with him touching her in this sensuous way. He was bad news. "A-a truce?"

"I'll try not to make you angry, and you'll try not to stalk away from me." Somehow both his hands now cradled her face.

She jerked back. "Touching me is not how to keep me from getting mad."

Noel's hands slid to his side. "I'm sorry."

"Stop saying that!"

"You're just so…beautiful."

He was only using those words to fluster her.

"I mean it. Do you want to see how you look to me?"

To him? "I-I don't understand." Did she want to?

Noel tilted the camera screen toward her and pressed a couple of buttons. He scrolled through over a dozen images of her, some where she'd been aware of him and others where she hadn't. Smiles, scowls, reflections. He'd captured the entire gamut of her emotions during their walk.

He'd looked straight into her soul and captured a piece of it. Her soul, not her heart. That she guarded, at least she always had before. Still, looking at these photos, the way Noel saw her, she felt exposed. He'd seen far more than she'd intended. "I think you should delete those."

Noel pulled the camera back, a shocked expression on his face. "Not a chance."

"I asked you for photos of the farm for the website, not an album of Claire Halford."

"Some of these would be awesome for your site."

Yeah, right. Good thing he didn't have the passwords to upload them himself. He'd do it, too.

"When do you need the images by? You'll want some from other seasons, too, won't you?"

She bit her tongue. How many more seasons would he be here for? The tree-planting contract had been for three months, with one gone. "Just email me the best ones as you have them, in the highest resolution possible. If you can take them over a longer period of time, that would be great." But she wouldn't count on him.

Not for photos, not for anything.

Noel's eyes gleamed. "I'll need your email address."

How had her tongue slipped up and given him that opening? She recited it for him and he closed his eyes for a second, his lips moving as he repeated it. "Got it."

He'd probably be calling to ask her to give it to him again when he had somewhere to write it down.

"So I have your permission to wander your farm whenever I like and snap photos?"

Claire hesitated, but that basically was what she'd asked him to do. She couldn't very well take it back now. "Sure. That would be great."

He pointed at the tree beside her. "Why don't you stand closer to that willow?"

"Why?"

"So my photo will be framed better." He grinned. "You did say I could take them whenever I wanted."

Chapter 11 --

A tap sounded on Noel's trailer door. "Who is it?"

"Me, Jess."

He couldn't very well turn her away, even though he didn't feel like talking to anyone. "Come on in." He dragged himself off his bed and plodded the few steps to the dinette.

Jess opened the door and peered around it. "You okay, boss?"

Noel sank into the upholstered seat and ran his palm over his unshaved face. "If that's all you want to ask about, I'll see you in the morning."

"Not a chance." She came in, shut the door, and slouched into the seat opposite him. "Talk to me."

It wasn't right that Jess should see him like this. Mind you, she'd seen worse, but never over a woman.

"You been drinking? You said you'd quit."

"No." He met her gaze. "I did quit. You know that."

Jess cocked her head. "Then what?"

"It's personal."

She barked a short laugh and slid out of the dinette. That girl could never sit still for ten seconds in a row. She went over to his sink and poured herself a glass of water then leaned against the counter, glancing around the untidy space.

Noel crossed his arms and leaned back, glowering at her. She was doubtless looking for empties. "I'll be fine, Jess. Thanks for caring. Now leave."

Jess straightened, her gaze fixed on his bed area across from her. She set the glass behind her without looking. Nearly missed the counter.

What was she staring at so intently, anyway? His bed was made, if somewhat a muddle because he'd been lying on top of the quilt. He'd been—

Noel surged to his feet as Jess took two steps forward and reached into the alcove. "Those are mine."

A stack of printed photos rested secure in Jess's grasp. She turned her back to Noel and riffled through them.

"Jess!"

She turned to face him, eyes sparkling. "You have got it bad, boss." Jess pushed past him and parked on the dinette seat, where she dealt out the images like playing cards. "Ooh, Dreamboat looks good there." She set a photo in the center of the table in a pile of its own. A photo of Claire leaning back against the rail fence, gazing into the distance.

The near distance, of course. Anything farther than the barbed wire fence a half-mile from the road was too far out to be on her radar.

Not that he was bitter. He snagged the photos from the table and pushed them back into a pile, letting the one Jess had singled out land somewhere in the middle.

It was his favorite, too. Jess had a good eye, but he'd never tell her so.

She scooted further into the dinette and leaned against the wall, tucking her knees up under her chin. "Do tell Mama Jess everything."

"There's nothing to tell." He slid the photos into their envelope and tossed it back on his bed.

"Nice try, boss. You have, what? Twenty or thirty pics of one pretty girl? And you're grouchy like a bear in springtime. Sounds to me like you need a listening ear."

Noel sighed. "She's a girl super-glued to this valley, to her farm." He spread his hands. "And look at me, a vagabond of the highest order. Does that sound compatible to you?"

Jess tilted her head, considering. "No."

His heart sank. Had he really expected a different answer from his foreman?

"You're right, boss. It's a bad idea. You live to travel and have adventures. You'd hate being tied to one place."

And Claire would detest his life, experiencing new places, new cultures, new languages. New thrills. But could anything be more thrilling than holding her in his arms every day for the rest of his life?

Whoa, Kenzie. Was his hindbrain considering permanence? He shuddered and straightened. "Thanks for coming in, Jess. I'm over it."

She cocked her head, lifting her eyebrows. "That simple?"

"Oh, yeah."

"So. Why don't I believe you?"

How could he prove it to her? "Here." He reached into the alcove and grabbed the photos. "You take them. Toss them in tonight's campfire, if you want." He slapped the packet into her hand.

"Whoa, boss. You haven't deleted them off your SD card, have you?"

He should probably do that, too. But no. Claire had asked him for photos for the website and if he didn't come through, she'd know she'd gotten to him. Well, she already knew, because he'd told her. But not following through on his promise would be juvenile and tacky. Besides, he'd have to see her a few more times because of Amber's wedding.

"I have them on my laptop still. But I promise I won't sit and stare at them. They're only on there until I get a package ready to sell Green Acres for their website. Then they're gone."

"Right. So you don't care about these photos of Dreamboat."

He shook his head so hard his hair slid over one eye. "Not a bit."

"So I can give one out to everyone in camp." Jess held up the envelope. "There's enough to go around."

Noel's insides froze solid. "What?"

She tapped it against her open palm. "Can't have it both ways, boss. Either you care or you don't."

o0o

A week had gone by and Noel hadn't emailed her any photos. Well, fine. Claire would take some herself with the point-and-shoot she'd bought during culinary school. It wasn't as fancy a camera as Noel's—it didn't have a foot-long lens—but it was hers.

Once the garden was planted she'd do just that, in fact. Forget Noel. She didn't need him.

Amber and Shawn would be out for Memorial Day next week. Come to think of it, Claire hadn't seen any pictures of Shawn yet. What did he look like? Tall, dark, and handsome? No, that described Noel, but she was getting him out of her head. Opposite—short, blond, and ugly. Well, no. She couldn't wish that on Amber, either.

It didn't matter. Shawn had met a rather lengthy checklist and conquered it. He was a hero, practically a Greek god.

Not a jerk like his soon-to-be brother-in-law.

A silver Mazda pulled into the driveway. Amber? Already?

Claire met Amber at the door. The younger woman's face

was puffy and her eyes red from crying. If she'd been sniffling like this all the way from Missoula, she must've gone through an entire box of tissues and been a menace on the roads.

Amber threw herself into Claire's arms. "It's off. The wedding's off."

"Oh, no. What happened? Are you okay?" Claire patted Amber awkwardly on the back. By the look on Amber's face, Shawn must've been caught with another woman. Or he'd turned out to be a wanted criminal in another state and the police caught him. What horrendous acts could he have committed? Serial killer, maybe?

"He stood me up for our date last night. I waited and waited for him."

Claire's eyebrows pulled together. "He must have had a reason. Did you call?"

Amber blew noisily into a tissue. "Eventually."

"And...?"

"His brother was there, and they were watching a baseball game. Can you imagine?"

"Um..."

"If I'm no more important to him than a stupid sports event—on TV no less—then he's just mean."

Claire racked her brain trying to think of something to say. "Does his brother come over often?"

"No. They're not even close."

"Well, then..."

"His brother lives in Butte."

"Let me get this straight. Shawn's brother from out of town came to visit him and they watched a ball game on TV?"

A new surge of tears. "Yes."

"And you're upset enough to drive for five hours to cancel your wedding in person? Without talking to Shawn about it?"

Amber hiccupped. "I talked to him."

"Oh?"

"I said if that's only how important I was to him, then fine."

A cell phone jangled. Amber put her hand on her purse then pulled it away. "It's probably Shawn. He keeps calling."

"Then answer it."

"N-no."

The phone quit after three rings. Amber heaved a big sigh.

"When you told him, what did he say to you?"

Amber's lower lip trembled. "He said I was being petty and immature."

Claire liked Shawn more by the minute. "And then?"

"And then I hung up and got in my car. I wanted to see Noel but he's not at the trailer."

"He's up the mountain." Claire had seen his truck go by a couple of hours ago herself. Completely by accident, of course. She'd simply happened to notice.

"Maybe Shawn would listen to Noel."

"A few weeks ago you thought Shawn was the most awesome guy on the planet. He could do no wrong." Unless one counted daisies instead of roses for a dating anniversary.

"I know him better now."

And Claire bet Shawn knew Amber a whole lot better, too. "Look, do you have that list on you? The one you showed me of how perfect he was?"

Amber rolled her eyes, flipped open her purse, and pulled out the dog-eared page. She thrust it at Claire. "Here. You can have it."

"Come on in." Claire stepped aside and crossed to the love seat. How did she get to be a marriage counselor, anyway? It wasn't simply to save the fee. She just couldn't ditch Noel's sister, though it would minimize contact with him. That would be good. Right?

Behind her, Amber kicked off her shoes and closed the

door. She slumped into the facing love seat.

Claire smoothed the sheet out on her lap and read the first item. "Tell me, Amber. Does Shawn still love God with all his heart?"

Amber glared at her. "Probably."

"Sense of humor?"

"Not so much."

"How about yours, girl?"

Amber narrowed her eyes. "What do you mean?"

"I mean—is there any way to look at this with more humor?" The girl couldn't possibly look at it with less.

Amber shrugged, though it must've been hard with her arms crossed so tightly.

Alrighty then. "Does he still have a job? Still love kids? Still respect his mother?"

Amber jerked up and stalked to the window. "What are you getting at here?"

"I'm saying that Shawn is the same guy you adored last week. The very same exact guy."

"I don't think so."

Claire passed the list to Amber. "Read it. Tell me what has changed." She put up a cautionary hand. "What's really changed, and not just because you're angry."

Amber's lower jaw worked as she scanned the page. Her hand trembled, and a lone tear dribbled down her cheek. She shot a daggered look at Claire then turned the paper over and read the other side.

Surely the stabs meant she heard Claire's meaning.

Amber flung the page from her and flopped back into the loveseat, eyes shut and arms spread dramatically.

Claire waited.

When Amber spoke, it was with a small voice. "So you're saying Shawn's right? I've turned into Bridezilla?"

"I never said any such thing." But she'd thought it.

"I'm making a mountain out of a mole hill."

"Are you?"

Amber leaned forward with her elbows on her knees and rubbed her temples. She heaved a big sigh. "It seems so."

"What are you going to do about it?"

Amber peered at Claire through her long lashes. "Call Shawn?"

"That sounds like a good idea. I'll go in the kitchen and put the kettle on while you do that. Give you two some privacy. Then, if you want, we can talk some more before you head back."

"I took the rest of the week off work. We were coming up this weekend anyway." Amber's eyes pleaded with Claire. "Is my room available?"

Claire nodded and patted Amber's shoulder, then headed for the kitchen to the tune of little beeps coming from Amber's phone.

o0o

Noel rubbed his sore shoulder as he pulled off the forest road up the mountain from Green Acres. Thankfully it had been sunny enough today that his solar shower bag should be heated. He could sure use a few minutes of soothing water without waiting for the generator to heat the tank.

Noel glanced at the farm as he passed, just as his cell phone came back in service. It beeped a message, but the silver car parked by the deck grabbed his attention. Amber's.

Had he lost a day? He would've sworn it was Thursday, and she wasn't coming until Friday, late.

By this time he'd passed Nemeseks' driveway and almost reached Elmer's. Noel parked beside his trailer and checked the messages on his phone.

A text from Amber: call me. Time stamped early this morning. Two more messages and several missed calls. She'd continued trying to reach him.

He leaned his head on the steering wheel. He absolutely did not want to get caught up in any drama, either Amber's or Claire's. And they were together.

He desperately craved a quiet evening. Maybe he could pretend he hadn't gotten the messages.

Nice try, Kenzie. They'd probably watched his truck go by two minutes before. No getting out of this, but he could have his shower first and get on some clean clothes. At least he wouldn't be at a disadvantage. As much of one.

Noel swung out of the cab and paused, sniffing the air. Something smelled burned. Polly hustled around under the tarped eating area while the vans carrying Enterprising Reforestation's crews pulled in and parked haphazardly around the area, his workers piling out.

No. He couldn't face the mutiny of hungry, frustrated workers. He had to deal with Polly, even before his shower. Before anyone else took it upon him-or-herself to do so.

He wiped the dust-encrusted sweat off his forehead with his denim sleeve as his cell phone jingled. He should leave the thing to ring. But Amber had seen him go by and would keep calling. Better get her over with.

He slid the phone on. "Noel here."

"Noel, it's Amber."

"Yeah, what's up? Make it quick, okay? Having some problems here I need to deal with."

Silence for a few seconds. That had come out wrong. Mean. Noel's heart sank.

"I'm sorry if I'm bothering you." Her voice had gone all stony. "I thought I mattered to you."

Noel sighed. "You do matter, but the chef is burning the

food, I wrenched my shoulder, and I need a shower. Can this wait ten minutes?"

"Fine. Whatever. Call me when you get a chance, if you ever do." She hung up.

He'd handled that perfectly once again.

Noel eyed Polly across the yard. What was she making anyway? What else could go wrong today?

Chapter 12 --

"Men!" Amber flung her cell at the love seat. It bounced, flew off onto the etched concrete floor, and skittered away in several pieces. She stared for a few seconds then burst into tears.

Claire leaned against the kitchen doorway, closed her eyes, and breathed a prayer. Where were her friends, anyway? Why did she have to deal with this emotionally wrecked bride-to-be?

She knew the answer. Jo wasn't technically Claire's roommate anymore, but she and Zach would be coming for supper, anyway. Jo worked as nutritionist at the old folks' home several days a week while Zach worked as a veterinarian. Sierra was in town setting up her naturopathic practice above the health food store.

No one would be home for another hour at least. And when they came, they'd expect food on the table. Good thing she'd put beef strips in marinade this morning. Chuck steaks needed all the help they could get.

"Come help me cook, Amber." Claire eyed the younger woman huddling on the love seat bawling her eyes out. "Go wash your face and blow your nose and give me a hand."

Hiccupping and nodding and sobbing all at the same time, Amber rushed down the hallway to the bathroom.

Claire set the Bosch to mixing dough for sundried tomato

and basil tortillas. If asparagus fajitas didn't fix things, she didn't know what would. Everyone would be in a better mood with good solid food inside them. Her included.

She selected a knife from the magnetic strip over the built-in butcher block and whacked the stem end off an onion. The blade needed sharpening. Again. If she'd stayed in Seattle she'd have replaced the whole set by now, worn as they were by decades of honing. They'd been Michel's knives when he started out, decent ones, but not the quality he'd aspired to. She could see why.

Amber reappeared with a freshly scrubbed face. "What do you want me to do?"

Claire set the onion and the blade on the chopping block. "Start with this. Careful, it's sharp."

"The whole thing?" Amber's eyes grew large.

Claire scrutinized the onion. "Think we need two?"

"No."

She shrugged. "Well, then. Slice it up thin." She'd have to keep an eye in case Amber had no clue what to do, which seemed likely.

Amber managed to get the peel off then sliced the onion in half.

The girl should do all right from there. Claire pulled a bag of asparagus from the fridge's produce drawer and began breaking off woody ends.

Amber glanced over. "What are we making?"

"Asparagus fajitas."

"Aspara-what? I've never heard of such a thing."

"My own invention. I believe the Texans would approve." She'd never know, being as she'd never go ask them.

Amber's knife clipped the chopping block with increasing speed. "Why are men such morons?"

Good question. "What's your dad like?"

Chopping noises stopped from behind her. "I've never met him. He left my mother before I was born, and has rarely been heard from since. Not for years now."

Claire turned to look at Amber. "Oh, no!"

"She said he had mental problems." Amber wiped tears from her eyes. "I hope I didn't inherit them."

The tears were from the onion. Right? "I'm sure you didn't." But it explained a lot about Noel. He was what, six years older than his sister? He probably remembered his father leaving the family. How traumatic for a small child.

Amber scraped the multi-sized onion chunks to the edge of the butcher block.

Hadn't Claire asked for thin slices? Would she be able to give those a few more chops without Amber noticing? Probably not today.

"Yeah, so I never knew my dad." Amber stared out the window. "Most girls dream of having their dad walk them down the aisle. I don't even know where mine is."

"I'm sorry." Claire reached into the fridge for two yellow peppers. "So you didn't really have any men in your life, growing up? Your mom never remarried?"

"She dated a few times when I was a teen, but she never really found anyone she clicked with. How about your parents?"

Surprising how easy Amber was to talk to, after all. "They split up when I was in high school. My mom got tired of being dragged all over the lower forty-eight when my dad thought he'd found the job that would make him wealthy beyond his wildest dreams." Wasn't just Mom who'd gotten tired of it.

"So your family is messed up, too."

"Oh yeah." But enough on that topic. "By the way, did you get through to Shawn?"

Amber nodded soberly.

"Is he still coming tomorrow?"

116

"Unless there's a baseball game."

Claire pivoted. "He said that?" Sounded like Amber was better off without Mr. Perfect after all. So much for checklists.

"No." Amber laughed, but it didn't sound like she meant it. "He said he's coming. Said he'd tried to call me last night but couldn't leave a message."

"If he has to cancel for any reason now, he won't be able to get through, either. Not with your phone broken."

A flush bloomed on Amber's cheeks. "Yeah. I guess I have a temper."

No kidding. "You can call him from mine and let him know, so he won't worry."

"May I?" Amber's face looked wistful.

Claire crossed the room and gave her a quick side hug. "It's right there on the counter."

Amber picked it up and punched in some numbers then explained to Shawn her phone was wrecked. She even managed to say it without a bunch of drama.

Maybe the girl could be taught.

"I should probably call my brother, too. I was—was kinda mad at him."

Understatement.

Amber took a deep breath. "I should probably apologize to him."

Claire hadn't listened to the conversation from this end, but she could imagine. "Go for it." She could finish making supper faster on her own. And maybe take a quick blade to that onion.

oOo

"The crew's complaining about the food, boss." Jess dropped onto the bench across the picnic table from Noel. "Have you noticed the lunch sandwiches have been kind of dry?

She must be rationing the mayo. And then the burned chili tonight, along with undercooked cornbread." She shook her head. "It's bad."

"I've spoken to Polly."

"You talked to her last week, too, but is she listening?"

"I told her she had a generous budget and I didn't see she was using it to potential. She needs to hire an assistant. Someone who knows what they're doing, unlike her kid."

"She's making a ton of money off us and feeding the crew dog food. They're not going to stand for it much longer. Wish Simon were here."

Noel spread his hands on the table. "It's not like I have options. Simon's not ready to come back just yet."

Jess's eyes lit up. "You called him?"

Simon had been the crew's chef for several years, but he'd begged this contract off to spend time with his cancer-ridden father. "Yeah, I called him. His dad passed away last week." Noel hadn't heard from his own dad in a few months. Dare he hope the man was still in Philly standing on his own two feet?

"Oh. I'm so sorry."

"Simon has to deal with the estate. He'll rejoin us in Montana."

"About options." Jess leaned forward. "You don't need a whole bunch of them. Only one." A little grin twitched at the corners of her mouth. "And I have thirty-two pictures of her in my camper."

"No." He met her gaze square on. "Don't mix my private life with my business."

"Your business, as you so eloquently put it, is suffering. Your private life, of which you told me last night you have none, holds the solution." Jess waved a hand to take in the silent, sullen crewmembers around the other tables. "You're going to cause these guys to mutiny."

He raised an eyebrow. "Mutiny?"

"Yeah. Half a dozen are eating in town tonight, grumbling because they don't have a choice. Essentially they're paying double, because you're already deducting Polly's meals off their pay. They're mad."

Noel took a closer look at his workers. He'd thought some had just finished eating before he came in. A quick glance around the parking area revealed some of the vehicles missing. He sagged. "Oh."

Jess nodded. "Exactly, boss. You've got a choice, and not too much time to make it." She climbed off the bench. "As for me? As foreman, I make a bit more than most of them. I bought groceries in town and I'm going to go cook myself some dinner in the camper right now." She narrowed her gaze as she stopped beside him. "And I'll admire some photos of a real chef, not some two-bit wannabe, while I do it."

He ought to protest, but what good would it do? Maybe he had another option. He could call that other guy from Wynnton back and see if he was still available to do the work, though he hadn't seemed all that qualified. Noel would need someone to step in ASAP though. Once he fired Polly, he'd better have somebody already on the property with groceries bought.

Noel watched one of his veteran workers scrape half a plate's worth of chili into the garbage can just as his cell phone rang. He glanced at the call display.

Claire.

Was she a Godsend or what?

He could pour some enthusiasm into his voice. He was going to need her. "Hi, Claire."

"What? Oh, it's Amber. I'm just using Claire's phone cause mine broke."

Noel tugged at his t-shirt neck. Seemed kind of hot under the tarp for a moment. What had his voice sounded like to his sister? Hopefully not too needy.

"About that. I'm sorry I yelled at you, Noel. That wasn't fair of me. I'm, well, kind of stressed out right now."

"Uh, it's okay." He couldn't remember Amber apologizing to him before, but that wasn't a huge thing. They'd have had to have real conversations to argue.

"But I really am sorry. I'm trying to be a better Christian and that should mean not blowing my temper all the time."

Noel shifted uncomfortably.

"Can you come over? I need some advice from a guy, and you're the only one in my life."

"What about Shawn?"

She hesitated. "It's about him. Please, Noel. I need a big brother."

"Why don't you come over here? We can talk in my trailer." Away from Claire until he could sort through the issues.

Most of the crew had left the eating area, and none of them looked content. Noel didn't have a lot of time to make a plan.

"I can't. Shawn's supposed to call me back on Claire's phone. Because mine broke."

He was a chicken. He did not want to face Claire. But did he really want to mess with both those women? He sighed. "Fine. I'll be over in half an hour."

Still needed that shower.

oOo

"Amber! Didn't expect to see you here." Jo gave the younger woman a hug. "I thought you were coming on Friday with Shawn."

Amber returned it with enthusiasm. "Something came up and I needed advice." She glanced at Claire. "Shawn's coming later. It's all good."

Claire set a platter of tortillas on the table next to the beef and asparagus mix. "Food's up. Where's Zach?"

"He had to work late." Jo pulled out a chair.

They all gathered around the table and prayed a blessing over the meal.

"Thanks so much, you guys," Amber gushed. "Being here is like having a bunch of big sisters."

Claire had always wished at least one of her younger brothers had been a girl. She could have used some girl-talk growing up. Guess it had been the same for Amber.

Jo laughed. "Zach says it's possible to have too many big sisters. At least when you're a guy." She set a tortilla onto her plate and reached for the asparagus.

Sierra passed the tortillas to Amber. "How was the drive?"

At least the evidence of Amber's major crying jag had dissipated, though the question seemed to catch her off guard. "Okay, I guess."

Best not to talk about Amber's early arrival. "How's it going, setting up your office?"

Sierra brightened. "It looks good, but I'm not sure it's the best location. I'm thankful to Doreen, of course. She's giving me a great deal on the space, but it will be a while until I don't think of Bethany every time I go up those back stairs. It weirds me out to think how she died like that."

"Doreen must be very sure Gabe won't ever want the apartment back."

"He signed on for a two-year stint at the orphanage in Romania." Sierra shook her head. "I wish he'd remember how much Doreen is hurting, too. Bethany may have been Gabe's wife, but she was also Doreen's only child."

"Grief isn't good at thinking of other people's needs or interests." Claire hadn't known the young couple as well as Jo and Sierra had, but the tragedy had rocked the small community to its core last summer. Worse yet, it had been Sierra's trucker dad that mowed Bethany's small car over. Tim Riehl had recovered from his injuries quickly, but Bethany was gone.

"Losing Bethany was hard for everyone," Jo said. "Zach and Gabe were best friends all their lives, so he knew her well, too."

"I don't know. I can't help but think Gabe won't be able to move on until he comes back here and faces things." Sierra added a sprinkle of shredded cheddar to her fajita and folded it up. "It's not my call to make. It's his life, but I wish he'd have more compassion on Doreen."

Claire nodded. "I bet she enjoys having you around."

"So she says."

The women chattered over dinner, with Amber finally relaxing some. As they finished up, a rumble grew out in the yard.

Claire glanced out the window as Noel's truck came to a halt by the deck. "Your brother's here, Amber." With any luck Claire could vanish into her room for the next hour or two.

"We've got clean-up." Jo pushed away from the table. "Right, Sierra?"

"Yep."

Amber snagged another tortilla from the platter as she stood. "Can we have these at my wedding, Claire? They're so good they don't even need a filling."

At least the wedding was still on. Or on *again*, depending how she looked at it. Claire prepared to beat a hasty retreat.

There was a rap at the door.

Amber stopped, her wide eyes focused on Claire.

"Go on. It's Noel."

"You come, too."

Claire shook her head. "He's your brother. You wanted to talk to him. He's all yours."

"But—"

Another knock, this one louder.

"Come on in," shouted Sierra, her hands full of plates.

The door swung open and there stood Noel, his dark hair still wet from a shower. A white t-shirt over worn blue jeans did little to camouflage his muscular torso.

Claire had a hard time pulling her gaze away, and it seemed he had the same problem.

Amber grabbed Claire's arm and propelled her to the door. "Let's sit on the porch swing."

Noel stepped back as the girls passed through the opening. His fresh soap scent filled Claire's nostrils.

This was crazy. What was she doing here? She didn't belong in their sibling discussion. She pulled her arm out of Amber's clutches. "No, I'll just be inside." She whirled around and collided with Noel's chest.

Both his hands came up and steadied her. Time held still though Claire managed not to look at him.

"Excuse me, please," she whispered.

"Come, have a seat," he said softly. "I think Amber wants you here. I promise I won't bite."

Chapter 13 --

Swing or Adirondack chair? If she sat on the swing Noel would probably join her. She sank into one of the deep chairs. Of course now he'd sit across from her and watch her. No winning this one.

She was right. Noel's gaze fixed on her, while Amber chose the swing.

He glanced at his sister. "What's up? Why did you come early?"

Amber poked her toe against the deck boards and started the swing moving. It seemed to take all her concentration for a moment. "I had a fight with Shawn."

He didn't look all that interested in her problems. "Oh?"

"His brother came up from Butte and they watched baseball on TV..."

A grin tweaked at the corners of Noel's mouth and he caught Claire watching him. His dimple deepened as he winked, and Claire felt heat rising on her neck. Ridiculous. She couldn't focus on Amber any more than he could.

"That doesn't sound so dreadful," Noel said at last.

"He stood me up. He didn't call."

Noel leaned his elbows onto his knees. "You should definitely ditch him for that. What a barbarian."

Claire barely kept her jaw from dropping at his sarcastic tone. She pressed her lips tight together.

Noel looked from one to the other. "Seriously? He didn't go on a bender or something like that? He sat home with his brother watching a ball game and you're mad enough to drive five hours to get away from him? And for this you need an intervention and a shoulder to cry on?"

Amber stopped the swing from moving with a firmly planted foot. "You're my brother! You're supposed to be on my side."

"I would be, if your side wasn't so dumb."

Uh oh.

Noel looked at Claire. "What? Don't tell me you think she gave a reasonable response?"

Claire's jaw clenched as she shot to her feet. "I didn't ask to be part of this conversation."

Amber jumped up and grabbed Claire's arm. "Please stay."

Claire shrugged her off. "I've already told you what I think. You've called Shawn and started talking to him again. I'm not needed here." Talking to Amber was one thing. Adding her ignorant brother was another.

"Wait." Noel sounded perplexed. "What do you want me for, Amber? I thought it was to tell you if you were over-thinking this. To which my answer is yes."

The tears Amber barely held back burst out again.

Claire took a deep breath and patted Amber's shoulder. "I don't think that's what she wanted of you."

"Then what?" He spread his hands.

He was a guy. Graham had never understood a thing she'd said to him, either. Good reason—as though she needed another one—to stay clear of Noel. "Amber needs a listening ear. Someone she believes has her best interests at heart."

"Of course I do."

Amber sobbed harder. Good grief. She'd abandoned Claire to do it all for her.

"That's not what your words sounded like to her." Or to Claire, either, for that matter. Wasn't she the dispassionate one here? The one with the least invested?

Certainly the least invested in Shawn, but it seemed a struggle to keep the same viewpoint on Noel.

Noel patted Amber awkwardly on the back. "I'm sorry, sis. Really. I think next time I need a set of cue cards."

"Cue cards?" Claire couldn't keep the disbelief out of her voice.

The conflicting emotions running across Noel's face would have been hilarious if Claire felt like laughing.

"I said that wrong, too, huh?" He released his sister and cast Claire a helpless glance. "Look. I'm trying here, honest I am. I don't know what I'm supposed to say to make things better."

Considering her own feelings a few hours earlier, Claire should've been able to sympathize. But his typical guy response made her want to throw things at him. A man that needed this much tutoring in how to speak with women wasn't ready for a serious relationship no matter what.

She rubbed her temple in an attempt to keep an encroaching headache at bay. "You're supposed to murmur sympathetic noises until you get a clear understanding of what she wants from you. Definitely no sarcasm to a crying woman, and no smart remarks until you know she's ready to handle it. No cajoling her out of a bad mood."

Amber slumped into the seat next to Claire and scowled.

Okay, maybe Claire shouldn't have put it that way, but she could tell Noel was considering and discarding a bunch of responses by his evolving facial expressions.

He finally settled on, "That doesn't make sense." His gaze shifted back and forth between her and Amber.

Claire raised her eyebrows. "It does to a woman, and that's

what we're talking about here."

"Not every woman." He paused, obviously thinking his contact list through. "Not Jess, for instance."

Claire crossed her arms and raised her chin. "That's nice." She'd forgotten about the other woman in Noel's life.

He was smarter than she'd given him credit for. "It's not like that, Claire."

"Isn't like what?"

"Jess is my friend and my foreman. She's never been my girlfriend and never will be."

Nice try. "How many romances do you think have started between people who were 'just friends'?"

Noel closed his eyes and let out an exasperated sigh.

"Is Jess gay?" Amber asked between gritted teeth. "That's about the only way to be sure."

"No."

"Well, then…"

"This is the stupidest conversation I've ever been part of in my life." Noel stalked to the deck steps. "First you ask my advice, then get mad when I give it. Then somehow I'm a dolt, and now you're dragging Jess into it. I'm out of here." He jumped off and strode the few steps to his truck.

If there'd been any doubt before it would never work with Noel, Claire knew it now. He was as much a jerk as any other guy she'd met, including Graham, who hadn't thought it important to consult his fiancée about where they'd live.

As Noel yanked open the door to his truck, he paused for an instant and his gaze met Claire's. He opened his mouth to speak then shook his head and clambered in. The truck roared to life and jolted down the driveway.

So much for that.

oOo

Jess materialized out of the shadows when Noel parked beside his trailer. He glared at her for a moment as his gut twisted even more. The impulse to turn the ignition back on and drive to... Baja California...anywhere...nearly overcame him. Preferably somewhere without women—chefs, sisters, or foremen.

He sighed and opened his truck door. "Hey, Jess."

"Hey, yourself, boss. What did she say?'"

Noel stared at her blankly.

"You did go over and talk to Claire about hiring on, didn't you? There's nothing else up the road besides the tree-planting site."

"Uh." He had to get a hold of himself. "Actually my sister called me from Green Acres to talk about her own stuff. The issue of cooking for Enterprising Reforestation never came up."

Jess's hands shot to her slender hips. "Dude! Where are your priorities? Look at the disaster Polly left behind tonight." Her fingers jabbed in the direction of the mess tent.

Aptly named. Even in the dim evening light, it looked a sight. The tables and benches weren't aligned, and objects lay in disarray on the serving table.

But still. "Claire isn't an option. We need another idea."

She scowled. "You said it hadn't come up. She applied for the job. She's qualified. You haven't even talked to her about it since. How can you say she isn't an option?"

"She just isn't. Drop it, Jess."

"Not a chance, boss. Not until or unless you come up with a better idea. Like by this time tomorrow at the very latest. Some planters threatened to quit today. I talked them into staying the week because I thought you—" her finger stabbed him in the chest "—were actively seeking a solution."

Noel took a deep breath while his mind scrambled through—and discarded—a dozen options, all of them named Claire. "I'll talk to you tomorrow. I need some time to think, and I'm desperate for some shut eye."

"Just so you know I'll take matters into my own hands pretty quick. I'm not willing to watch our loyal crew walk away."

He closed his eyes for a second. "Me neither. I'll deal with it tomorrow. I promise."

Jess's posture relaxed slightly in the moonlight. "Okay, boss. You cover it."

oOo

Noel practiced his speech the whole way down the mountain the next afternoon. He could call Claire, but it would be better coming in person. Besides, how could he know Amber wouldn't answer, since she borrowed Claire's cell?

He didn't want to get into another discussion about Shawn with Amber. Man, he'd tried to defend the guy a little and both women practically bit off his head.

Only Amber's car sat in front of the straw bale farmhouse, but that didn't mean anything. Those girls swapped out their one car like public property.

Noel turned into the driveway and parked. He sat for a second. He'd even done a bit of praying about the dilemma. Maybe he'd get brownie points for that, or whatever kind of point system God used. Everything was kind of surreal. Begging Claire for a favor after she'd made sure he knew where he stood with her.

That is to say, nowhere.

Well, then, seeing each other at breakfast and dinner every day shouldn't be an additional problem. He needed a chef. He climbed out of the truck and made his way to the deck. Still no sign of life anywhere on the farm.

He rapped on the door. No answer. He knocked louder. A

few minutes went by before he heard the scuffing of feet on the floor. He took a half step back.

Amber opened the heavy carved door and stared at him, blinking. "Hey, what are you doing here?"

He'd better say the right thing this time. "Two things. I've come to apologize to you for being an insensitive jerk."

Her face softened slightly. "I don't know why I expected anything different from you."

Noel's jaw dropped before he could quite control it. "Pardon?"

Amber shrugged. "You're a guy. You can't be expected to understand how women think."

"Is that some kind of counseling by Claire?" Because if it was—no, he didn't have the luxury of stomping away one more time.

"Just reality."

That caught him off guard. "Uh, well, I am sorry."

She nodded. "Accepted. What's the second thing?"

"I need to talk to Claire. Is she around?"

"She's at work."

Noel stared at his sister.

"The Sizzling Skillet? I thought you knew she worked weekend evenings."

"Right. I did know." How could he have forgotten? Of course, she had a job. He'd even eaten there a couple of times. Yeah, she'd applied to cook for the crew two months ago, so she obviously didn't love her position. That didn't mean she'd be willing to ditch it for a six-week gig.

A sly smile played around Amber's mouth. "Something wrong, big brother?"

He sighed. "The woman I hired for Enterprising Reforestation is a lousy cook and my crew is in revolt."

"So it isn't just that you want to see Claire again? Cause

methinks you're somewhat smitten."

Noel narrowed his eyes, but his sister grinned and waggled her eyebrows at him as though she was the brightest star in the night sky.

"I think she's very attractive, yes." He'd have a hard time denying that, anyway. Amber had seen him tongue-tied around Claire. "But that's not what I'm here about."

"When are you going to settle down, Noel? This would be an awesome place for you. So much wild land and far from the city lights."

"I like my life, thank-you-very-much." If only he could convince himself.

"You couldn't do better than Claire. I think you really care about her—as much as a guy knows how to care about a girl."

Noel shifted from one foot to the other. "Thanks for your opinion. What time does she get off work?"

Amber shrugged. "It varies, depending on how busy the restaurant is tonight. They close at ten, but sometimes she's still not home before midnight."

He couldn't offer her any better hours to speak of with a four-thirty breakfast for the crew so they'd be on the mountain at first light. But he could keep an eye on her and make sure she didn't work too hard.

He wished.

Noel turned away. "Okay, thanks. I'll try and catch her later or tomorrow, then." Jess would blow a fuse if he came back without a confirmation from Claire, and soon. Maybe he'd go sit in the parking lot at The Sizzling Skillet after ten. He thought about Polly's cooking. Maybe he'd catch dinner while he was at it.

"Noel?"

He glanced back. "Yeah?"

"I've been praying for you."

"Oh? Well, thanks." Maybe thanks.

"If you're not on speaking terms with God, you might want to change that."

"Sure. I'll get right on it."

Nosy little sister.

Chapter 14 ---

"You should've known we'd need more lasagna tonight." Nevin stood at Claire's elbow as she scrubbed the black rock over the grill. "It's not acceptable to run out."

She blew hair out of her eyes to no avail. Sweat made each strand stick to her forehead. Oh, for a shower. "Didn't run out until after eight."

"That's no excuse."

Claire set her jaw and continued the cleaning. The day chef would find the kitchen spotless as she did every weekend morning.

"Plan a little better tomorrow."

"Canvas the town ahead of time to see who's coming for dinner and what they're planning to order?"

"Don't be smart with me."

"Leave her alone."

Oh, Tony. He'd be better off keeping his mouth shut when the boss's mood soured.

Nevin pivoted. "Mind your own business, kid. You done all them dishes?"

"Almost."

"You do your job and leave the managing to me."

Claire paused leaning partway across the grill and caught

Tony's eye over her shoulder. She shook her head slightly, took a deep breath, and continued the scrub.

"You're a lousy manager. You don't care enough to remember anybody's name and you pick on people for things they can't help. How about a little encouragement around here?"

Claire closed her eyes, her ears ringing as she waited for what would surely come. She wasn't disappointed.

"You're fired."

Tony barked a short laugh. "Do you even know who I am?"

Claire straightened and turned, leaning against the grill. Her back had all but seized tonight, and the stress of the aftermath wasn't helping.

Nevin slipped on a bit of oil on the floor but regained his balance as he stalked to Tony. He waggled his finger upward under the kid's nose. "Trust me. I can figure out who to fire. You're on the schedule, aren't you?"

"Yeah. As DW4."

There wasn't anything Claire could do for Tony. She'd kept him an entire month longer than he'd wanted to stay, but he'd made his choice tonight and would have to deal with it. At least he still lived with his folks. He didn't have to put up with Nevin. Lack of income would put a kink in his social life for a while, but that was about it.

If she did the same, she'd be back in Seattle in a heartbeat. It was still almost tempting.

"Don't talk back to me, young man."

Don and the waitresses were smart enough to stay out of the kitchen right now, though Claire could sure use Don tidying the counters. She turned back to the grill, blocking Nevin's raised voice. A few more grinding swipes and she'd be done.

The swish of the swinging doors to the restaurant brought silence in its wake. Claire wiped her forehead with her sleeve.

Now for the griddle.

"He's got no right to speak to you that way."

Claire glanced up at Tony. "Oh, you're still here?"

"Yeah, I'm staying until the last load of dishes is put away. Just a couple more, but I know you'd do it yourself if I walked out now."

She looked at him with new eyes. "Wow. Thanks, Tony." She was going to miss the kid but could hardly blame him. "If you need a reference for another job, let me know."

His blue eyes lit up. "For real?"

"Yeah. You've been a good worker."

"Hey, thanks, Claire. What do you need me to do before I go home? Besides the dishes, I mean."

Don wandered in from the dining room. "Everything under control back here?" He looked Tony over. "Thought you were fired."

Tony beamed at him, looking a bit like the Cheshire cat. "Sure was, and proud of it."

"Don, if you can get the other side of the kitchen, we'll be out of here in twenty minutes." She shouldn't have to tell him. He'd worked here longer than she had, but hated being an assistant. If she could only get her nerve together to quit—she'd better not get fired, like Tony—Nevin might move him up.

"Got it, boss lady." A tinge of sarcasm colored Don's voice.

From the corner of her eye, Claire saw Tony straighten and open his mouth. She shook her head. She couldn't handle any more of his defense tonight.

Tony's jaw clenched, but he turned back to the dishwasher and slid another load in.

Don busied himself in the prep area, freeing Claire to mop the floor in her section.

She'd be awake a long time after she went home.

oOo

Noel drummed his fingers on the steering wheel as a couple of more people left The Sizzling Skillet's side door and hurried to their waiting vehicles. If he weren't parked right next to Claire's car he'd figure she must've gone home already.

Finally the door opened again, silhouetting Claire and someone behind her as the light went out.

Noel pressed the button to slide down his window. "Claire?"

She turned, and so did the tall skinny person.

"Who is that?" a young male voice asked.

"It's okay, Tony. Thanks. Go on home." She locked the door.

Man, she sounded beyond exhausted. She moved toward his truck window with a speed—or lack thereof—that matched her voice.

The kid leaned against the restaurant door, his arms crossed.

Noel couldn't help the grin that spread across his face. Nice to see Claire had someone who looked out for her.

"What are you doing here, Noel?"

"I came to talk to you. I see you're tired, but it really can't wait. Is there someplace we can go for a coffee?"

Her back stiffened. "I don't know that I have anything to say to you. And no, The Sizzling Skillet is open later than anyplace else in town. Everywhere else closed hours ago."

On a Friday night? Wow. "Okay." He slid out of his cab.

Her white coat gleamed in the darkness except for where food had splattered on it. Her short hair, usually neatly swept to the side, hung in clumps. Noel longed to wipe the smudge off her cheek.

He should have caught her in the morning, but too late now. "I'm sorry about yesterday. I really blew it with Amber."

Claire crossed her arms. "You'll have to take it up with her."

"I did, this afternoon. But you were there when I opened my mouth and were witness to my boneheadedness."

She nodded and glanced toward her car. She took a wobbly step toward it. The kid zipped there in no time flat, holding her elbow.

"Thanks, Tony. Go on home. Noel won't bite. Really."

Noel leapt to open the driver's door for her and she slid behind the wheel.

"If you're sure..." The boy sounded dubious.

Claire nodded, and Tony gave Noel the once up-and-down before striding out of the parking lot and down the street.

Noel squatted beside the open door. "Mind if I get in the passenger seat and talk to you a minute?"

"Whatever." Claire leaned against the headrest and closed her eyes. "I thought you'd said your piece."

"That was only the prelude." He jogged around the car and slid into the other side before she had a chance to change her mind.

"What's up? And please, why can't this wait until tomorrow?" Her eyes sprang open. "Did something happen to Amber?"

He rested his hand on her forearm. "No, she's fine. Shawn got in a few hours ago and they're all right."

"Good."

"A couple of months ago you applied as chef to Enterprising Reforestation. I, uh, didn't hire you."

"Uh huh."

That didn't sound encouraging.

"Things have come up. The woman I did employ is doing a poor job. She swings between burning the food and undercooking it. She's repeating the cheap parts of her menu much oftener than the other stuff, and she's sloppy and surly."

Claire slipped her arm from under Noel's hand. "I'm sorry to hear that."

"Not half as sorry as my crew is to be experiencing it. They're threatening to walk off the job."

She rubbed a tired hand across her forehead. "So what do you expect me to do about it?"

"I want to fire her and hire you."

"You what?" Claire turned toward him in her seat. "You want me to give up my job for six weeks of full-time cooking? Because I sure can't do both."

Noel tried to plead with his eyes. "You once wanted to. I hoped you still did."

"That was for three months of work. We're down to like half that. When do you need somebody by?"

He hesitated. "Monday morning for breakfast?"

She slammed her hand against the wheel. "You're kidding me, right? I have to give two weeks notice or be black balled in this town. There's no way on God's green Earth I can do both jobs. You're too late, Noel."

He'd messed up. "But—"

"Look, I need to go home and get some sleep. Would you mind getting out of my car?"

She couldn't make him. But what good would it do to antagonize her further? Nothing.

Noel pulled on the door handle, and cool air swirled into the car. "Claire, please. Tell me you'll think about it." A stroke of genius shot through his brain. "You need to pray about it, right? You can't just go making a snap decision without consulting God."

She sat there for a second, her brown eyes boring into his. "I pray about everything."

"See? Give it until tomorrow. No need to make a final decision tonight."

"Do you?"

Noel stared back. "Do I what?"

"Pray about things. Amber told me you were raised in a Christian home, so I know you understand the concept."

Ouch. "Sometimes. Okay, not as much as I should."

"If you feel you 'should' pray, it's not the right attitude."

"Pardon me?"

"A relationship with God isn't based on what we should do. It's based on want to. It's based on Him loving us and us loving Him, and both of us wanting to do things for each other. I want to follow God's will, not because I should, but because He's been so awesome to me and made me happier than I'd ever dreamt." Claire's back straightened. "He has. So when I pray, it's because I really care about His answer and want to follow His leading."

"But that's…"

"That's what, Noel? Crazy talk? It's the way I live my life."

And all this while he'd been shoving God off into a corner. "You honestly think God has made you happier?"

"I know it."

"But how? How can you know that? You might've been happier…" He waved a hand around. "I don't know, snorkeling in Australia, or being a pharmaceutical rep in Missoula."

She grinned, but the tired lines stayed on her face. "I'll leave that one for Shawn. Trust me, I know the peace I have when I'm in God's will. It's worth everything to me."

There wasn't much he could say to that. He climbed out of the car, walked around it, and leaned back in the driver's side window. "How do you know it isn't God's will for you to work for Enterprising Reforestation if you don't ask Him?"

She opened her mouth and closed it again, those brown eyes catching the light from a nearby streetlamp.

"Claire? You're—" No, he shouldn't go there.

Her eyebrows went up.

He reached out and slid his fingertips down her cheek, just once. "I'll talk to you tomorrow. Okay?"

Claire bit her lip, her eyes fixed on his. "Okay."

o0o

She tossed and turned most of the night. After that horrid confrontation with Nevin, had Noel's offer been some kind of a sign? But she'd been braver a few months ago. She hadn't known his company from Adam then. Didn't know Noel Kenzie was a crazy attractive man with the potential to make her heart go wonky.

She couldn't make enough money in six weeks to be worth dropping The Sizzling Skillet. She'd also need an assistant. Back then she'd have had time to find someone.

But there was Tony. The boy wanted to learn how to cook, but he was still in school for a couple of more weeks. Could she manage breakfasts on her own if Tony worked for her after class every day? He could pack lunches and help with supper prep and clean up. It might be enough.

The moon peered in Claire's window. This was crazy. She shouldn't even be considering it. She'd told Noel "should" had no part in her life. Was it better to say she was dumb to think about it?

He'd challenged her to pray...and then said he didn't pray himself.

She couldn't marry a guy like that.

He hadn't asked her. He'd asked her to cook for six weeks. No one had said a thing about lifetime commitment.

It had been in his eyes, though. And he'd bitten off more than one sentence without speaking them. And his touch...

A tremor ran through Claire's body even now, remembering. She longed for more from him, more than the times he'd touched her cheek so gently. She wanted to feel his lips on hers, to run her hand over his perpetually unshaven cheeks and chin. She wanted to feel his arms around her, tightening, pulling her close. She wanted to do the same to him. And more.

Claire flung the blanket off, stuffed her feet into slippers, and padded down the hallway to the bathroom. She splashed cold water on her face and stared at herself in the dim glow of the nightlight.

The real question was, could she work for Noel and not dissolve at the sight of him every time he came near? Could she keep her work and her...love life...apart?

But it wasn't a love life. Her list was much shorter than Amber's, but the very top item was the same. *He must love God with all his heart.*

Noel didn't. So he wasn't marriage potential.

Period.

But did she? She talked a good spiel about following God. What if it had been God's will for her to marry Graham and travel the world with him, helping people in need? What if she only followed when she liked where God led?

Her mind slid to the second item. Being devoted to life here on the farm. Noel talked about snorkeling in Australia. He'd mentioned other places as though he traveled frequently.

She wasn't into that.

Period.

What if those things changed?

Claire turned from the bathroom mirror. There was no reason to expect they would. She couldn't bank on it.

She should pray God would change Noel. Maybe God wanted to use her to do that. Maybe she should accept the position.

Maybe she should stop using the word "should."

Chapter 15 --

Someone had flipped the coffee pot on before Claire made her way into the kitchen on Saturday morning, rubbing sleep out of her eyes.

"Hey, Claire!" Amber sounded way too perky for so early in the morning.

Claire squinted at the clock. Scratch that. Ten. She'd slept in after a miserable night.

Amber jumped up from the table where she'd been seated around the corner from Sierra. "Come sit down. Let me get you breakfast."

Claire shook her head. "I just want a piece of toast is all. I'll get it, but thanks."

"If you're sure…"

"Yeah, I'm good." She focused on the girls at the table as she pushed the toaster button. "What's up?" She hated working afternoon shift and rarely connecting with the others all weekend long.

"Shawn went to see the log cabin with Zach."

Claire poured a coffee and inhaled the deep aroma. She needed this in the worst way. Jo had gone off coffee, cold turkey, choosing locally grown herbal teas rather than supporting distant businesses and freight lines. Claire understood the sentiment, but wasn't ready to make the choice. Simply choosing fair-trade organic would have to do for now. At least in the mornings. Mint tea worked fine the rest of the day.

"Anyone check email lately?"

Sierra shook her head. "Just my own."

Claire took the mug over to the computer desk and logged onto the Green Acres email. Her eyes bugged out. Three more inquiries? One wedding, a family reunion, and a retreat group?

This couldn't be right. Surely she was only seeing what she wanted to see. "Sierra, come here. Please."

Both girls came to look over her shoulder. She should mind about Amber, who was only a client after all. But more. As their first—and as Noel's sister—she'd become a friend. That relationship had crept up on Claire, but it couldn't be denied.

Sierra let out a low whistle. "Things are taking off. So cool."

Claire opened the calendar and transferred the three new dates into it. In pencil, as they weren't confirmed. Every event requested a weekend. Nevin would never allow her to stay at The Sizzling Skillet if she asked for this much time off.

Maybe she should say yes to Noel.

"Your toast popped," said Amber. "What do you want on it? I'll get it."

Claire blinked. "Butter and some of that organic cheese, thin sliced. Thanks."

"No problem."

Obviously Amber felt like one of the family. She'd been here enough weekends lately, and though Green Acres charged her room and board for her stays, they weren't getting rich on her by any means.

One of the family. Claire's gaze followed Amber to the kitchen. What would it be like to have Amber for a little sister all the time? Claire gave herself a mental shake. She knew better than to go there.

"We've got Amber's wedding roundtable right after lunch. You good with that?"

Sierra's voice pulled Claire back to the sun-streaked great room. "Right. That sounds fine." What was she supposed to have done by this meeting? Menu choices? She'd made some notes the other day. "Did we ever hear back from Isobel and Greg?"

Sierra nodded. "They're on for the second weekend in September, but we won't start working intensively with them for another month or so."

Claire looked the calendar over. By then she'd be nearly done working for Noel, if she took the job. They'd be heavy into planning these upcoming events. New possibilities landed in the inbox several times a week. Of course, some of them—possibly many—wouldn't come to fruition, but lots would.

She took a deep breath. "I'm quitting at The Sizzling Skillet."

"You're what?" Sierra grabbed Claire by the shoulders and twisted her in the revolving chair. "Seriously?"

Claire pointed at the calendar. "Every event is on a weekend. Nearly every planning meeting is on a weekend. The restaurant isn't a job that's compatible with what we're trying to do here, unless Nevin puts me on weekday shifts. He'd never do that. Beatrice has worked those forever."

"But—"

"I know what you're going to say. I've been worried about money." She glanced at the kitchen, where Amber hummed to herself as she prepped Claire's toast. Claire lowered her voice. "I still am. But Noel asked me last night to finish the season with the planting crew, and I'm going to take him up on it. It'll be crazy nuts for six weeks, but it will match many months' worth of shifts at The Skillet, dollar wise. Then I can focus on the farm."

"But what if…what if it doesn't take off?"

Claire shook her head. "I'll cross that bridge when I come to it and pray I don't need to."

"But you can't do all that by yourself. You said you'd need a helper, and I've got office hours now."

"I'm pretty sure I can find someone."

"Like who? Maybe Jo part time, but she can't do every day."

Jo. *Bingo*. She'd probably be able to fill in around Tony. "I need to call Tony and offer him a job."

"Who's he?"

"Kid Nevin fired last night. Been washing dishes at The Skillet for a month or so."

"Seriously, don't you need someone with more experience? Someone who hasn't been fired? And besides, a kid? Doesn't he need to be in school?"

Amber set the plate beside Claire's elbow. "What's up? What kid?"

"Tony. He's keen on learning to cook, and always a good help when I needed him for a few minutes between dishwasher loads."

Amber frowned and took a seat nearby. "I don't get it."

Claire took a deep breath. "I'm going to work for your brother."

o0o

Noel pulled into the Green Acres driveway. This was getting crazy. Every time his sister beckoned, he was supposed to run to her rescue? If he didn't want to see Claire so badly, he'd have told Amber he was too busy to come this morning. And if Claire turned him down—and she almost certainly would—he really *would* be too busy. He couldn't handle the job himself, though. He was a decent cook for an occasional small party, but he knew his limits.

This better not be more wedding stuff. It was bad enough when a few of his friends had gotten hitched. They'd ditched the easy lifestyle in the blink of an eye and claimed to love every minute of it. Bewitched by some girl.

Maybe if it were Claire it would be worth it.

Almost, but not quite.

Claire sat on the deck swing alone. No Amber in sight.

Noel frowned even while his heart sped up. Was this some kind of set up? Was Amber capable of noticing someone else's attractions when she was so deep in with Shawn? He swung out of the truck and approached the deck. "Good morning, Claire."

She got to her feet and leaned on the railing, clad in blue jeans and a plaid flannel shirt. "Hey there."

"Where's Amber? She asked me to come over."

"Yeah. She did that for me."

Erratic heartbeats were supposed to be a negative thing, something people went to the doctor for. Noel kind of liked the feeling in his heart. He stopped right below Claire and looked up at her. The deck sat only a couple of steps up from ground level, so he didn't have to tilt his head far. "Oh?" He parked one hand on either side of her on the railing.

Those brown eyes. They got to him every time. Her jaw worked for a few seconds. "I've decided…yes. If you still want me, I'll work for you."

"Really?" He couldn't help the wide grin that crossed his face. "Really?" He bounded up the steps and grabbed Claire, whirling her around. "Oh, man, you're saving my bacon."

She put her hands on his arms, steadying herself as he let her feet hit the planks again. "Not sure how I'll come up with groceries for the first few days. All the careful plans I showed you banked on having time to get suppliers in place."

"I'll help you. We can go grocery shopping together at Super One, and I'll show you what Polly is leaving behind, plus the orders she's already placed with the restaurant supply company. I can make the switch work." He'd actually volunteered to go shopping? That was a first. Normally he avoided it like a rabid bear.

Claire let out a long shuddering breath but didn't pull out of his hold. "I just don't know when. We're supposed to meet for Amber and Shawn's wedding right after lunch, and I have to go to work at four."

Noel's eyebrows shot up. "You're keeping your job? How will you manage?" She couldn't. What did she have up her sleeve?

"I can't quit with five hours notice, Noel. I have to work tonight and tomorrow. Even then I'm giving Nevin less than a week to replace me."

And she looked exhausted already. "You're going to be able to serve breakfast at four thirty in the morning after working until midnight?" Noel's hands slid around her and pulled her closer. "It's going to be ugly," he murmured against her hair. "I'll help you make the transition any way I can."

She pushed back a bit at that, but not enough he needed to release her. "Did you say that to Polly, too?"

Noel chuckled. "Not hardly. You going to have help in the kitchen?"

"I need to call Tony. The kid who came out the door with me last night." She sighed. "Nevin fired him."

And that was a recommendation? "Rough evening?"

"You could say so." She gently disengaged from his arms.

He felt chilled without her tucked up against him. "Is that what led to this yes?"

She rubbed her hands along her arms. "Partly. And also this morning we got a few more enquiries about doing events here

147

at the farm. They're all on weekends, and I can't do weekends if I'm working at The Skillet."

"If you're honestly going to work your next two shifts, when will you prep for Monday? Need to hold off coming until Tuesday?"

"You give your crew Sundays off, right? And they don't get meals that day, either?"

He nodded. "They cook for themselves or eat in town. Which is why this is a good time for me to switch, but I can see it isn't for you."

"I'll have to do more with Amber via email and skip today's meeting to get groceries before work. And get in touch with Tony so we can do as much prepping as needed tomorrow afternoon. If he'll come. I better call him." She dug into her hip pocket for her cell phone and turned away.

Noel wouldn't spring the news on Polly until cleanup later tonight. He didn't want to take the chance she'd quit before the evening meal. He'd even avoided Jess earlier this morning, not wanting to face her bombardment of questions, comments, suggestions, and complaints. Jess. One issue that'd come up with Amber and Claire yesterday. Why didn't anyone believe they were only close friends?

o0o

Claire tapped the button to hang up from her call with Tony, and turned slowly around to face Noel. He leaned his elbows back against the railing when she approached. The smile in his eyes reached his mouth. "All okay?"

She forced herself to focus on his eyes, not his lips. This would be a challenging six weeks. "Yes, Tony's willing and his mom says it's okay. It's a good thing the school year is nearly over. He'll come over right after church tomorrow and we'll pack all of Monday's lunches and do the breakfast prep. I think we can do it in three hours before I have to go to work."

And if she didn't need any sleep Sunday night, because she wasn't likely to get more than four hours in bed, tops.

His eyes tried to read hers, and he held out his hands to her.

What a temptation to walk into them and be held. She had to resist. She reminded herself of her checklist, and how he didn't meet the major criteria. She reminded herself it was a bad idea to be romantically involved with her boss. She reminded herself...

She pasted on a bright smile. "When can I get a look at the facilities? I guess Polly is there now."

Noel reached out and captured her hand. "Come over to Elmer's with me, and I'll show you around as best I can. She's usually gone for a few hours after lunch, so we can do a more detailed survey then."

Claire pulled her hand out of Noel's. Again. How she wished he'd earned the right to capture it...and her heart. "I need to let everyone inside know they'll have to do the planning meeting without me." She grimaced. "I hate letting them down."

"What about you?" he asked softly. "I'm only offering six weeks."

Claire paused. The rest of her life would be desolate and empty without Noel in it.

"You won't be able to go back to The Sizzling Skillet, will you?"

She shuddered. "No. And I don't want to. It looks like we have lots of events coming up here, if everything comes through. With any luck—and God's blessing—I'll have enough earnings from that."

Relief swept his face. "I'm glad. I was worried I'd asked you to bail me out. I know you don't owe me anything. If I'd been smart enough to hire you in the first place, we wouldn't be in this mess right now."

Being as he'd mentioned it... Claire tilted her head. "Question for you."

"Yes?"

"Why didn't you? You made fun of my menu. Was that it?"

"Did not."

She laughed. "You did, too. But I got the feeling there was more to it. You were looking for a reason to hire somebody else."

He swallowed so hard she stared at his bobbing Adam's apple. He closed the gap she'd only just placed between them. "Claire, it's all you. Your presence filled that little room and blew me away. I knew I'd never be able to focus on my work if you were around."

Claire couldn't believe he'd admit it so freely. Her palms turned clammy. She wanted to tease him and ask if it would be any better now than it had been then, but the words wouldn't come.

Noel's right hand entwined her fingers, but his left swept the length of her face.

He kept doing that, creating an insatiable longing inside her. In this instant, it didn't matter. His eyes and hands had captured hers, and in only a few seconds, his lips did the same.

Claire melted into his embrace.

Chapter 16 --

Noel pushed the grocery cart while Claire loaded it with various items. An awful lot of vegetables for his liking, but Noel kept his mouth zipped. Might be a nice break from pasta. He had no doubt she knew what to do with the ingredients to make them tasty.

Her lips had been tasty. That kiss hadn't lasted long, but there would be more of them. He needed to hold back, though, or risk losing a second cook. Not that he'd ever been tempted to kiss Polly. A shudder ran through him.

Claire glanced his way. "You okay?" She crouched to examine a case on a bottom shelf.

"Want me to get that?"

"Sure."

He lifted the heavy box into the cart with ease. This must be what normal couples went through, picking up groceries. He and Claire looked like they belonged together. Maybe he could sweep her off her feet and take her with him when he left.

A niggling voice told him it wasn't likely, but a guy could dream.

"Why, hello, Claire! I haven't seen you in a long time." An older man snagged Claire to his side.

"Ed! Nice to see you." She smiled up at him. "Did you have a nice cruise with your family?"

"We did. Just got back in town a few days ago." The man looked Noel over and nudged Claire. "Anyone you want me to meet?"

A flush crept up her neck. "This is my friend Noel. We're doing an event for his family out at the farm."

He rated being a friend. That was nice, sort of. He reached out to shake the older man's hand firmly. "Pleased to meet you."

"The name's Ed Graysen. You may have seen Ed's Plumbing Shop out on the highway. That was my business before I retired, but they kept the name."

Noel glanced at Claire then back at the man. "That's great. I'll keep it in mind if I need any plumbing done." Kind of unlikely, but he could keep the old guy happy.

"Ed did the water system at Green Acres for us last year. He was a big help."

The old dude grinned.

Claire patted Ed's arm. "Not only that, but he organized a crew to help us the day the trusses came. I'm not sure how we'd have managed without you, Ed."

"You're too kind."

"Not at all." Claire shifted out from under the man's arm. "Anyway, it was nice to run into you."

The old fellow looked Noel in the eye. "You'll be in church tomorrow, then?"

Now why did Noel get the idea he was being measured? And what business was it of Ed's, anyway? Still, he didn't want to make things awkward for Claire. He smiled. "Possibly."

It couldn't hurt, could it? It would make him look better in Claire's eyes. She wouldn't be fooled for long. To win her he'd need to *be* better, not only look better. Was it worth it?

The old guy wandered away and Claire returned her focus to the shelves along the aisle.

When he was near Claire, she was worth giving everything else up. When they'd been apart for a while—say, a few hours—he still felt the pull but knew it was a temporary infatuation. He'd get over her when he moved on. It might take a while, but he would.

oOo

Claire followed Noel into the cook trailer at Elmer's farm. Everything needed a good scrubbing. She'd assign Tony that task tomorrow, if still needed after the other woman moved out. If Polly left it like this between meals, Claire doubted it would look any better once she'd left in disgrace.

Still, with the groceries stowed, Claire was pretty sure she had things in hand for the first couple of days, at least.

She was crazy, throwing away a regular job for an intense month and a half and the hope of random events later. Was it because Noel asked? No, she was fed up to the hilt with Nevin and Don. But it didn't hurt Noel had been the one to ask.

They exited the compact space.

"Hi, Claire. Remember me?"

Claire turned to face the petite blond woman. Oh, yes, she remembered her from the interview day. Jess, the unknown entity.

"I'm Jess, Noel's crew foreman. I'm so glad you'll be joining us here at Enterprising Reforestation." The girl stuck her hand out.

Claire took it. She couldn't very well not. While Jess's gaze measured Claire from top to bottom, it didn't seem in a jealous way. That ought to be a relief, but somehow it wasn't. "Yes, I remember. Good to be here." How she hoped that wouldn't turn out to be a lie.

Jess indicated the tarped-off eating area. "I think you'll find the crew quite welcoming and not too picky. They just want hot, tasty food."

"That doesn't seem too much to ask," Claire ventured.

Noel's hand touched the small of her back, and Claire shifted away. He was such a physical person. That kiss had caught her totally off guard. Her face heated again at the memory.

Jess must've noticed where Noel's hand went. A smirk toyed with the edges of her mouth as she focused on Noel. Like they had a secret language about Claire or something. Not cool. She didn't like the thought they'd discussed her, but it seemed inevitable.

It's just a job, Claire. A well-paying temporary position that would both exhaust her and set her up for months to come. She didn't have to take Noel personally.

But his kiss had been very personal, yet not insistent at all. As sweet and gentle as the times he'd touched her face. She almost wished he'd demanded more, that she'd been the one to pull away. But no, she'd still been seeking more when Noel lifted his lips and cradled her face in his hands for another brief instant, gazing deeply into her eyes.

She took a couple of steps away from Noel. "I need to get going. I have to be at work in an hour. I'll talk to you tomorrow." She looked from him to Jess and back again, then nodded abruptly and fled.

o0o

"No, I don't have time to watch the dishwasher." Claire met Nevin's gaze. "Who's hostessing tonight? She can keep an eye and run an occasional load. Let the wait staff seat their own customers."

Nevin narrowed his eyes.

The bell pinged with another order. Claire stared at Nevin for a few more seconds, daring him to argue with her, before turning to see an order for six entrees.

"You're in charge of the kitchen, so we'd better not run out of plates or glasses."

"You're the one who fired my dishwasher and didn't replace him. Keeping dishes clean is not my job."

"Everything that happens in this kitchen is your responsibility."

Claire bit her tongue before saying something she'd regret. Some people were just worse to apologize to than others, and there was no way she'd put herself in a situation where she'd have to say *sorry* to Nevin.

She took a deep breath. "Actually, everything is not my job. Furthermore, I'll be giving you a piece of paper when we close tonight tendering my resignation. My last shift is tomorrow."

Nevin's eyes bugged out. "You can't do that to me."

"I sure can, and I will."

"You have to give me two weeks notice."

"No, I don't. I realize it is polite to, but I can't. It is six days, though. It's the best I can do."

He pushed himself in front of her. "Is it because I fired that little twerp last night? He was mouthy."

Another order came in. "Nevin, can we talk about this later? Folks are looking for their meals now. If you've got all this time to stand around and talk, how about you run the dishwasher?"

By the look on his face, she'd gone too far. She only had to put up with him two more evenings, and if he fired her now for her impertinence, it wouldn't be much loss. In fact, she'd welcome the chance to both cook *and* sleep in the next forty-eight hours.

"Watch it, missy," he snarled and stalked away.

Oh, yeah, that terrified her. Claire turned to the row of orders and glanced over the meals she'd already started. Thankfully nothing had burned while Nevin messed with her routine, but she couldn't count on getting everything plated at the same time.

Focus, Claire. She could do this. She'd done it a thousand times before.

"You're testing him, aren't you?"

Trust Don to be holding back just out of sight, listening. "Nope. It's for real. Please peel more potatoes and defrost more eight-ounce steaks. Busy out there tonight."

He trudged across the kitchen and dumped a bag of potatoes into the peeler. "You're serious? You're quitting over that kid?"

"I'm quitting. It isn't about Tony." Though that situation hadn't helped. She shot a sidelong glance at Don. "Maybe this will be your big break. Ask Nevin to put you on the grill."

His face lit and then clouded. "I doubt he will."

"You don't know that. You need to get a bit pro-active." Did Don have it in him to grasp the opportunity? It seemed he always needed to be told what to do, and even then he whined.

Anyway. That was his problem, and Nevin's. It wasn't her responsibility anymore. For now, she simply needed to keep cooking and hope her stack of clean plates didn't run out.

o0o

"What are you doing up so early, boss?" Jess sat behind her camper with a thermal mug in hand. "It's Sunday. You always sleep in on Sunday."

"Yeah, I know. Thought I'd try something new today."

She tipped her head. "Want a coffee? I've got a whole pot brewed."

Noel glanced at his watch. "Sure, that'd be great."

Halfway to her feet, Jess frowned. "Going somewhere?"

He hesitated. "Yeah, maybe. My sister's been after me to go

to church. It's been a lot of years since I last went. Thought I might give it a try."

A knowing look crossed Jess's face. "Your sister, eh? And here I'd have bet it was Claire. Seems like you'd do nearly anything for her."

Noel hitched a shoulder. "She hasn't asked me, but Amber has." Claire had sure paid attention when that old guy had talked to Noel about church, though. And honestly? If Claire was giving up some of her day to go when he knew what a lot she had to get done, he had to wonder if there wasn't more to it than he remembered.

Maybe the little church in Galena Landing wasn't the same as the stuffy one he'd attended in Missoula, though Amber still went whenever she wasn't at Green Acres. How could he know unless he checked it out?

Jess came back out with a tall, fat mug. "Poured some cream in it for you."

"Thanks, Jess." He popped open her spare lawn chair and collapsed into it, inhaling the dark, rich brew. Ah, yes, this should help.

"So you're going to church with Claire. Never thought of you as the churchy type." Jess leaned against the picnic table. "No offense meant."

"None taken." He took a sip. "And I said Amber, not Claire."

Her knowing gaze met his. "Right. And Claire won't be there, I suppose?"

"She'll be there."

Jess reached into the kangaroo pocket of her hoodie. "You might want these back, then." She tossed him a thick envelope. "I grabbed them when I got your coffee."

The photos of Claire. He caught the packet instinctively and fought the urge to open it and thumb through the familiar images. Not in front of Jess.

She laughed. "You're welcome. So things are all going hunky dory now, eh? She's gonna cook for the crew and be here onsite most of our waking hours." She quirked an eyebrow. "Maybe sleeping hours, too?"

"Nope. You know better than that."

"Yeah, I guess it would make working together tough if you had a fight or something."

"That's not what I meant, and you know it. I respect Claire. She's not the kind for a fling."

"You've turned over a new leaf?"

Noel held Jess's gaze steady. "You know I did that quite a while ago. More than one. I'm a new man." Wasn't there something in the Bible about that? Seemed like he remembered it from Sunday school back in the day. Only he'd renewed himself without God's intervention, so it probably didn't count.

Jess sighed. "Not sure I'm ready for you to add religion to all the rest. You were more fun back in the old days." She collapsed into her lawn chair.

"Waking up hung-over wasn't the most fun part of it."

"Well, no. I guess not. But still, you were always ready for a good time."

Noel took another sip of the coffee. Jess made it nearly strong enough to corrode his gut lining. Good things she'd added the cream. "I'd like to think I still have a good time, but my definition has changed somewhat. I think it's made me a better boss."

Jess propped her feet up on the camper steps. "Can't deny that." She shot him a sidelong look. "I can't help but wonder how things would be different if you and I had gotten together when we first met."

"We've been over it, Jess. It's better this way."

"I nearly always believe that. Then I see what you turn into when you really fall for somebody and, well, I don't mind saying it makes me a little wistful."

"No way, girl. You're not jealous?"

She sighed. "Not full on jealous, no. Just…makes me wish I had somebody who wanted to look at me that way, you know?"

He did know. "You're something special, Jess. Some guy is going to come along and sweep you off your feet. All I can say is I hope he doesn't take you away from Enterprising Reforestation, because I'm not sure how I could ever replace you."

Jess looked about to say something then shook her head. "Nah. That won't happen."

It wasn't Jess's fault he didn't see her romantically. She was fun and attractive. She was also comfortable, more like a sister the past few years than Amber had been. And a guy just didn't go having those kinds of thoughts about a sister. The idea of Shawn touching Amber intimately made Noel queasy, though Shawn would soon have the right. The guy better be worthy.

"Why don't you come to church, too?"

Jess's head was shaking before he'd finished the question. "No, I won't interfere with you and Claire like that. You think she knows what to make of me? I doubt it."

Chapter 17 --

Claire glanced out the passenger window of Amber's Mazda as they pulled into the parking lot at Galena Gospel Church. She caught her breath. What was Noel's truck doing here? He jumped out of the cab, dressed in clean jeans and a button-up short-sleeved shirt.

Amber zipped into the spot beside her brother's truck, and Noel reached out to open the door for Claire. Good thing she wore pants, or it would be difficult to get out without showing too much leg.

"Good morning, Claire."

She reached back in to grab her purse and Bible. "Hi." What was she supposed to say? Her heart sped up every time she was near him. Especially when it was unexpected, like now. She couldn't help the surge of delight that he might come to value spiritual things.

"Hey, bro. Didn't expect to see you here." Trust Amber to come right to the point.

Noel looked across the roof of the car at his sister. "Good morning to you, too. And why not? Maybe there's more to me than you knew."

"Maybe. But I doubt it." She eyed Claire speculatively.

This was uncomfortable. Claire took a few steps away.

Maybe the two would follow her. Zach's car pulled in on the other side of Amber's, with the other members of the Green Acres team. Claire couldn't face the knowing smirks from everyone.

She glanced over her shoulder to see if Amber and Noel were coming, just in time to catch Noel's gaze travel down the length of her body.

He caught her watching him and winked. In two long strides he caught up and bumped her shoulder with his arm. "You're looking gorgeous today. That color really suits you."

Claire looked down at her red and gray striped top and gray slacks. Her face felt like it'd match her blouse any time now. "Um, thanks."

"Got a question for you." His voice remained low.

Behind them, Claire could hear the rest of the group chatting as they all moved toward the church doors. This couldn't possibly be a good time for a private question such as he hinted at, but she couldn't help herself. "Oh?"

"Has there been no one in your life to tell you how attractive you are? Every time I tell you, it seems I embarrass you, and you don't believe me. What do you see when you look in the mirror?"

He couldn't possibly want to know she thought her mouth was too large and her nose too short. Then he'd start seeing the same flaws and stop complimenting her. And she didn't want to talk about her mouth. Not after yesterday's kiss.

They'd reached the church steps. "This isn't the time, Noel."

He stretched to open the door, and his eyes caught hers for a brief moment. "Trust me. You're beautiful."

She swept past him and heard him say something to Amber and Sierra. He'd held the door for all of them, then, like a true gentleman. Why, oh why, had he come to church? The one sanctuary she had to gather her strength for the upcoming week, and now she'd have trouble focusing. With her luck he'd sit right behind her and she'd feel his eyes on the back of her head the entire service.

Claire didn't linger in the foyer but filed into a pew between Sierra and Amber as quickly as she could urge them to come.

"He's fallen hard," Sierra whispered.

Claire shot her a frustrated look. Noel made no attempt to hide his attraction. Of course, Sierra picked up on it. Too bad no one could help Claire deal with it.

Though this might remove the X from beside number one item on her list and turn it into a check. Not just for coming to church, of course, but if this was the beginning of Noel turning to God. Returning, she corrected. He'd grown up in the church.

Sierra nudged Claire again, but this time her gaze went past Claire's head. Claire glanced up.

Noel edged his way past Shawn and Amber, gesturing for Amber to scoot over.

Claire closed her eyes and breathed a prayer as heat flooded up her face. No way could she look at Sierra—or at Noel, who now wedged himself tightly between her and Amber.

He presumed so much. It seemed to be his nature to believe he was wanted wherever he went. That she desired his presence as much as he seemed to want hers.

The problem was, he wasn't precisely wrong.

o0o

Church was the same and yet different from how Noel remembered. Some of the hymns sounded familiar, and other songs had a decided contemporary edge. There sure never had been drums on the stage—dais—whatever they called the raised thing in a church—when he was growing up. He ought to remember. Platform?

The shocker came when the middle-aged drummer read the scripture and then delivered the sermon. It caught Noel so far off guard he actually paid more attention than he'd expected.

The guy—the paper in his sister's hands said he was Pastor Ron—talked about plans, and how everybody made them, just some more detailed than others.

Noel scooched down in the bench and crossed his ankles then his arms, shifting slightly away from his sister and closer to Claire. He liked the warmth of Claire's shoulder and hip pressed up against his. If he were really into planning stuff, he'd arrange for that, and more, to happen a whole lot more often.

The pastor guy said folks should be paying a lot less attention to their own plans and spending more time asking God for His. Nice thought. That seemed to indicate God could be trusted, and Noel wasn't convinced.

"We say to one another, let us go to this town or that and stay for a year, creating wealth for ourselves," the pastor said. "But it is all meaningless. The author of Ecclesiastes got that right. If we're ignoring God's plan for our lives, that's all we have. Chaff the wind can blow away at a moment's notice. Nothing valuable, nothing lasting. It looks good for a time but, when all is said and done, our lives have been spent on worthless things."

Yeah, well, Noel had been there and done that. Like he'd reminded Jess, he'd already changed from party animal to someone who thought things through a bit better. He'd never have turned Enterprising Reforestation into the kind of business he had if he hadn't grown up a little.

Still, his plans sounded a lot like what the pastor dude said—a plan to stay in one place for a predetermined amount of time to make money. Hey, so what? It was the nature of his chosen field. A guy couldn't live in one spot and plant trees year round for decades on end. And somebody had to keep the forest healthy. Why not him? He loved the outdoors, the sound of wind in the trees, the smell of rocks and dirt heated by the sun, the glimpse of deer and bears and chipmunks, the taste of wild huckleberries and strawberries warm from the sun.

He was made for nature.

The pastor's voice drew him back in as he gave examples of people who had planned well and done great things, yet on their deathbeds realized that nothing they'd done had eternal value.

Noel was young, barely thirty. There was plenty of time for serious thoughts later, when he'd lived a little. He shifted uncomfortably.

Claire glanced his way then returned her gaze to the pastor. Her lips were parted as she soaked in the teaching and jotted an occasional note into a pad open on her lap, beside her Bible.

She lived and breathed this stuff. And no amount of Noel sitting beside her in church would fool her into thinking he believed like she did.

Right. She was here, for now, and so was he. He'd let things happen as they were meant to, and see how things unfolded. Wasn't that what the guy meant? Not to live on his own plans?

"A life lived for God has true purpose that will last beyond this blip of time," the pastor said.

Claire nodded.

Noel was sunk.

o0o

Only five days into the regimen and already Claire wondered what she'd signed on for. It took a solid four hours in the morning—starting at 3:30—to cook breakfast for the crew and scrub up the kitchen and mess area. By mid-afternoon she was back, this time with Tony, creating a delicious meal and dessert, plus prepping up sandwiches. As soon as Jess dropped off the large empty coolers, Claire and Tony packed them with fresh ice and the next day's lunches, ready for Noel to swing into the bed of his pickup and haul back up the mountain in the morning.

Noel ducked into the cook shack. "Hey, gorgeous. I brought you something."

Tony snickered.

Cheeks flushed, Claire glanced up.

"Not talking to you, kid." Noel cuffed Tony's shoulder.

Tony looked at Claire, a smirk lining his face. "I figured."

Had everyone in camp noticed Noel had a crush on her? That's all it was.

Noel hovered over her. "Don't you want to know what it is?"

"Um, sure. What did you bring me?"

He rolled his eyes. "You didn't sound the least bit curious. Can't you do better than that?"

She pushed hair off her face with her forearm. "Nope. I'm busy making rhubarb crisp for tonight. I don't have time to play games."

"Well, then." Noel reached over and tucked the errant strand behind her ear. "I guess I'll just have to show you."

Claire's temple tingled from his touch as she shifted away and renewed the effort to cut butter into the sugar and oats. "Guess so."

He pulled a paper bag from behind his back. "Look what's in here."

Curious, she obliged. Her eyes widened at the sight of the cone-shaped fungi. "Morels? Where'd you find them?" Those had to be her favorite wild mushrooms.

"We're planting in an old burn area. Can you use these?"

Claire shook her head. "Not for the crew. First off there's

not enough, but more to the point, the health inspector would have something to say about them not coming from a distributor."

Tony peered into the bag. "Wild mushrooms? Those things are dangerous. They can kill a person." He backed away.

Claire shrugged. "Sure they can, if you don't know what you're picking. Morels are pretty distinctive, though." She pulled one out of the bag and held it up for Tony. "See how the flutes look like little sponges?"

He'd backed up almost to the door as though the very presence of one might kill him.

"Get a grip, kid." Noel blocked Tony's getaway. "Restaurants pay a premium for these babies. A few of my buddies spend months every year following the mushrooms and selling them to brokers. Some even get shipped to Japan."

"Really?" Tony looked from Noel to Claire and back again. "You're kidding me."

"He's right, Tony. We used them in the restaurant in Seattle, bought them from reputable brokers. Morels and oyster mushrooms and shaggy manes. Occasionally some other kinds, too. Nobody ever died."

"So you're saying I'm not reputable?"

Claire looked at Noel. "Didn't say that. Personally, I'd eat them no problem, I'm just not allowed to serve them in a commercial kitchen." She waved a hand to indicate the assembly line meal prep she and Tony had been involved in.

"Got a few minutes to spare?" Noel stepped closer. "Maybe we can fry these up in a little butter and have a snack, just us."

It seemed really important to him. Claire ran a mental checklist and nodded. "We could take five."

"Count me out." Tony eyed the mushrooms warily.

Noel upended the mushroom bag onto a clean cutting board and brushed dirt off the fungi. He parked a cast iron skillet onto a burner, cranked the heat, and dropped a generous pat of butter in. Then he turned back to coarse-chop the mushrooms.

Claire's eyes widened. It had never crossed her mind he'd know his way around a kitchen.

He glanced up, catching her staring, and winked as he scraped the mushrooms into the frying pan.

The enticing woodsy aroma of the sautéing morels all but dissolved Claire's knees. She'd have to get him to tell her where he'd found them so she could keep an eye on that spot in upcoming years.

After he was gone.

Tony edged closer, peering into the pan. "They smell good."

Claire couldn't wait any longer. She stabbed a couple of slices and lifted them to her lips, blowing so her mouth wouldn't scorch.

"Wait a sec, let me salt and pepper them. You can't eat them that way."

She pulled the slices off the fork with her teeth. The delectable, earthy flavor nearly melted in her mouth. She reached out to snag some more. "I can, and I will."

Noel blocked her while seasoning the remains in the pan. He jerked his chin at Tony. "Grab a fork, kid. Give it a try."

Tony eyed Claire as she reached around Noel to stab more. "You're not putting me on?"

Noel laughed. "Not a chance. You've just got to leave half of them for Claire." With that he turned down the heat and forked a few into his own mouth.

"Okay." Tony watched them both for a couple of more seconds before making a tentative try. A beatific expression crossed the boy's face. "Oh, wow."

"Exactly." Noel nodded, tucking his arm around Claire as though he only meant to pull her closer to the skillet. "Here you go, have some more."

Maybe she should add one more item to her list. Must know how to find and cook wild fungi. Only, who but Noel would ever be able to check that one off?

Chapter 18 --

The email at the top of Noel's inbox taunted him. He'd been blocking his next contract from his mind, but this missive required an answer.

A basic reply, really. Simply a confirmation of his crew's expected start date higher in the mountains further east. Three weeks.

Photographs of Claire, sticky-tacked over his workspace, smiled at him, glared at him, or looked pensively away. He hadn't fulfilled his promise of getting more photos taken for her website. She hadn't mentioned it since the day he'd kissed her.

True, the farm greened up a lot since then, looking far more like the English garden setting engaged couples probably sought. Photos now would do a much better job of showcasing the natural and tended beauty of the place. And it *was* beautiful.

Maybe next Sunday afternoon he'd talk Claire into a photo excursion around the place then follow up on Jess's suggestion. A picnic. Claire had been shocked he could cook, though she'd tried to hide it. He'd do a whole dinner for her, maybe take her up to the planting site and show her where all her food was being turned into fuel.

That didn't help him with his email from Ben Brower.

The spring contract was coming to an end, right on schedule. For the first time in Noel's life, he wasn't craning his neck to catch a glimpse of what would come next. No, he wished these days could linger on, possibly forever.

With a heavy sigh he clicked *reply*.

Simon would be rejoining the crew in Montana. He was a great cook, far better than Polly, but lacked some of the touches the crew had grown used to with Claire.

Homemade cookies. Fresh produce. Tasty whole-grain breads—some made by Claire. No anemic white for this gal.

Right. She'd be staying here, and he'd be moving on. He'd keep one foot moving forward, but he'd enjoy every minute of Claire's company that could be had before he must leave.

Yes, Ben. We'll be there the first week of July.

He stared at the words on his screen and wished he could delete them. Then hit *send*.

oOo

"How about a shot of the sweet peas growing up the arbor?" Sierra pointed out.

There wasn't much Claire could add to this situation. Sierra had the eye for all this, knowing what the online photo album should include. Noel had the photographic skill to make Sierra's vision a reality.

He moved his tripod closer and zoomed in for a macro.

What could Claire do? Yeah, she could cook. She could make her plates look amazing, but they weren't doing food today. When Noel had suggested the afternoon for a photo shoot, she'd offered a meal, and he refused.

"I'm whisking you off for dinner," he'd said, his brown eyes glinting with mischief.

Why couldn't she say "no" to him? Why couldn't she

remember her checklist, now tucked under her pillow and as tattered as Amber's, proved Noel was not the right guy? Sure she'd added a few items, tailor-made for him, but those didn't counter-balance the first few lines.

Not just the mushroom thing, but the light in his eyes, his gentle touch, his amazing knack of finding her eyes across the crowded mess tent—even his perpetually unshaven face.

"Claire? What do you think?" Sierra waved a hand in front of Claire's face.

Claire blinked to orientate herself. She kept spacing out daydreaming about things that could never be.

"Think about what?" Then she realized Sierra had threaded a panel of lace through the latticework supporting the sweet peas. "Oh. That looks really nice." And it did. It romanticized the pastel blossoms even further.

"Honestly, I don't know where your brain is at." Sierra, standing slightly behind Noel, tipped her head toward him, and winked at Claire.

Thankfully Noel's attention focused on her, not Sierra. He gave her the gentle, private smile she'd come to treasure.

Claire gave her head a shake. "I'm sorry. I'll try to concentrate better."

Noel put the cap on his camera lens. "That's probably enough for today, anyway. I'll get more next Saturday during that retirement party."

The one Claire would be missing due to cooking for his crew. There was something wrong about that.

"We could do a few more still. I have some ideas." Sierra looked from Noel to Claire.

Noel crossed to his customized backpack and nestled the camera inside. "Nah, that's good. Claire and I need lots of time for our dinner date."

Heat infused Claire's cheeks. Had she agreed to a date?

He'd asked her for dinner. She supposed that was a date. Probably.

He glanced at her and grinned. "There's one problem, Claire. You're way too dressed up."

She looked down at her tan capris and frilly tank. This wasn't precisely formal wear. If only he'd tell her where they were going. But no. All he said was it wasn't The Sizzling Skillet. A good thing as she hadn't really been on speaking terms with Nevin for the past month. She cocked her head at Noel. "What's suitable, then?"

"I'd suggest jeans and hikers. Or those cute pink boots. Possibly a hoodie in case it gets cool later on."

She narrowed her gaze at him. "I don't know any restaurant for which that's the preferred dress code."

Noel's brown eyes held hers. "Who said anything about a restaurant?"

Claire's hands found her hips. "Usually assumed when going out for dinner."

That wicked grin swept his face. "You assumed incorrectly." He poked his chin toward the house. "Go get changed. Time's a-wastin'."

She bit her lip and headed for the deck steps. The least he could do was tell her flat out, but no. Everything with Noel had to be a game.

A few minutes later he gave her a hand up into the cab of his truck. He'd already stowed his camera bag behind the seat in the extra cab. He had some other stuff in there, too, with a striped blanket tossed over the top. Gear for his job, no doubt. Before Claire had time to ask more about their destination, he turned left at the end of the driveway. In seconds the truck jounced up the logging road.

Claire crossed her arms and braced her legs, sinking deeper into the leather seat. Up the mountain? Though she'd never admit it, she wanted to see the tree-planting site. Had he read her mind? No wonder he'd been in a hurry to leave Green Acres, though it was only four o'clock. It would take some time to get up and down the mountain then drive into town for the diner. No wonder she didn't need to be dressed up.

Noel glanced her way, his eyes twinkling like he was the best thing since sautéed mushrooms. That could even be true. She kept focused on the mixed conifers outside her window, watching while fir trees and hemlocks swept by.

He shifted into four-wheel-drive and eased the truck up the rutted trail with apparent confidence. "No more questions?" he teased.

Claire shook her head. "I'm completely non-curious. You'll tell me everything I need to know when I need to know it." The food at the diner wasn't heralded to be that great, but in Noel's company, anything would be wonderful. Or taste like sawdust. It had nothing to do with the quality of the food.

He'd be leaving in just a few weeks and would probably never think of her again, at least not after Amber's wedding, if he even returned for that. There'd be somebody new in another town, somebody he could flirt with for a few months and then leave behind.

Her list did not include love 'em and leave 'em as a winning character trait.

"Penny for your thoughts."

Claire made an effort to shake off her dark feelings. Enjoy an evening with her handsome, fascinating boss. Be thankful for the confidence he'd restored in her, that someone could see her as attractive. She'd gotten over Graham. She could get over Noel, too, and maybe down the road there would be someone just for her. Someone that matched her list in all the ways necessary. "I think they're worth a dollar at least."

"Whoa, inflation has hit the thought category. Not sure if I have that much change on me."

"Then you'll have to take a rain check."

He slid down the truck window and leaned out, looking at the sky. "Not in the next few hours, I don't think."

"Funny boy."

He flashed his grin at her. "I try. Seriously, though, there could be a storm later. I checked the forecast. Get it? Rain check?"

"Ha-ha." Claire didn't even try to make it sound like she found him humorous. A guy like him didn't need encouraging. Then what was she doing in his truck, loving and dreading his presence at the same time?

He pointed out the window past her. "This block is where we started planting in April."

Ten-inch-tall seedlings sat in roughly even rows across the steep slope.

Claire imagined digging holes in the rocky hillside to plant the trees. She could feel the chilly rain and the oppressive heat and the annoying sting of a million mosquitoes. She shuddered. Not her way to enjoy the outdoors.

Noel's face glowed. "I love it up here. The peace, far from traffic and sirens and vehicle exhaust." He pushed a button to lower her window, too. "Lean out. Smell the forest."

She sniffed in the aroma of sunlight on moss and decaying logs. The humid warmth caused her to peer at the sky, where clouds roiled in the distance. That rainstorm seemed likely.

"Rough part in the road here, but we're not going too much farther up."

The truck lurched through a low spot and climbed over rocks to regain a smoother track. Smoother only by comparison. Claire couldn't imagine choosing to drive this to work every day.

Every day for three months. Not forever.

174

She blocked the thought out of her mind. She wasn't going there. Not today. For now she'd just enjoy the moments she had.

The road curled around the mountain, and the hillside dropped away out her window. A splashing stream tumbled down on Noel's side and disappeared, though she heard the waterfall at what seemed to be under her feet.

She pulled away from the window.

Noel looked over at her. "Not a fan of heights?"

She clung to the door's elbow rest, willing him to pay attention to the road, not her. "Not much."

"Nothing to be afraid of."

"Easy for you to say."

"It'll be worth it. We're nearly there."

How could *there* possibly look any different than any other place they'd driven past since leaving the farm? She managed a sharp nod and tried to loosen her grip on the armrest. Show some trust. If only she weren't aware of hawks flying along below her, yet way above the trees. Claire closed her eyes and turned her head so Noel wouldn't notice. Maybe he'd think she was admiring the view.

The truck jolted to a halt and the engine cut out.

Claire took a deep breath and peeked out between her lashes. They were surrounded by sky.

"Ready?" he asked.

For what? To get out and rid herself of the shaky feeling the height had given her? She nodded.

Noel sprang out of the truck and came around to her door. He opened it with a sweeping bow. "Come and see."

Claire gingerly slid out of the vehicle and reached for him, glad of strong hands to hold her up. He didn't seem to mind as he led her to a rock not far away.

Across in front of them lay the entire valley. Galena

Landing glowed in the late afternoon sun, the lake placid and calm at its feet. The river glistened as it wound toward Wynnton. Fields patchworked a quilt along the valley bottom, rows of cottonwoods and willows outlining various farms.

Claire sank onto the rock, not daring to stand lest she tumble off the edge and roll down the steep hillside where her battered body would eventually be found, picked at by crows.

"Isn't it beautiful?" Noel knelt beside the rock and rested his arm behind her. "It makes me feel like the king of the world."

She should mind, but his support was welcome. Claire managed a nod. It was impressive. He was right about that.

King of the world? A stray thought wandered through Claire's mind and came out her mouth. "I wonder if this is like what Jesus saw when Satan tempted him. He showed Him a whole panorama and said He could be ruler of it all if He'd only acknowledge Satan's supremacy."

Noel jerked back. "Pardon?"

Claire shook her head. "I didn't mean it that way. You're right, it's absolutely breathtaking." In more ways than one. "I guess what I meant to say was it's a terrific reminder to worship the Creator, not the beauty itself."

Chapter 19 --

Right. Claire had a ton of faith in the Big Guy. Noel kept forgetting because she didn't talk about it a lot. She didn't need to. She lived it.

The whole Christian thing was familiar from childhood, so Noel supposed he might be somewhat immune to random comments. She may have said more over the months they'd known each other than he'd picked up on. But the comment about Jesus's temptation…what was a guy supposed to say about that?

She might be a little strange, but in an endearing way. How could he leave Idaho without her?

Noel shot a glance at her profile as she gazed out across the valley. The view was spectacular, but not compared to her. "Stay right here."

Claire looked up, her eyebrows pulled together. "I don't know where else I'd go."

Noel laughed. "Then it shouldn't be a problem." He strode over to the truck, opened the back door, then pulled a cooler from under a Hudson's Bay blanket. Tossing the blanket over his shoulder, he turned back to Claire and hefted the cooler.

"A picnic?" Her voice even squeaked a little at the end.

Yep, he'd surprised her. He carried the cooler to a nearby

flat rock and set it down. "And it isn't from the ditzy diner, either."

She bit her lip and her face reddened. Cute. He was right on the money.

"Aw, your lack of faith in me causes serious pain, Claire." He opened it up, removed the checkered fabric from the top, and spread it on the rock.

"Even a tablecloth?" She sounded incredulous.

"Yep." Jess to the rescue.

He spread the blanket beside the tablecloth then swept a bow to show Claire she could move to the new location.

Claire sank to the edge of the blanket with her hikers amidst the tufts of grass.

"Let me get you something to drink." Noel pulled out two plastic wine goblets, along with a bottle of sparkling raspberry. After pouring, he handed her one of the goblets.

She took it from him with trembling hands, her eyes fixed on his.

He clinked his cup against hers. At least it would have clinked if it had been glass. "To us."

Her jaw clenched. "Noel, I don't think—"

Noel pressed his finger against her soft lips. "That's the spirit. No thinking. Let's just enjoy today." He settled down beside her, shoulders brushing, and took a sip.

After a moment, she did the same then shifted away and set hers beside the blanket. She stared off into the distance.

"Hungry?" he asked.

"A little bit." A small smile crossed her face. "More curious, though."

Noel winked at her. "I'm full of surprises."

"You seem to be."

Their eyes caught for a long moment then Noel turned to the cooler and brought out a baguette, a tub of herbed cream cheese, and a butter knife. "Just so you know, I didn't make this."

She eyed him speculatively, as he'd intended. He tore off a small chunk of bread, spread it with cheese, then handed it to her. His eyes held hers captive while she chewed the morsel.

oOo

Claire had never been this intimately aware of a man's presence. It was dangerous to meet Noel's eyes, but she couldn't help herself. She wanted more of him. But the only kind of more she could give and accept was the image of Noel filling her eyes, her mind—her memories.

There couldn't be any other kind of more. Not today, not ever. Still, she couldn't regret being here.

He opened a container and set it on her lap. The aroma of herb-spiced chicken tickled her nostrils. The brown speckled drum and thigh lay nestled next to potato salad with a few cubes of yam in it. No deli in town sold anything like it.

"You really made this yourself?" Not Jess, she wanted to ask, but that was unfair. Besides, Jess wasn't here. Whatever existed between them, Noel had chosen to spend his day with her, not his foreman. Jess had always treated Claire as a friend.

"I did." Noel's fingers gently swept her bangs to the side. "For you."

Her skin tingled from his touch. She'd thought she was hungry, but her appetite for food had dropped with each touch. Her every nerve ending was tuned to his body, yearning for more.

For an instant she thought he'd kiss her again. She wouldn't push him away. But then he broke contact and opened a second container, and took a bite of his own chicken leg. He winked at her. "Pretty good, if I do say so myself."

Claire should try to eat something, not sit here on this mountain like a lovesick fool. She lifted a drum and nibbled it. Her eyebrows shot up. This was no store-bought mix. The man was an excellent cook. "This is delicious. I might need the recipe."

His shoulder bumped hers. "Every cook keeps his secrets." He picked up her fork and captured a piece of yam. "Here, try this."

She opened her mouth, allowing him to feed her. The slightly sweet taste of the unusual dressing melted in her mouth. She grabbed his wrist. "What is that?" And more importantly, why was the guy planting trees instead of cooking in some swanky restaurant?

He shrugged, looking pleased at her response. "Just a little twist I started making a year or two ago. Honey mustard, a bit of fennel."

That slight licorice flavor. Fennel. She should have recognized it. When she loosened her grip on his wrist, he caught her hand. With his other, he stroked her cheek.

Claire closed her eyes, savoring the sensation, knowing she shouldn't encourage it. She felt him move a second before his lips, tasting of chicken seasoning, met hers.

She fumbled with the container on her lap, getting it out of the way so she could twist to meet him more fully. Her fingers tangled in his hair, holding his face at the right angle for their deepening kiss.

This time she'd be the one to pull away first, but not yet.

Definitely not yet.

He released the hand he'd held and slid both of his around her back, cradling her against him.

Dear God, why was it again that she couldn't have this man until death would them part? Claire clung to Noel, even when his mouth released hers and he rocked her tightly across his chest, nuzzling her neck.

"Come with me," he groaned into her hair. "I need you with me always."

Was that a marriage proposal? It didn't quite sound like one. And where exactly did he want to take her?

Far from Green Acres.

And if she were paying any attention to her aroused senses, possibly far from God as well.

She'd never been so tempted in her life to toss everything she valued, everything she believed in, right over a cliff like the one in front of her.

The devil had offered everything to Jesus, too. Nothing he'd offered had been evil in itself—in fact, all of it already belonged to Jesus. It wasn't the timing, and it wasn't the way. To agree under those circumstances would have made God less God, and Satan would have become the ruler of the universe.

Loving Noel wasn't wrong, either. But giving in to him under these circumstances was. For another few seconds Claire soaked in his nearness before she drew back.

He allowed her some room while keeping his hands linked around her. He rested his forehead against hers and looked deeply into her eyes. "Please?"

Her fingers tightened in his hair. "Oh, Noel, you know I can't. Green Acres is my home, my life."

"Home is wherever a person is with those they love."

But he hadn't quite said he loved her, no matter what his eyes told her. She slid her hands down to his shoulders, flexing her fingertips into his back muscles. "This is where God wants me."

"How can you say that? Doesn't He want us to be happy?"

Claire pulled away a little more, a cool breeze passing her forehead where she no longer touched Noel. Did God want her happy? It wasn't His stated purpose. She shook her head a little.

"He wants to give us peace."

Noel's eyebrows arched. "Peace?"

"Don't you feel it?" The conviction within her grew, even as her heart seemed about to break. "When I surrender everything to God and ask Him to do His will—not mine—He provides perfect peace that soothes my soul." Even now the balm was being applied. It gave her strength to put her hands on Noel's arms and gently push him to release her.

"How can you say this isn't God's will? Why would He bring us together only to tear us apart?" Confusion and hurt mingled in those brown eyes that had come to mean so much to her.

Claire sucked in a deep breath. She had a feeling those exact thoughts were going to haunt her for many sleepless nights.

"Is it that you don't want to leave Green Acres? A farm is more important to you than I am?"

He hadn't asked her to marry him, only come away with him. Did he even realize the words he'd used? "This place means everything to me, but not just because I love it here. It's because I truly feel God called me to be a part of it. I'm sorry, Noel. God will always be the most important person in my life. I want to please Him more than anyone else."

Noel rocked away from her. "I can't believe I'm losing to some invisible guy in the sky."

Yes, she was making the right decision. "You told me you believed in God."

He raked his hands through his hair where, just moments before, her own fingers had been. "I do. Really, I do. But all this talk about His will and stuff—it's old person talk." His eyes widened as they met hers and he realized what that must sound like. "I mean no offense, Claire, but isn't there plenty of time for religion later? We're young. With any luck we'll have fifty or sixty good years yet."

Noel flung his hand out and waved it, encompassing the valley behind her. "Yeah, I believe in God. I even believe He created all this beauty. But why do it if He didn't mean people to enjoy it?"

A chill came over her. A bit of wind, no doubt. "Who said anything about not enjoying it? There's been nothing unenjoyable in my life when I walk with God." Except for Nevin. And a few other minor inconveniences. "Don't you understand? He's my foundation. Anything I build without His support is sure to collapse. That's where the dissatisfaction will come in, every time." She should know. Look at Graham.

The sky seemed to darken, but wait. That might not be her imagination. She twisted on the striped blanket and looked behind her at the sky.

Ominous clouds boiled over the mountains across the valley. A streak of lightning flashed through the dark mass, followed by a distant rumble.

Noel surged to his feet and snapped the lid on one of the containers. He tossed it into the cooler and reached for the other. "If you're hungry you can eat on the way back down. We need to get going."

Hungry? The tastes had been tantalizing, but she had no desire for food left now. Even the mingling of dissatisfaction and peace fled in the presence of the lightning. Another flash lit up the darkening sky. A plume of smoke lifted from the distant mountainside.

Fire.

"Claire? Can you get the blanket?" Noel grabbed the cooler—when had he gotten everything in it?—and ran for the truck.

Claire struggled to her feet, still staring at the smoky wisps. A small explosion puffed as a distant tree went up in flame. "There's a forest fire." Rain began to spatter around her as clouds choked off the last bit of sunshine.

Noel stood beside her and stared for a moment. Then he reached down and shook out the blanket. It fluttered beside her as he bundled it up. He grabbed her arm. "Come on! We don't want to be on the mountain top when the storm hits over here." He threw the blanket into the truck's back seat.

She stumbled behind him to the vehicle where he hoisted her into the passenger seat then slammed the door.

Claire's eyes found the flames again as another tree caught fire.

Noel shoved the truck into gear.

She clutched at his arm. "Look!"

"I see it. Can't do anything about it from up here, but I'll call it in when we get off the mountain. Hang on, I'll be going fast, at least until we're down into the forest."

The truck jolted down the rutted road, rivulets of water already finding a twisted path down, racing the vehicle.

Thunder rumbled, closer now. Lightning split the darkening sky again and again.

Claire cowered in her seat, waiting for it to strike nearby. A fire further down could block them up on the mountain, recklessly devouring everything in its path.

"Claire? Talk to me."

She squeezed her eyes shut. "I-I'm afraid."

"Hey, it's going to be okay. Nothing to worry about." Silence for a moment while the truck jounced about. "Really. That was just a little fire, unlikely to get much bigger. Maybe the rain will even put it out without a crew."

Such a man as this—how could she let him go?

Chapter 20 --

"I thought you'd like to know the fire up the mountain is under control." Noel paused as he dished up his plate the next evening.

Claire pushed her hair off her forehead with her wrist, but didn't meet his gaze. "That's good. I was worried about it."

"I could tell." He watched her pensively. "Anything you want to talk about?"

"Not really." She turned away to refill the vegetable tureen.

He couldn't let her walk out of his life like this, could he? How could he convince her of all the fun things they could do in other places? She just didn't know, didn't understand. It wasn't that she didn't care for him as much as he did for her. That had been pretty obvious yesterday on the mountaintop.

"Hey, boss. Some of the guys have a few questions for you."

Claire's back stiffened at Jess's voice.

Noel swallowed the lump in his throat. "Be right there." He watched Claire a moment, but she didn't turn. "Claire?"

At that, she did turn, pain evident in her eyes. "Yes? Is there something wrong with your meal?"

His meal? He glanced at his half-filled plate then back at her. "No…"

"Good. Then finish dishing up, because you're holding up the line."

He reached for the next scoop mechanically. Who could ever have thought things would go downhill this quickly? He'd always known it was dangerous to date an employee, but his hands had been tied. Not on the dating, he supposed, but the employee part. And they hadn't even been dating. Just one beautiful drive to the top of the world. Two kisses he'd never forget. One plea that had come from the bottom of his heart. One heart-wrenching discussion about the will of God.

And one rejection.

He didn't get it.

"Noel! Over here." He followed Jess's voice to a small table with several of his experienced planters present.

He'd known better back when he'd felt that flare of attraction for Jess a few years back. She'd been dating his best friend then, and by the time they'd broken up, Jess was his new best friend and his crew's foreman. After some rocky weeks, they'd decided to remain friends no matter what. And it had worked.

Why hadn't he kept Claire at arm's length until he'd gotten used to the position with her? He set his tray on the table beside Jess, where he could keep an eye on Claire behind the serving counter.

"Hey, guys. How goes it?" He met each pair of eyes in turn as he swung his legs over the picnic bench.

"There's some bear sign not far up from our current planting site," James said.

Noel nodded. "Griz?"

"Nah, probably a black."

"How fresh?"

"Few days maybe."

"Make sure your gun's ready when you're up there. Take a

bit more time to ensure everyone's safety. Everyone have a can of pepper spray?" Thirty noisy planters ought to be enough to scare off any bear, but if one went rabid and attacked, it wouldn't be on his watch. "Show me tomorrow, okay? We'll do a bit of scouting."

James nodded and dug into his meal.

"Good food," Wade said. "Thanks for getting rid of Polly and finding us a real cook."

Jess's elbow found its way into Noel's ribs. He shifted slightly away, not wanting to respond. If Jess hadn't noticed the strain between him and Claire today, he wasn't going to point it out.

"A woman of many talents," Jess said, teasing evident in her voice.

Noel buttered his dinner roll and had a bite. Somehow it reminded him of that baguette yesterday. Suddenly the roll tasted like sawdust. He set it down and picked up his fork to dig into the pork stew. At least it was nothing like fried chicken or potato salad.

He still had all the picnic leftovers in the fridge in his trailer. If he couldn't face it in the next day or two, he'd turf it in the garbage. He hated the waste, but...

Jess's elbow dug his ribs again.

Startled, he looked up. "Pardon me?"

"Just talking about how dry the spring has been," Wade said.

"Been great for planting. I hate getting rained on." James glanced sideways at his friend.

Wade shrugged. "Me, too. But I'm worried after yesterday's storm. This whole area is like a tinderbox, ready to explode into flame, and there wasn't enough rain to make a difference."

"We'll be out of here before the fire season gets underway. It'll be some other crew's problem, not ours."

He became aware of Jess's eyes on him and glanced her way. "There's been more rain on Montana's eastern slopes than here." Not that his words would deflect her any.

They didn't. "I agree with Wade. Could be a big issue this summer. Think things will be as green as your sister would like for her wedding?"

Noel's eyes sought Claire, but she was focused on Tony as he set out desserts. He still had a lot of times he'd need to deal with Claire, but once Amber's wedding was over, so was he. If he couldn't win her back by then, he'd be done. Forever.

"Boss?"

"The spring Green Acres gets its water supply from runs deep. Zach doesn't think they should have any water shortages." He turned to Wade. "Yesterday's strike—they did get that burn contained, didn't they? That's what I'd heard."

"They're water bombing it. It's a bit steep for a ground crew, but if there's no wind, it should be okay."

Maybe his assurance to Claire was premature. If that fire did take hold, it was still miles away across the river and across the valley. Thousands of acres of farmland stood between it and Green Acres.

James elbowed Wade. "Rhubarb bars for dessert." Both guys jumped off the bench, overturning it, then rushed the counter.

"Hey, boss, what's up?"

Noel should have known Jess was paying closer attention than it seemed.

"Something feels off between you and the chef. Dreamboat didn't like your picnic yesterday?"

Why did he tell Jess so much? It became really annoying when he wanted her out of his business, but he had no one to blame but himself. "We barely started eating before the storm hit." Didn't have to tell Jess which storm, did he?

"Pretty nasty up top?"

She had no idea. Well, maybe she did. "You could say so."

The guys wended their way back but stopped to visit at another table.

Noel turned to Jess. "Look, she really infatuated me. But I'm over it. Things between me and Claire could never work. We don't have the same goals in life, and besides, she can't stand me."

Her kiss had said otherwise.

Laughter played in Jess's voice. "Really?"

Noel frowned. "Yes, really."

"Then why does she keep watching you when you're not looking?"

Noel jerked his head up but Claire was focused on scraping out a pan.

Jess doubled over with snickering. "Gotcha."

o0o

It had been the longest shift of Claire's career. Okay, maybe not the longest. Some of those nights at The Sizzling Skillet compared with many years ago when she was an apprentice. But still, tonight ranked right up there if one counted a dragging clock.

"Got the lunches packed up?" she asked Tony.

He pointed at the coolers stacked on the west side of the mobile kitchen's door, where they'd still be in the shade as the crew loaded up in the morning. "Breakfast is prepped, too."

"Thanks, kid. I don't know what I'd do without you."

He flashed her a grin. "It's a lot of fun helping you. I only wish this job wouldn't be over so soon."

Yet the season couldn't end fast enough for her. "There will be other options for you at some point."

"I suppose." Tony took a deep breath. "I'd like to go to

189

culinary school."

She mustered up a smile. "That's awesome. You can probably start applying early in the New Year, but don't narrow your options too soon. Keep up all your grades."

"Yeah, yeah, I know. You sound like my mom."

Today she felt old enough to be the mother of a teen. She felt positively ancient. If she let Noel go, would she ever find someone else, or was her biological clock ticking so rapidly that he was her last chance to have kids of her own?

She needed to stop that line of thinking. It wasn't *if* she let Noel go. She'd already told him in no uncertain terms they had no future. She'd even meant it, though the entire conversation had replayed all night long. Whenever it could shove over the memory of that blissful kiss. There she went again.

A few minutes later she let herself into the straw bale farmhouse just down the road. Jo and Sierra sat curled up in opposite ends of one love seat and looked up as she entered.

"How are things going?" Sierra asked.

Why did they have to be curious now? Why not two days ago, when everything floated by on silver clouds? Or next week, when she had regained her composure?

Claire shrugged and padded into the kitchen.

"Teapot is full," Jo offered without moving.

How well these two knew her. They'd been there for each other through thick and thin.

Claire poured a cup and sniffed. Mint. Should help soothe her. Maybe tonight she'd be able to sleep. She set her cup on an end table, sank into the easy chair, and plopped her feet on the ottoman. How could she ever admit to her closest friends what a fool she'd been, falling for a guy that was completely unsuitable?

"I hear you went out for dinner with Noel yesterday," Jo said.

No preamble? With Jo, that wasn't much of a surprise. Claire cut a glance at Sierra, who wiped polish remover across her purple-streaked nails.

"Sort of. He packed a picnic and took me to the top of the mountain behind Green Acres."

"Up where they're tree planting?" Jo cradled her mug of tea.

"Further. The planting site is only about halfway up the mountain where it had been logged last year. There's actually quite a fantastic view from the very top, clear across the valley." If one could handle heights.

"Tell me about Noel."

A fierce pang pierced Claire's heart. "There's nothing to tell."

Sierra glanced up for a second then returned to her fingernails.

Jo watched Claire over the rim of her cup. "Nothing? That's not the tale I hear."

"Okay, so he's a guy." A totally hot guy. "He's Amber's brother. He owns Enterprising Reforestation. He's my boss. He likes to travel all over the world in the offseason. And there's nothing to tell." She may have said that all a little too forcefully to be convincing.

"I've heard he's cute and funny."

Claire barked a laugh. "You shouldn't pay attention to rumors like that. You're a married woman."

Sierra snickered.

"Nice one, Claire." Jo cracked a grin. "So there's nothing to the way you two have been eyeing each other?"

Claire opened her mouth to deny everything but her conscience stabbed. "I could fall for him if we had more in common." There, she'd said it.

"Could fall? Not, as in, have fallen?"

Claire recrossed her ankles the other way. "Whatever there

was, whatever there might have been—it doesn't matter. It's over."

Sierra screwed the cap on the nail polish remover and set it aside. She tucked her knees up under her chin and eyed Claire. "Have you been praying about it?"

Claire narrowed her eyes. "Yes."

"So you're saying there's enough there to be praying about." Jo leaned forward.

There couldn't possibly be a need to answer that, so Claire didn't.

"A year ago I never thought things would work out with Zach, in case you don't recall."

Claire remembered. "That was different."

"It's always different." Jo shrugged. "He was fixated on returning to the city to be a pet vet. Didn't want to spend his life doctoring cows and horses."

"But he grew up here." In fact, the girls had bought their farm from Zach's grandmother, who was now in a nursing home, and his parents owned the property right next door, where Jo and Zach were living at the moment.

"He did, but he didn't want to move back here again. Not only that, he wasn't walking with God." Jo glanced at Sierra, a little smile peering out. "And besides, I thought he'd gone and fallen for Sierra."

At least Noel was only fixated on her, Claire. No doubt about that. But how long would it last now that she'd turned him down? "It's still different. Home for Noel is Missoula, but he's been living in his little vacation trailer for years, traveling from job to job. Zach wasn't established anywhere yet."

"You're saying Noel's more settled in his unsettledness?" Sierra asked with a laugh.

"Something like that. And where Zach had been an active Christian as a teenager, Noel wasn't. Oh, he says he believes in

God, but figures there's plenty of time to think about religion later, when he's old."

Jo leaned forward, elbows on her knees. "The thing is that God answered prayer about Zach, making him willing to stay right here and take over Doc Taubin's practice. Calling him back into a closer walk with God."

"Yeah, well, that's great. I was really happy for you then, and I still am. I just don't think we can expect God to work the same kind of miracle again."

Jo's eyebrows arched. "Why not? Doesn't He want His children to be happy?"

Those words again, the same way Noel used them.

"Every good and perfect gift comes from above," Sierra mused, staring at the ceiling as though a gift-wrapped box would drop in her lap any second. If anything fell, it would likely be a spider.

"It's like I told Noel, our happiness isn't God's main goal. You know that." Claire surged to her feet. "He expects our obedience, and the peace He gives when we're walking in His will is worth everything. It's better than happiness."

Jo cocked her head to one side. "That's what you said to Noel?"

"All that and more. Trust me when I say we don't have a future." She drew her lips into a pensive line. "A long time ago I said I'd be content to be Auntie Claire to you guys's kids. I still mean that." Okay, content might be the wrong word, but if that was her destiny, she'd trust that God would give her the grace—and yes, the peace—to be the best aunt those children could ever have.

"Well, that's good at least." Sierra stood and stretched. "Though I'm less likely to have kids than you, for what it's worth."

Halfway to the kitchen for another cup of tea, Claire turned back. "Why would that be?"

Sierra grimaced. "Not seeing any guy looking my way. You at least have something to patch up."

"Patch up." Claire snorted. "It needs more than a patch, I'd say."

"Well, I'm glad you two are up for it. You're getting the chance to be aunties."

Claire pivoted on her heel and stared hard at Jo.

Jo looked like a cat presiding over a puddle of spilled cream. "Zach and I are expecting a baby."

Chapter 21 --

Barely awake, Noel fumbled with his ringing cell phone. "Hello?" Not even a hint of daylight peered through the trailer's mini blinds.

"Son?" The voice slurred.

Noel lay back against his pillow. "Dad. It's the middle of the night."

"Don't wanna talk to your old man?"

No answering that one honestly. "I have to get up and go to work in a couple hours. What's so important at—" he squinted at his watch "—two a.m.?"

"Need a few bucks and thought you might be willing to help me out."

Not again. Noel closed his eyes. "What happened?"

"I just don't have any more. It's gone."

"You mean you gambled it away."

"I nearly had it that time. I was winning."

He'd heard it all before. More than once. "And then you went double or nothing?"

His father's voice took on a sour tinge. "I said I was winning."

"You didn't call me to borrow money because you're ahead of the game." It wasn't precisely borrowing. He'd never seen a nickel returned for all the times he'd bailed Dad out.

Silence.

His dad was good at that guilt thing. Noel hadn't ever figured out what exactly he was supposed to feel guilty about, but that didn't stop the emotion from barreling through him. "What do you need, Dad?"

"That's more like it. Just a few Ben Franklins will do me until I can get things moving forward."

Nothing had changed. "You still at Della's place in Philly? I'll pay your room for next month and get you some grocery vouchers."

"Philly?" Confusion shadowed Dad's voice.

Noel let out a whoosh of air. "Where are you?" Of course Philly had been too good to be true. He'd lasted, what, a year or two there? It was almost like he'd settled down, which wasn't the same thing as keeping a job.

"St. Louis. You know, with that arch. Thought maybe I'd swing back west and see your mother."

Uh, that would go over like a bear in a planting site.

"Then maybe see you. Where you at these days?"

"Idaho, but I won't be here much longer. Got another gig after this one."

A drunken chuckle met Noel's ear. "You travel the country like your old man."

The words escaped before Noel could censure them. "Not exactly like you, no. I actually work and pay my own way."

Bewildered, now. "I used to do that."

And then he'd hit the bottle a few too many times. Watching his father, even from a distance, had been a huge motivator when Noel decided to quit the booze. Once his dad had been a traveling salesman. Now he was just a drunk on the move.

"I haven't seen you in a while. Maybe I could stay with you a bit."

Oh, please, no. "My trailer is very small, Dad. There isn't room for anyone else. And my jobs take me way into the mountains." No one to con or bum a drink from. Might that be a good thing? "No towns, no people except my crew. It wouldn't work."

His dad huffed. "Well, I know when I'm not wanted."

No doubt that's why he wasn't at Della's any more.

"But I hear my baby girl is getting hitched and it seems her old man ought to be there to give her away, doncha think?"

Noel's gut chilled. "Did Amber ask you?" No way would she have done that. She didn't even know Noel kept in loose contact with their father. When she'd asked Noel to walk her down the aisle, she hadn't said anything about wishing for the father she'd never known instead.

"She probably don't know how to find me. So I'm ambling over to see what's up." There was a significant pause. "Leastways if I can come up with the fare."

Noel had never been so tempted to deny his father funds. Could he justify ruining Amber and Shawn's big day by providing means for Dad to come west? On the other hand, could he live with his conscience if he kept the man away if he wanted to make amends? Dad hadn't claimed that as his goal. But still. There was more chance of it happening if he saw his family than if he stayed away. Maybe.

He probably should ask Amber before giving Dad money this time, but that would lead to more questions than he wanted to answer. What were the odds their father would actually get all the way from St. Louis to Galena Landing in time? Pretty much zero.

He sighed. "How much do you need?"

o0o

Amber and her mother came to Green Acres the next weekend to finalize some arrangements.

"Do you know anyone who might want to buy a house in Missoula?"

Claire swung to face Eileen Kenzie. "No, why? You're not moving, are you?"

She glanced at her daughter. "I might be, if all goes well."

It didn't look like Eileen and Amber had argued. They sat there side by side with no visible animosity. So could it really be that Eileen wanted to move to get away from her daughter?

Amber elbowed her mother. "Mom, you're scaring Claire."

Was it that obvious?

Eileen looked startled. "What?"

"Shawn is being promoted. And transferred."

Claire felt like the bus had left without her. "Oh, no! I mean, the promotion is great. He couldn't convince them to keep him in Missoula?"

Amber shrugged. "It doesn't matter. His grandparents live in Flagstaff, and the family goes down often. He's happy to move nearer to them."

"You're moving to Arizona?" Claire heard the incredulity in her own voice. "And it doesn't matter?"

"I'm pretty sure I can get a job there. If it takes a while, Shawn will be making enough to keep us comfortable for the time being. I think it will be kind of fun."

She couldn't be serious. "But Missoula is your home." Claire cast a glance at Amber's mom. Noel hadn't mentioned ever living someplace else while he was growing up. Not that he'd given her the details of his life.

Amber laughed. "It's really not a biggie. All I care about is being with Shawn." Her eyes grew large and her hand came up to cover her mouth. "Oh. I didn't mean it that way."

Eileen looked puzzled. "Mean it what way?"

But Claire knew. "I once was engaged to a man who decided to join Dentists Without Borders. He was certain I'd be happy to gallivant around the world with him." She grimaced. "He was wrong."

"I didn't mean to make it sound like you should've been. It truly doesn't matter to me." Amber took a deep breath. "I mean, we're different, and so are the circumstances."

The girl should stop talking already before she dug herself a deeper hole. Claire stared at her for a moment before turning to Eileen. "So you're thinking of moving to Arizona, too?"

"I can't very well do without my baby."

Claire noticed no one had said a thing about Noel's whereabouts. They probably didn't see him often enough for it to be a big deal, and he traveled so much—her gut soured—that Arizona was as likely as Montana to be on his way to or from a destination.

"Aw, Mom. You know we'd love to have you live nearby."

Which could never be said of Claire's mother, who was best off left in Denver where she'd migrated when she finally dumped Claire's dad.

"Well, you surprised me, is all." Claire put a cheery voice to it. "Here I thought your family roots went deep into Montana soil. I assume no one is moving before the wedding?"

"Oh, definitely not. That's only six weeks away. Shawn is flying south next weekend to look for a house for August first."

"You're trusting him to find you a place to live, sight unseen?"

"Relax, Claire. It's only a rental. We can move again later if it turns out to be not the best part of the city or something. It'll give us time to look for a place to buy."

That kind of trust was foreign to Claire. She'd thought Graham was the weird one, expecting her to love him enough to fall in line with his plans. But if she believed Amber,

199

Graham's expectations had been normal and her own response strange. For a moment she tried to imagine leading Graham's life. Failed. No, she couldn't have done things any differently. If nothing else, this conversation told her she hadn't loved Graham. Not truly. Yet how was that a surprise? Hadn't she come to the same conclusion three years earlier?

Maybe she had no idea what love really meant. The only other recent example had been Jo and Zach, and Jo had won out about staying on the farm. A niggling memory poked at Claire's mind. Hadn't Jo so desperately loved Zach she'd been willing to move to Coeur d'Alene before she'd found out he'd accepted a position at Landing Veterinary?

Noel hadn't asked Claire to marry him. He'd only talked about her coming away with him. Had he meant marriage? Because nothing else was on the table. Claire gave her head a shake. A wedding wasn't, either.

o0o

His mother's high heels clipped to a stop on the church's bottom step. "Noel?" She fanned herself, though it wasn't that hot out. "Is that really you?"

He crunched across the parking lot toward her, but she didn't need to make a production out of her surprise.

The Green Acres car hadn't pulled in yet. Maybe Mom wouldn't figure out this was all about Claire. What did he really want his mother to think? Either that possibility or the one where he was seeking God looked equally unattractive.

Noel leaned over to peck her cheek. "Good morning, Mom." He tucked his hand under her elbow and practically lifted her up the steps. He nodded at his sister. "Hi, Amber."

She winked at him then glanced at the parking lot.

Noel could hear vehicles and voices but no way was he

turning to see what had her attention. Not with their mother's interest firmly focused on him. "Shall we?" He took Amber's arm and escorted both women into the foyer.

"Good to see you again, Mr. Kenzie." The gray-haired church elder beamed and reached for Noel's hand, not seeming to notice both were occupied.

Noel released Amber to shake Ed Graysen's hand. "Good morning, sir. I'd like you to meet my mother, Eileen, and my sister, Amber. Mom, this is Mr. Graysen."

The elder winked at Amber. "I've met the pretty young lady before." He turned to Noel's mom and closed both his hands over hers. "It's an honor to meet you, Eileen."

Noel could only hope the guy was happily married. It wasn't like Mom needed anyone in her life, especially not in Idaho if the rumors of her move to Flagstaff held any truth.

"You have such a lovely family," Mr. Graysen went on.

"Thank you." Mom pulled her hand free and gave the older man a slightly puzzled look. She took Noel's arm again, tugging him to turn aside. "Who is that?" she whispered after a few steps.

"One of the church elders." Noel glanced over his shoulder just in time to see Mr. Graysen give Claire a hug. He squelched the jealousy that rose at the sight.

Mom hadn't noticed. "This isn't a very large building."

"Galena Landing is a lot smaller than Missoula." Amber tugged her purse strap higher on her shoulder.

Those things always looked like they were a nuisance, and women seemed to jam enough into them to put their backs out of whack. Even Claire, and she wasn't a city girl like Amber.

There'd be no way to pull off his stunt of last Sunday and wait until Claire sat down. Not after how badly the day—and week—had gone. But he could steer his sister and mom into the back pew so he'd be able to watch Claire throughout the service.

"I like to sit a bit closer to the front, son." Mom shook her head and pointed to a spot halfway up the sanctuary. "There's an empty row."

Noel leaned down. "I'm not that comfortable in church, Mom. I'd feel kind of awkward way up there in the middle."

"But I can't see or hear from here. You sit wherever you like. Amber, are you coming?" Mom turned on her spiked heel and marched down the center aisle.

Amber shrugged and sent a look of appeal at Noel then followed their mother.

"Whatever." He hadn't meant to say it out loud, but a nearby older woman looked at him with a frown. Sit with his family or at the back? Blast his mother anyway. He gritted his teeth and followed her into the middle of the empty pew. She could've let him sit on the aisle so he could escape if he needed to, but no. A few people edged in from the other end, and more filed into the row in front of them. Sierra. Claire. Mr. Graysen with a smiling older lady. Even he would have trouble wedging himself in beside Claire with the number of people claiming the seats.

He glanced up as a shadow loomed over him, and Zach and Jo slid in beside him. Great. He'd managed to avoid Zach since the guy had taken too close an interest in his relationship with Claire a couple of months back. Still, he had to be polite. "Good morning, Zach." Noel leaned forward a smidge to see Jo beyond her husband. "Hey, Jo."

"Hi yourself!" Jo grinned at him then tapped Claire on the shoulder. Claire turned—away from Noel. The two girls whispered for a moment then Claire faced the front as the worship team came on stage.

Noel hunkered down in the pew, crossing both ankles and arms. The only bright side was Clair's profile.

Chapter 22 --

Claire squirmed on the crowded pew. Pastor Ron's words arrowed straight at her heart and Noel's gaze scorched the back of her head. This would've been a fine sermon any other time. Everything had become awkward since meeting Noel. How dare he rock her world?

Still, why did Pastor Ron have to choose this particular Sunday to enthuse on the temporariness of life on Planet Earth? Only a stranger here, he said. Only camping out. And in the light of eternity, he was right. It shouldn't matter where she lived since it wouldn't last anyway.

But when she closed her eyes from Pastor Ron's gaze—why couldn't he look at someone else while delivering this message?—she could see only Noel's face. His dark eyes as he looked at her. His appreciation of the beauty of their surroundings. His delight in the morel mushrooms and the herbed chicken. What did Green Acres matter in comparison with a love like his?

Not that he'd asked her to marry him. No, those memorable words hadn't crossed his kissable lips. Come away with me, he'd said. What did that mean?

Belatedly Claire realized Sierra and Mrs. Graysen, on either side of her, stood as the worship leader urged everyone to turn in their hymnal to "This World is Not My Home." Just passing through? Where *did* she have her treasure laid up? Could she sing this song? Either way, Noel watched from behind. He'd see if she did...or didn't.

Oh, God. Why this message? Why today?

o0o

"Wasn't that a lovely sermon, son?" Mom spoke rather loudly into the quiet sanctuary as she gathered her purse and Bible after the service.

"Wonderful," Noel murmured. He took Mom's elbow in hopes of steering her straight out the door to the vestibule and beyond as quickly as possible, but she'd have none of that nonsense.

Zach Nemesek turned. "Thought-provoking, for sure." He glanced from Noel to Amber then at Mom. "Mrs. Kenzie, I presume?"

Noel beat his mother to the punch. "Yes, this is my mother, Eileen. Mom, meet Jo's husband, Zach."

"Lovely to meet you." She placed her soft hand in Zach's for a brief instant then withdrew. "Josephine is a wonderful young woman."

The skin around Zach's eyes crinkled. "She is definitely something special." He glanced at Noel then back at Mom. "Even though we're just passing through a bit of time on this planet like Pastor Ron said, I'm thankful God drew me back to Galena Landing to spend whatever time I do have with Jo."

Mom pressed her fingers against Zach's arm. "You grew up here, then?"

"Sure did. Right here in this church." He grinned. "Next door to Green Acres, actually. The girls bought my grandparents' land."

Noel hadn't known that. There was a lot he didn't know.

He'd been so focused on leaving before Claire could lure him into staying he hadn't bothered really getting to know anything about her past. He glanced at her, but she was deep in discussion with Sierra, their faces turned away from his. Like a cloud coming between him and the sun, cooling him.

"You're coming for Sunday dinner, aren't you, Noel?" Jo interjected, leaning around Zach. "Your mom and sister are. Sierra put chicken soup in the slow cooker early this morning. It won't take long when we get home. We'll just make a batch of biscuits and dish up."

"Uh." The sermon confused him. Did those thoughts mean he had a better chance with Claire or a worse one? Could he stand being in her presence? Or vice versa?

Amber elbowed his ribs. "Of course he's coming. What else would he do? Reheat a tin of ravioli in his trailer over at Elmer's?"

"Hey, I'll have you know I can cook."

"Since when?" Skepticism loomed in his sister's eyes. "I've seen no evidence."

Good point. He never bothered in Missoula with Mom and Amber. Nobody ever asked him to contribute and he hadn't volunteered. "I make a mean taco stew."

Amber's narrow eyebrows met. "News to me."

Claire and Sierra turned toward the conversation behind them.

"Taco stew?" asked Sierra. "Sounds delicious."

Amber swatted Noel's arm. "You're making that up since there's no way you can prove it."

He opened his mouth in protest but Sierra beat him to words. "Oh, I don't know. What do you need for ingredients, Noel? We probably have most of it. Maybe you'd like to make supper at Green Acres tonight. You know, in thankfulness for us feeding you lunch."

"What, no one believes me?" His eyes caught Claire's.

She took a deep breath and looked away. "Noel's a good cook."

"That's very interesting, my dear." Mom all but purred. "How might you know this?"

Noel's heart sank. He'd managed to keep his mother from suspecting the strength of his feelings for Claire and had sworn Amber to silence on the topic in their matriarch's presence. Now the cat was out of the bag.

Claire met his mother's gaze. "He's come through the mobile kitchen at Elmer's a time or two. He knows his way around."

A breath slid out he hadn't realized he'd been holding.

"Sierra has a great idea, though," Jo put in. "You up for chef tonight? You'll get all the prep help you could possibly want. I think I hear Zach volunteering."

Noel's eyes snagged onto Claire's. "Sure, I'd like that. I can swing by Super One and pick up what I need."

"Like what?" asked Sierra. "We have stewing meat or ground if you need that. Or is your recipe chicken-based?"

"Stewing beef is great. But I need a few other things to do it right." He ran through Simon's Aunt Linda's recipe in his head. Cilantro. Avocados. Peppers. Hadn't he noticed a good variety of peppers at the store that day with Claire? If he was going to tingle her taste buds, he'd need poblanos.

"Sounds good, even if Jo did volunteer me." Zach's deeper voice broke into his thoughts.

Sierra grinned at Zach. "Co-ol. Guys' afternoon in the kitchen. You better teach Zach some useful tricks, Noel. He can't cook his way out of a mac-and-cheese box."

Trapped. Noel allowed a half grin on his face as he looked at Zach. "Guess it's me and you, brother."

Zach slid his arm around his snickering wife. "Guess so."

oOo

It was all Claire could do to stay out of the kitchen that afternoon. It was her domain, after all. The two masculine voices rolled back and forth, accented by the thunking of knives against cutting boards and the scintillating aroma that rose from the sizzling Dutch oven on the cook top.

Too bad she couldn't relax on her one day off. Four weeks of ten-hour workdays six days a week were taking their toll.

"Your move." Amber waved her hand in front of Claire's face.

Claire focused on the Settlers of Catan game spread out in front of her. It proved she couldn't concentrate. Why had Sierra's parents thought the girls needed a game that demonstrated the allure of colonizing far-off places? She more needed a game that emphasized nesting, not expanding her territory. She set a small wooden house down. Placing a settlement on a space with low probability for ore but high probability for wood might—or might not—be a good direction. What did it matter?

"Sierra says you've signed off on the full menu for the reception?" she asked Amber. Maybe she could divert the conversation some.

"Oh, yes!" Amber beamed. "It all sounds so delicious. Those chicken roll-ups will be a perfect finger food."

To say nothing of making use of the dark meat from all the birds whose breasts would adorn another platter. Beyond Amber, Sierra winked for Claire's eyes alone. "Good thing, as we've had to order the chickens already."

Claire's cell phone vibrated in her pocket. "Excuse me." She surged to her feet as she tugged the phone out. With any luck this call would free her from the ongoing game. But the name on the display stilled her heartbeat for an instant. *The Sizzling Skillet.* Her heart sank as she thumbed the call on. "Hello." And it didn't matter who was calling. She had nothing left to offer them.

"Claire? Nevin here. How would you like to pick up a shift or two?"

He made it sound like it would be so much fun there was no way she could resist. Yeah, right. "Hi, Nevin. No, I'm sorry, I don't have time."

"I've heard you're cooking for that reforestation group. That won't last much longer, will it? If you can pop in for this evening's shift, I'll consider offering you your old job back when you're free of that commitment." He said the last as though it were a dirty word.

Claire's back stiffened and her hand tightened around the small phone. With Isobel and Greg's wedding called off, she could almost wonder whether she'd been too hasty quitting at The Skillet. But for her to go back and work for Nevin? She wasn't that desperate. Not yet. "That's really big of you, Nevin." A little smoothing might go a long way. "There's simply no way I can come in today, though."

"I can't hold the position open forever, you know."

She gulped back the retort that wanted to surface. "I understand. You just go ahead and hire someone permanently for those shifts."

Silence for a few seconds. Which seemed to prove he hadn't found it so simple to replace her. Now why wasn't that a surprise?

"I think you've made a big mistake, Claire. If it's money you want, I can offer you a raise. Say, fifty cents an hour?"

At this moment, he could double her former wage and it would barely entice her. "Sorry, no. Money isn't the issue."

He pounced on that. "Then what is? This can't be all about

that kid, whatever his name was."

"His name is Tony. And no, it's not about him." Though it might've been, if Noel hadn't brought things to a head first.

"Nevin? I don't wish to talk about this any longer. I have company I'm ignoring to take your call. I need to get back to them." If only they weren't playing that stupid game. "Why don't you give Don a chance? He always figured he was chef material."

Nevin uttered a rude word then mumbled a few things about burned food and annoyed customers.

"Thanks for calling, Nevin. I need to go now." She thumbed the cell off in the midst of his renewed pleas.

Sierra glanced up from the game as Claire approached the table. "What was all that about?"

"Nevin is willing to forgive me for quitting. He wants me to come back."

A shadow filled the kitchen doorway in Claire's peripheral vision.

"And?" Sierra prodded.

Claire sat at the table, smoothing her pant legs. "Is it my turn?"

o0o

"Interesting sermon this morning." Zach clumsily turned tortilla strips in the sizzling peanut oil.

Noel's hands itched to take the tongs and do the task himself. "Uh hmm." He stirred the stewing beef. Nearly browned enough.

"Everything in life is such a fine balance. I used to make those kinds of plans Pastor Ron talked about. You know, I figured I'd do so many years of veterinary practice in Coeur d'Alene, then buy a house, then start my own business." He laughed, but not as though he found it funny. "I had a ten-year plan all mapped out. All I needed was to get my foot in the door somewhere and they'd see what a genius I was. They'd wonder how they ever managed without me."

Noel's plans had been a lot looser than Zach's. Of course, he'd already achieved Zach's final one of owning his own business. Even that was barely an end in itself, though. He still needed to find several contracts every year and fill out the staff. Seasonal work didn't lend itself well to loyal workers beyond a few years. Other than Jess. She'd want something more, too, sooner or later.

He glanced at Zach. "I take it Landing Veterinary wasn't high on your list?"

"Not so much. I'd decided I preferred being a city boy. Having all the conveniences around me and the money to enjoy them."

"I'm not that fond of cities, in general." Noel suppressed a shudder. "Give me a mountainside and a couple of bears any day over concrete and people. At least you can guess what a bear might do in any given situation."

Zach chuckled and lifted the last strips onto a kitchen towel. "I see your point. I wanted to run my own life, I suppose. I'd drifted from God."

Here it came.

"What's your church background, Noel?"

So Zach was the designated person to get to the bottom of things, was he? A few weeks ago, it might have offended Noel. Now, not so much. "Mom made me go to church when I was a kid in Missoula. Went my own way in high school. It didn't seem all that relevant, you know?"

Zach leaned back against the counter, arms crossed. Waiting for more. Good thing he'd already turned off the oil.

Whatever. The guy wanted the scoop, he'd get it. Both

barrels. "Got into some dope, some booze. My old man ditched the family when I was a little kid, and he started contacting me from wherever he was at the time. Texas, Kentucky, Maryland, wherever. He just drifted." Noel dumped chopped onions into the pot and added the spices.

"You ever see him?"

"Five, six years ago. But he keeps in touch." Noel scraped the pot's contents around, not willing to see pity on Zach's face.

Silence for a moment. "I can't imagine," Zach said at last. "My dad was always here for me. He got sick last year. Guillain-Barré. Ever hear of it?"

Noel shook his head.

"It's neurological. If untreated, your body starts paralyzing from the extremities in. Sooner or later it gets to your core muscles, like your heart, and kills you."

"He didn't die, did he?" Surely Noel would remember hearing if Zach had been recently bereaved.

"No. They figured out what it was and got him on meds to stop the progress before it got that far, but it certainly whopped him a good one. We're not sure if he'll ever regain full health again. He and my mom are in Romania right now, helping out at an orphanage my best friend's parents operate there."

"Right. I remember hearing something about that."

"They should be back sometime in the fall. I've never gone more than a few weeks without seeing my parents until this year. I can't imagine what it must've been like not to have a dad around."

Noel checked his recipe notes and added the peppers and tomato paste. "It's just how it was. I managed."

Zach leaned closer. "Jo and I are expecting a baby in late winter. Had you heard?"

Something stirred in Noel. "Congratulations."

"I guess…it makes me think all the more what a responsibility it is to be a father. You know? I want to be around for my child. Take him fishing, kick a soccer ball around, teach him to drive the tractor."

The words themselves made sense, but the concept was foreign. Noel couldn't pass on what he'd never known. Well, other than fishing. He knew how to do that, but it wasn't his dad's fault. Whatever skill sets he'd acquired over the years, they didn't include anything close to parenting. Even Mom worked mainly on the guilt principle, which, as far as Noel was concerned, didn't serve as grounds for a great relationship.

A kid deserved more, didn't he? More than a bum of a dad who phoned for money in the middle of the night? He couldn't be a different kind of father. He didn't know how. He'd already taken after his dad in wanderlust, though he paid his own way, unlike Dad.

Claire would want kids some day. Her kids deserved a real dad. Somebody who could give them security.

For her good, and that of the kids she'd surely want to have, he needed to get out of her life.

Chapter 23 --

The supper dishes cleared away, the group settled into the lounge furniture out on the deck to enjoy the pleasant June evening. Claire chose an Adirondack chair. No chance of Noel tucking in beside her, though his face across the table over two meals already today had been nearly unbearable. He'd been rather quiet over supper, even when everyone raved over his taco stew. She needed that recipe. Rich flavors. Just the right amount of spice.

She glanced his way, but he stared off up the mountain. Longing for distant places, no doubt.

Why couldn't this have been a peaceful Sunday afternoon for meditation instead of company, so she could reflect on Pastor Ron's message without Noel's face haunting her? Like his presence made a difference. But what did it all mean? Could it be that she was too attached to this farm, only temporary in the grand scheme of things? But then so was love. The Bible gave no indication that human relationships would continue in heaven, so maybe love wasn't worth anything either.

A surreptitious glance at Jo nestled in the crook of Zach's arm on the swing, Domino sprawled at their feet, negated that thought. God created love, created marriage. Encouraged humankind to find mates, to have a family, as her friends were doing.

Sierra, Eileen, and Amber discussed wedding decoration details with great animation. Even without Shawn here, the glow of his love and commitment to Amber shone around the group.

It seemed to Claire that her and Noel's silence must be like a flashing light over their heads. "I need to turn on the sprinklers."

Heads jerked to look at her as she rose.

"It's been so dry this spring," she said to their unspoken questions. "It's not like we'd normally consider wasting water on the lawn, but with all the weddings and parties we're hosting here over the next few months, it kind of has to look nice."

"Not to worry." Zach kept the swing moving in a lazy circle with the toe of one sandal. "There's plenty in the spring, and the sprinkler water soaks back into the ground."

He always said that. Claire wasn't sure if he was right or if she just wanted his explanation to be accurate. Either way, it didn't pay to let the flowers die from lack of moisture.

She should've known Noel would follow her to the tap beside the pole barn where the seeping hose twined through the flowerbed.

"Claire?" His voice sounded more hesitant than she'd ever heard it. Where was his robust self-confidence?

She crouched down and cranked the handle open then watched the black rubber bubble from oozing water droplets.

"Claire? I've been thinking."

Maybe he'd finally realized how presumptuous his earlier invitation had come across, and now would ask her to marry him. She didn't have an answer, but maybe she was closer after Pastor Ron's sermon. She clambered back to her feet and hugged her arms around herself as she peered up at him. Would he step in for a kiss? Would she let him?

But he held back, his expression unreadable. "Come for a walk?"

She nodded. What was on his mind?

Domino heard the words and bounded down the steps, wandering between them as they strolled out the driveway, like they needed a chaperone or something.

They'd turned onto the forest road before he spoke again. "I haven't really told you anything about my father."

Claire jerked to look at him. So not what she'd expected this conversation to be about. "Amber said he'd walked out before she was born, and that your mom raised you two alone."

A nerve in his jaw twitched. "That's true. But Amber doesn't know how much contact I've had with him."

He said it with such heaviness that Claire halted in the middle of the road and put her hand on his arm. She yanked it away as soon as she realized it was there. He hadn't made the first move. It wouldn't do for her to come on strong. "But that's good. Right?"

Noel's fingers twined around hers with the strength of a spelunker gripping a lifeline and pulled her into step beside him. "He's a drunk, Claire. He gambles the little he can spare from booze, and wanders around the country looking for someone gullible enough to give him more."

She caught her breath. No wonder Noel hadn't talked about his father. "I'm sorry."

"Yeah, me too." By now he was striding so quickly Claire could barely keep up without breaking into a jog. "It's no use."

She tried to get her hand free, but he didn't let go. "Noel, slow down. What else do you need to tell me about your dad? It's okay. It wasn't your fault. You were just a little kid."

He seemed to become aware of his speed and tapered it to a point where she could keep up without panting. "But he's my father."

Which meant what, exactly?

"Don't you see? I'm just like him. I can't get enough of seeing the world. It's like an itch inside me."

Something froze in Claire's gut. "Do you drink? Do you gamble?"

He shook his head so vehemently his wild hair flared out around him. "Not any more. Never got into gambling, thankfully, but I used to drink to excess. I figured out after a while that it didn't help my business head any, and I quit. I didn't want to be like him."

"So your dad drinks, gambles, and wanders. You don't drink or gamble but you like to travel. Is that right?"

"Yeah. I guess."

Did she mistake the lilt of hope in his voice? "Traveling isn't a sin, Noel." It nearly choked her to get the words out.

He whirled around on the gravel road and grabbed her other hand tightly in his. His eyes searched her face. "Claire, it wasn't supposed to be like this."

She bit her lip and forced herself to hold his gaze. "Like how?"

"With you. I wasn't looking for love. Just someone whose company I could enjoy for a few months."

She'd always known that, but it still slapped her like a frozen dishcloth. She tried to pull her hands free, but his grip intensified. "I wasn't—I'm not—looking for love either. Green Acres is enough for me."

Noel's eyes bored into her soul. "You deserve better than me. Your-your kids deserve a devoted father. One without all the baggage I'd bring."

Whoa. His mind had gone way beyond, "come away with me."

"You're not the only one with baggage."

Domino plopped down on the road and burrowed his nose

into his paws.

Claire clutched Noel's hands. "My dad hauled us all over the country while he chased the pot of gold at the end of the rainbow. My mother got fed up with it and stayed put in Denver when I was a teen. Dad kept going. My brothers are a mess—nowhere near as grounded as your sister."

Noel looked into her eyes as though he could see down to her toenails through their portal. "So your father loused up his sons, too. You and Amber are strong. Maybe it's easier for girls when their dad takes off."

Nice try. "I doubt it." Claire tugged her hands free and stuffed them into the pockets of her capris. She sidestepped him and continued up the road, hoping he'd follow.

"You deserve someone better than me."

She whirled to find him rooted to the gravel right where she'd left him. "Not better."

He narrowed his eyes. "Different, then."

Tears threatened to boil over. Hadn't she thought the same thing? That he was an awesome guy if only... If only. "What you're saying is I'm not worth sticking around for."

Noel clenched his teeth. "I didn't say that at all. I'm trying to be honest about my own shortcomings, not yours."

The pain was too great. She had to protect herself somehow. "But you're admitting I have some." *Oh, Claire, don't go there. You know you have issues. Everyone does.*

"You're putting words in my mouth." His hands twitched at his sides and for one brief moment it looked like he'd close the distance between them and kiss her senseless.

It scared her that she wanted him to.

"I won't be taking my meals with the crew for the remainder of the season. Please route any requests through Jess. She's more than capable of handling things." He turned on his heel and strode toward the farm.

Claire's feet were one with the road for too many seconds. "Noel, wait! You can't mean this." She started toward him.

"It's better this way. You'll thank me later."

She stared after him. She wouldn't chase him down, cling to his arm, cry on him. Not when he'd clearly rejected her.

She dropped on her knees beside Domino and buried her face in his coat.

So this was how it felt to be on the other end of the stick.

o0o

"You're a fool, boss." Jess's hands sat firmly planted on her slim hips.

How could a girl barely five feet tall take up all the available floor space in his trailer? Noel stared at her. Only one beer. He'd bummed it off one of the guys while he'd been smart enough to know that if he went to the bar, he wouldn't stop at one. He'd been right. One wasn't enough. "Don't talk to me that way."

"I'll talk to you any way I want. You know better than this. You quit drinking, remember?"

He shrugged and tipped the can back, but he'd already drained it. "Your point is…?"

Jess planted her hands on the dinette and leaned into his face. "You asked her to marry you, and she turned you down."

Laughter snorted out of him. "In your dreams."

Her eyes narrowed. "Then what?"

"It's none of your business. All I ask you to do is handle everything with Claire and the kitchen until we leave Galena Landing. I'll take some of the other stuff off your back to balance things out."

"And if I say no, deal with Claire yourself?"

"Then you're fired. I'll get Wade to do it instead. All of your duties."

She smirked. "Nice try, boss."

"I mean it."

She searched his face, and he could only hope she didn't see the battle going on inside his head. "I was hoping you called me in here to offer me dibs on buying Enterprising Reforestation."

Noel scowled. "Now, why would I do that?"

"I thought maybe you'd come to your senses." Jess grabbed the empty can from his slack hand. "Turns out I was wrong." She headed for the door.

"Jess. Will you do it?"

She swung around with the knob in her grip, her eyes blazing at him. "It's not like I have any options."

"Sure, you do."

"Right. Help you hide from the only woman who's ever gotten under your skin or get fired? What kind of choice is that?"

He tried for the crooked smile that usually won his way with Jess. It'd worked on Claire, too. That smile didn't seem to be anywhere in his repertoire at the moment.

Jess huffed. "Okay, I'll do it, but under one condition."

Like she had room for demands of her own. He raised his eyebrows. "I'm all ears."

"If you change your mind—"

Noel couldn't keep the sour laugh from bubbling up.

"I mean it. If you change your mind any time in the next year and decide Claire is worth it, which I'm here to tell you she is, then you will sell me Enterprising Reforestation for a really good price." She named a figure.

"You want me to lose my shirt?"

"I'm not that stupid, boss. I know what you bring in and what the expenses are. I know you're banking money on every job." She raised her hands as though in self-defense. "And that's as it should be. You take the risks and it's your company."

"But that's—"

"No risk to you to shake on this deal, boss. You made up your mind you're walking away from this town never to return. You'll never have to make good on it."

She had a point there. He slapped his hand on the table. "You got it."

Jess's hand plucked his off the dinette and gave it a firm shake. "Don't forget. You're a winner either way." A moment later the trailer door clicked shut behind her.

Noel sank his head into his hands. He'd never expected winning to feel like this.

Chapter 24 ---

The mess tent lay silent, even with a couple of dozen people in it. After weeks of listening to the chatter and the laughter, Claire could hardly believe it was the same place.

Tony peered out of the mobile kitchen and glanced back at Claire. "Did somebody die?"

Claire shook her head and finished tossing the salad. "You done with the veggies?" Normally she delighted in the potatoes, parsnips, and turnips mashed together. Today they looked as blasé as she felt, like off-white mush. Yummy.

"Yeah. Want me to start loading the serving counter?"

"Please. The meatloaves are ready to go out, and so is the roasted asparagus."

"I'll be glad when asparagus season is over. Seems like all we've had since we started cooking here."

She cut him a glance. "You'll soon get your wish. It's the vegetable in season. What's in the cooler is the last of it."

Tony scooped the mashed tubers into rectangular tubs that fit in the heated serving counter while Claire carried the rest of the meal out. She whisked the cloth off the plates and cutlery then clanged the gong.

Tired workers drifted toward the counter.

A diesel engine roared to life. Claire's jaw tightened. She

would not stare after Noel's truck as he left the camp for Galena Landing. No way would she make their spat any more obvious.

"Hey, where's the boss going?" Wade asked.

A couple of guys shrugged.

Jess elbowed her way closer to the front. "He needed something from town." She eyed Claire.

She had to know something by the look on her face. Claire tried for a smile, but it wasn't forthcoming.

Tony plunked the last serving tub in place.

Claire backed up. "Tony, can you keep an eye on the counter tonight? I'll start the cleanup."

In her peripheral, Tony's chest puffed with pride. Claire pulled her gaze away from Jess and fled back into the cook trailer. Normally she dealt with the crew and let Tony clean the kitchen. Not today.

Outside, the scrape of metal spoons in metal tubs accented the quiet talk amongst Noel's employees, normally a raucous bunch.

She turned the tap on full blast, not even caring about wasting water, and leaned over the sink. Tears threatened to flow. She blinked them back, hard. Tony might have something he needed to fetch. He couldn't find her in here blubbering.

Jess's voice rose above the rest, saying something about Noel, and Claire strained to hear. What was the official story? The crew certainly knew of the spark between their boss and their chef. Wade, James, and the others had grinned knowingly at her more than once.

Claire squeezed her eyes shut. Oh, God, what should she do? Two more weeks of this avoidance treatment? She'd never asked to fall in love with Noel Kenzie in the first place, but once she had, her life filled with exotic flavors. Now it seemed as insipid as an unsalted egg and as monotonous as day-in-day-out asparagus.

She hadn't even had the opportunity to refuse him herself. The mountaintop didn't count. They both knew that wasn't a real rejection. His words had rushed the fledgling relationship. She'd needed time. He'd needed to figure out exactly what he wanted.

But this. This smacked of permanence. It would be entirely possible for him to avoid her for two weeks. Even if he returned for his sister's wedding, it wasn't like he needed to talk to the caterer. She was staff. Hired help. Just like here.

The pots would not wash themselves. The crew's lunches for tomorrow would not fix themselves. It wasn't fair to Tony to make him pull her weight as well as his.

Claire brushed her bedraggled hair away from her eyes and began to scrub.

oOo

Florescent lighting bounced off the yellow walls of the diner. Noel stared at the hamburger in the plastic basket in front of him. A guy really shouldn't have to put up with meals like this, not when he'd gotten a whiff of meatloaf mixed with other tantalizing aromas moments before. Would it have been so impossible to get Jess to bring a plate to his trailer?

But that was halfway to admitting he was wrong, and he couldn't do that. Claire would notice and read something into it. Jess would crow. The crew would wonder more about dinner trays than a trip off Elmer's property. Maybe.

He picked up a few French fries, dunked them in ketchup, and tossed them back. Lukewarm, grease-soaked, and coated in twice too much salt. Oh, the cost of his pride.

A shadow loomed over his table and he looked up, startled.

"Noel Kenzie?" The gray-haired man held out his hand.

Noel wiped his on a paper napkin from the dispenser before reaching out to shake. "Yes, sir. Mr. Graysen?"

The old guy's eyes crinkled when he grinned. "That's me. Ed. From Galena Gospel Church." He hefted the tray he held in his left hand. "Mind if I join you? The wife's gone to visit her sister for a week, and I got tired of cooking myself bacon and eggs."

"Sure." Noel waved at the brown plastic bench across from him. "Have a seat." What else could he say? He didn't really want the guy's company, but it seemed rude to deny it. And it was pretty obvious he'd just parked here himself, with his burger still whole.

Bacon and eggs. Well, that was another solution, probably a better one than the diner offered. He'd raid the Super One and cook for himself for a couple of weeks. That would sure beat the alternatives.

He eyed the burger distastefully and took a bite. Lukewarm congealed fat. Could he even finish this meal?

Ed Graysen had a big bite of his burger. He wiped his mouth with a napkin and winked at Noel. "Just what a fellow needs every now and then, eh, Noel? But we have to keep the likes of those Green Acres girls from finding out."

Noel raised his eyebrows.

"They're all over the healthy food, you know. They get most of their stuff from other farmers around here." Ed grinned. "They're good cooks, too. At least Claire sure is. They invited me and Mona out a few times for a Sunday lunch."

Did everything come back to Claire in this town?

Noel took a large bite, hoping that if he filled his mouth, it wouldn't seem rude not making small talk.

"Say, isn't Claire cooking for your work crew?" Ed frowned over his burger. "I must have misunderstood. Mona says my hearing isn't as good as it once was. It must be from all the practice I've had tuning her out over the years."

Noel supposed Ed meant to make a joke, a comrade-type thing. He forced a chuckle and ate a few fries.

"No, I'm pretty sure that's what I heard. Didn't I see you helping her get groceries for your crew that one day?"

The guy was like a bulldog. Much as Noel did not want to talk about it, there didn't seem to be much choice. "Yes, she works for me." He started a mental count, wondering how long before Ed put two and two together.

Ed's bushy eyebrows shot up to where his hairline used to be. He leaned back against the plastic seat and squinted at Noel. "There seems to be more to this tale than meets the eye, son. Do you want to talk about it?"

When had a man ever called him "son" in a voice like Ed's? Never. His dad only whined and manipulated to get what he could from having a boy. Ed's voice rumbled with concern and honesty.

For an instant Noel wanted to spill it all on the old guy's shoulders. Pour out frustrations about his dad, share his jealousy over Zach's relationship with his father, and Zach's delight in the coming baby. Zach wanted to do the whole circle once again.

But what was Ed to him, really? Just an old geezer he'd never see again once he left this town. And he could guess Ed's answers. All about letting God run things. That was fine when you were eighty and had one foot in the grave, but not for him. Noel still had plenty of aspirations for life. He wasn't ready to settle down in one place, with one woman—with God.

He'd taken so long in deciding whether to form an answer that Ed began eating again, though the man watched him with a worried expression. Finally Ed said, "Can I tell you a story?"

Noel shrugged. He balled up the remainder of his burger in its greasy wrapper and pushed the plastic basket away, fries and all.

"I was born in the 40s, during the war."

Noel did the math. Ed wasn't quite as ancient as he'd assumed.

"Things were pretty good in the 60s. The world was wild and free if a man was willing to seek out opportunities. I spent a while in Alaska, drinking hard, partying hard, but I couldn't get Mona's sweet face out of my mind. I still didn't want to come back to Idaho though."

Despite himself, Noel was intrigued. "Why not?"

Ed grimaced. "She wrote me every week, you know that? She had such elegant penmanship and wrote on stationery with flowers pressed between the pages. Smelled mighty fine."

Noel waited.

"At first I thought I was running from her. That I didn't love her as much as I ought to. Maybe if I stayed away she'd find somebody else, somebody that deserved her more. I had this ideal man in mind for her, someone hardworking and respectful. Someone who would honor her."

The story seemed to hit close to home, only in Noel's case it was true. Claire really would be better off with some other guy. As for Ed, obviously he'd been meant for Mona.

Ed parked his elbows on the table and leaned closer. "The problem wasn't Mona. It was God. I didn't want to admit I needed Him in my life. Oh, you know, it's not that I didn't believe in Him. I did. Nowadays many folks think He's a fairy tale. I happen to know that's not the case."

The old guy's eyes creeped Noel out. Like they peered into his soul or something. He feigned nonchalance. "Oh, yeah. I believe in God. No problem there."

"The demons also believe, and tremble."

Noel reared back.

"I startled you, I see. It's a verse from the book of James.

God requires more from us than simply acknowledging His existence."

Here it came. Aiming down both barrels.

"He loves you. He died for you. He wants to give you peace and meaning."

Claire had said the same thing. Peace. Could the old guy in the sky really provide that? Because Noel could use some.

"Have you ever prayed for God's forgiveness, son? Given everything over to Him? If not, He's waiting for you."

"Uh, yeah. About that. Thanks for—" He almost added, "nothing." Noel surged to his feet and picked up the tray with the remnants of his meal. "Nice to run into you this evening." If God were real, Noel ought to get zapped for lying.

"I'll be praying for you, son."

Noel gave Ed a curt nod and strode for the door. Just what he needed—somebody else interfering in his life.

o0o

A knock sounded on the mobile kitchen door. "Claire? You okay?"

Jess.

Was she ready to talk to Noel's foreman? Not really. If she were being honest, she hoped Noel would come in when he returned. Maybe tell her he'd thought things through and that he really loved her. Maybe that's why she'd sent Tony home early and told him she'd finish up.

It certainly hadn't been for a heart-to-heart with Jess.

"Claire? You still in there?"

She sighed and moved toward the door. "Yes, I'm here." When she pushed the door open she was surprised to see dusk had fallen. Morning would come way too quickly. She needed some sleep.

Oh, elusive sleep.

Jess blinked at the brightness and pushed past Claire blocking the doorway. "Noel asked me to get your supply list for next week." Jess leaned against the sink and crossed her arms.

That stung. Yeah, he'd said he'd turn everything over to Jess, but she hadn't really expected him to mean it. "I'll have it for you tomorrow. First thing." Which meant, of course, she needed to take stock of the kitchen before she left tonight. Good thing the menu was already written and posted on the corkboard.

Claire reached for a pen and paper and opened the first cupboard, her back to Jess. If Noel's foreman planned to park in here and stare, she might as well get started right now.

"It's none of my business what you and Noel fought about."

Claire didn't even turn around to acknowledge that one.

"He's a really good guy. A keeper."

"He's all yours."

Jess laughed. "For the right girl. That's not me."

"Apparently not for me, either. Thanks anyway."

There was a little scuffling sound from the sink area. "Two more stubborn people I've never met."

"Oh, I doubt that." Even as the words came out of Claire's mouth, she knew she was wrong. Noel certainly was stubborn, but maybe—just maybe—she had a bit of a streak in there herself. Not that it mattered, because Noel could out-stubborn her like she was a bowl of Jell-O.

Jess sighed. "So both of you are planning to stay miserable."

Claire turned around.

The girl was no taller than Jo. Must be something with those J-people. They also both wouldn't let go of something once they had it in their teeth. "Look, Jess. Thank you for caring. I'm not sure why you do, but I appreciate it. Except it doesn't change anything, all right? Noel's made his decisions and the rest of the world gets to abide by them. You want somebody to talk to, go find him."

Jess narrowed her eyes. "Okay, that tells me a lot. It's Noel being pig-headed, as usual. What did you say to set him off?"

Claire's hands slipped to her hips. "I honestly don't see that it's any of your business." Maybe this wasn't the most Christian way to act, but what was Jess's problem, anyway? "I'm sure he's like this every place you guys go, right? Finds some girl, makes her feel special for a while, then dumps her. Too busy moving on to the next job, the next big thing. Well, you know what? I'm not playing his game. I'm just not. I'll get you that list in the morning, and when Enterprising Reforestation moves off my mountain, I'll be glad. You get that? Glad. Because my life will be back to normal and I won't have to put up with this anymore."

Claire whirled back to the open cupboard and her head collided with the door that stood ajar. Man, that hurt. Like she needed physical trauma on top of emotional pain. The tears she'd managed to hold back—just barely—began to pool and flood her eyes. No. She was not going to cry in front of Noel's foreman. Not happening. She stiffened to keep her shoulders from trembling. Waited for footsteps across the floor and the sound of Jess letting herself out of the kitchen.

Sounds she did not hear.

When Jess's voice came, it was soft. "Wow. I don't think you'll be glad at all when he's gone. I didn't know anyone could love Noel enough to have such a strong response to him. Misery loves company, so patch this thing back up and quit spreading your gloom around to the rest of us."

Chapter 25 --

On the road again. The trailer towed smoothly behind Noel's big pickup truck. Everything would be better in Montana. There he'd have a male chef who'd cooked for his crew several seasons before. There'd be no reminders of Claire. There'd be no Ed Graysen staring thoughtfully at Noel over stale diner fries.

Because it simply wouldn't be right to start thinking seriously about God and religion at this point in his life. It'd be like doing it for Claire, and he was pretty sure that was the wrong reason. Worse, it might not be a strong enough motivation. Once upon a time, his dad must have loved his mom, too, or they wouldn't have married and had two kids. Or so a person would think. It sure hadn't lasted long.

Noel couldn't do that to Claire. He *wouldn't* do it. She deserved better than him. Now that they wouldn't see each other every day, they could both forget. Time would lessen the pain.

Noel gripped the rawhide-covered steering wheel with both hands. *Pain?*

His cell phone rang, and he reached up to his visor and pressed the Bluetooth button to receive the call. "Noel here."

"Where are you, son?"

That his dad was calling in the daytime was a good sign. Sort of. "On the road to the new camp in Montana. How about you?" Noel clenched his teeth. This better not be another plea for cash.

"Denver. Been here a few days." A short pause. "You think your mother would take me back?"

"I doubt it." The words spilled from Noel's lips before he could censor them. "But there's no way I'm mediating for you. You want to talk to Mom, it's all in your hands."

"She ain't home. Or at any rate, she's not picking up the phone."

Noel stared at the curvy highway in front of him. "She's in Idaho for the weekend with Amber. Give her until Monday evening."

"It ain't a long weekend." Dad hesitated. "Is it?"

"No, but I don't know what time she'll be home and then she works tomorrow."

"She has a job?"

Anger boiled close to the surface. "She certainly does. How do you think she managed after you left? You think she's become a no-account bum who sits around on government assistance all the time?" He managed not to add the words, "like you." "She went to college and got a job and paid off her loan and raised Amber and me to be productive members of society."

"Wow. I never knew she had it in her."

Noel passed a sign for the upcoming town of Libby. "That's because you rarely bothered to check in with her, and when you did, it was all about you." All about asking for a handout, and Mom had told him in no uncertain terms to get lost. Too bad Noel wasn't strong enough to do that.

And his dad had done it thinking Mom was on welfare? That was just sick.

Noel's CB radio crackled. "Pulling over in Libby to check the tires on the kitchen, boss."

He glanced in the side mirror, where Jess's truck loomed with its overhanging camper. "You got it, Jess."

Everyone in the convoy would have gotten the message along with him. They might as well make it a lunch stop while they were here.

"Who's that? Your girlfriend?"

Right, his father would have heard the conversation. "Jess? No. She works for me." Claire had worked for him, too.

Dad chuckled. "Keep her close, that's the way."

The man made Noel want to hurl. "I'm done talking to you. I'll be stopping in a minute to deal with things on my crew."

"But I haven't told you why I'm calling."

Noel's teeth clenched.

"I just need a bit more dough to make it to Missoula. How about you help out your old man?"

Something inside Noel snapped. "No. You want to get there, you figure out how. I'm done bailing you out."

"Didn't that mother of yours teach you no respect?"

"She sure did. She raised me the best way she could as a single mom. She taught me how to be a man, because you weren't there to do it, and you're not much of an example, are you?"

"Hey, now. Is that any way to speak to your old man?"

"All you've ever done is ask me for money, and I'm done giving it to you. I wired you enough to get you clear out here, so it's not my fault you're stranded halfway." A service station with an attached restaurant appeared on Noel's left and he pushed down his turn signal. "I've got to go. Call me if you ever straighten out your life." He reached up and turned off the call then negotiated the turn into the parking lot.

After he cut the engine, he leaned his forehead on the

steering wheel, sickened by the disgust he felt for his father. He'd been busy thinking of all the ways he was like his dad. Maybe it was time to start focusing on the ways they were different.

oOo

Claire scooted the stepladder a little further to the right and put more paint on her roller before climbing back up.

"Thanks so much for helping." Jo glanced up from cutting in around the doorframe with a brush.

"What day are Zach's parents getting home?"

"Sixteenth of August. They were going to stay in Romania longer until they found out I was pregnant."

Claire laughed. "It's not like they were going to miss the birth by staying two more months."

"I know. But Rosemary is anxious to start sewing for the baby's room. You know, quilts, curtains, wall hangings."

Claire climbed down to reload her roller and looked around the small space. "You sure this cabin is going to be big enough for a family?"

"It's bigger than the old trailer was, and we can always add a room or two off the side later if we want."

"If you have a pile of kids, you mean."

"Yeah." Jo patted her still-flat tummy. "Zach has a bunch of sisters so he thinks a big family is normal."

"You guys will be good parents, like Rosemary and Steve were for him."

"I hope so. It's not like my mom was a great role model." Jo cast Claire a sidelong look. "Where are you going to live when you get married? In the straw bale house?"

An unladylike sound escaped before Claire could hold it in. "I thought we'd been over this. No wedding in my future."

"You haven't heard anything from Noel since he left?"

In three days? "No." Claire rolled furiously for a moment. "I like this mossy color meeting up to the log walls."

"Yeah, me too. Zach wanted the interior walls to be logs like the rest, but I voted him down." Jo stretched and rubbed her lower back. "It's good to spend some time with you. Seems I hardly saw you when you were cooking for Noel."

"It was exhausting. I barely know what to do with all my free time now." For one thing, it gave her far too much time to think about the good days with Noel. The days before the final two weeks.

"Is he coming back for his sister's wedding?"

"How should I know?" Claire sent Jo an irritated glance. "If he shows up, he shows up."

"But Amber will be disappointed if he doesn't come."

"Yeah, it matters to her, not to me."

"Claire?" Jo paused, her voice so soft Claire had to turn and look. "Denial doesn't work. Talk to me."

"Really? You were once queen of denial yourself. It's over, okay? A couple of weeks of nice dreams, and that's it."

"You know, eventually I had to stop running from God."

Claire allowed her eyebrows to flick up. "You certainly gave Him a run for His money. You basically stuck your fingers in your ears and sang *lalalala* when Sierra or I tried to say anything to you about Zach."

"You're right. Am I glad I stopped doing that? What do you think?" Jo pointed her brush at Claire, and a dollop of green paint landed on the sealed concrete floor.

"It's different."

Jo rolled her eyes then bent to wipe up the splotch. "It's always different. I know you love Noel. You may not have admitted it to yourself, but it's obvious. And I'm pretty sure he loves you too, from what Zach said about their conversation that afternoon. So don't give up."

"Look, I know you were ready to waltz off to the city with Zach if he'd have asked it of you."

"Because I finally figured out he was worth it."

"Don't give me a bunch of nonsense. I've always been worried that the dream of this farm was too big, that it would be snatched from me yet. Right now my biggest worry is that I won't be able to make my share of the payments without The Sizzling Skillet."

"So you'd rather go crawling back and work for Nevin than call Noel up and tell him he means the world to you? Noel's not asking you to live in the city. He loves the wilderness, like up our mountain."

"You know he doesn't even have a home address, right? With Eileen moving to Flagstaff with Amber and Shawn, all he has is that little trailer. Do you think I want to be a vagabond for the rest of my life? Can you envision me living someplace else—even here—while he traipses off into the bush for weeks at a time? Because that's not happening. "

"Well, no. That doesn't seem fair to a woman. Do you really think he wouldn't make some changes for a wife?"

"How should I know? He never said. He never asked me."

Jo stared at Claire. "So that's the problem."

"What do you mean?"

"I had the impression he was more serious about you than that."

"Yeah, well, so did I. At least for a while. But I was wrong, okay? And now he's gone. And if you don't mind, I'd like to move on."

"Move on to what?"

Claire stared in frustration. "To living my life without dreams of romance. To being practical, and figuring out how I can make a go of this farm without Noel *or* Nevin. To putting one foot in front of the other and dealing with the hand God dealt me."

"That's where I think you're wrong, Claire. God dealt you a hand, and you stuck it in your back pocket. You're pretending it doesn't exist. Do you think there's a reason Noel didn't ask you to marry him?"

"Why? What do you know that I don't?" Claire narrowed her gaze. "I suppose he talked to Zach."

Jo flinched. "No. Not that I know of."

"Well, that's good then, because he sure never proposed to me. In fact, a few hours after he and Zach were all buddy-buddy in the kitchen, he told me he was getting out of my life for good. Some nonsense about it being better for me and our unborn children."

"Whoa! He said all that?"

"Yes, he did. I have to say that Pastor Ron's sermon that morning had me thinking about that whole *this world is not my home* thing. I could almost imagine a life without Green Acres there for a few hours. But going for a walk with Noel that evening certainly derailed that train of thought."

Jo set the paintbrush down, crouched cross-legged onto the concrete, and patted the spot next to her.

Obediently, Claire hooked the roller over the end of the paint tray and sat, too.

"Okay, I'm listening," Jo said quietly. "What did he really say? How did your unborn children come into the conversation?"

"His dad is a bum. Noel figures because he likes to travel, he's exactly like his father. He doesn't see the ways he's different. But honestly, Jo? Even if he came to grips with that, there's still a huge problem."

"And that is?"

"As far as I know, he's not a believer. I know Eileen and

Amber are, and I know Noel was raised in the church. But he evades questions about his faith. Jo, you know I can't marry someone who doesn't follow God." She let out a sad laugh. "Thanks to Amber, I made a checklist of the qualities I want in a mate. Noel does pretty well against that list except for the big ones. If he doesn't love the Lord, I know you don't want me to marry him anyway."

"He was in church a few times. I think God's working on him."

"Sitting in church doesn't make someone a Christian. You know that, Jo."

"Give him a little time?"

"He's the one who walked away and said it was over. It's up to him to work through things and let me know." Yet it had seemed so final. "I can't do it for him."

Jo blinked a few times and brushed her hand across her cheek.

Tears? Jo had never been particularly sentimental. Pregnancy hormones?

"You're right. I'm sorry, Claire." Jo heaved herself to her feet and held out her arms.

Claire walked into them. "Now you understand?"

Chapter 26 --

"Good to see you, Simon!" Noel gripped his old friend's hand. "I was so sorry to hear about your dad."

Simon nodded. "Thanks for giving me the time to be with him. It meant a lot to both of us."

"My pleasure." After his own father's phone call earlier that day, it was hard to remember some guys liked hanging out with their dads. All his life most of his buddies had dads that came to their games and took them fishing. It'd be fun to teach a little guy stuff like that.

"It's cool you were able to find somebody to cook that set for me. Everything work out okay?"

Jess snorted indelicately as she strolled up.

Simon glanced from one to the other, his forehead furrowed. Then he focused on Noel. "Not so well, I take it?"

What to say? "She was an awesome cook, Simon. You've got your work cut out for you to win the crew back."

Jess laughed. "It's true, Simon. Wade begged her to come along." She slanted a sidelong look at Noel.

"So, then, I don't get it. What happened?"

Jess raised both hands. "Not my story to tell. Besides, I've got camp set-up to oversee while boss man talks to you." She winked at Noel and backed up a step. "Tell him about Claire."

"What was all that about?" Simon watched Jess stroll away.

Noel clapped a hand on Simon's shoulder. "Nothing. Claire had advantages you don't have, with the camp situated right near a town and a bunch of farms. You don't have the freedom to create menus like hers considering the ordering schedule back here."

"Why do I get the feeling that's not the whole story? Claire, eh? Tell me, was she ugly and sixty?"

Noel tried to meet his chef's gaze without letting anything on. "Nope, not at all."

Simon raised his eyebrows. "So ...thirty and cute?"

"Other combinations do exist, you know. Come on, let's get camp set up. Can't let Jess do all the work."

Simon fell into step beside Noel as they strode toward the mobile kitchen. "I need to find out more about my competition."

Noel laughed. "No competition there."

"That's not what it sounds like. Of course I'm not female or cute."

"Exactly." Oops. That may have let out more than he'd intended. Oh, well. He'd known Simon a long time.

But Simon's gaze was on Jess as she backed the mobile kitchen into a clear spot.

Interesting. "Do you want to help Jess get things set up there?"

"Uh, yeah." Simon had already left Noel's side. "I'll make sure it's all level. Pull out the tables."

Noel leaned against a tree and crossed his arms. Jess jumped down out of her truck, pulled a construction level out from behind the seat, and flourished it in Simon's direction. Together they checked both sides of the mobile kitchen before declaring it level.

Simon made good money in the winters as weekend chef at

a resort in Colorado and skied the rest of the time. Noel couldn't help but wonder if he'd be interested in buying a business, like Jess was. He shook his head. Enterprising Reforestation was his. He'd started it six years before, bought the kitchen, the vans, and all the equipment. He was in the prime of his life. This was a bad time to sell.

Was it a bad time to start settling down? Claire's face wouldn't leave his mind. No matter what he did, what he tried to think about, she was right there.

With a start he realized he hadn't emailed her the last batch of photos for her website. He owed it to her. Now why did the thought of contacting her make his heart rate rise a bit? Once camp was set up, he'd have a look through his files and see what to send her when he drove into town, back in Internet range.

oOo

Sierra leaned back in the computer chair. "Two fall weddings confirmed, plus one for next May. A family reunion on Labor Day weekend." She bit her lip and glanced at Claire. "That one will be a lot of work. Thirty-four people in something like ten camping units for three meals and two snacks per day."

Claire laughed. "But it's only three days. Don't forget I did pretty much the same thing for six weeks straight, with just Tony to help."

"Oops. So you did." Sierra stretched both hands over her head until her back cracked. "I'm sorry I couldn't help you more."

Claire shrugged. "It was my gig. No worries." If only things hadn't soured with Noel that last bit. He still haunted every thought two weeks later. What could she have done differently, said differently? But, no. This was his battle to fight and win. It was mostly between him and God.

She became aware Sierra was still talking. "Pardon me?"

"You're way off somewhere." Sierra eyed her, chuckling. "Montana, maybe?"

A flush crept up Claire's neck. "Nope. Right here." Maybe on memory lane over at Elmer's, but definitely not Montana. "It's time to finalize our first courses here at Green Acres for next season and start advertising. Are we going to start with a cob outbuilding for your clinic, or what? How settled in are you in that town office?"

"I don't know." Sierra pursed her lips. "Doreen gave me a great deal on rent, and a few people have made appointments. Mostly they aren't too sure about a naturopath. A town office may be a colossal waste of my time. Besides, who knows when or if Gabe will return and want his space back."

This was new. Claire dropped into a seat at the plank table near the computer desk. "Waste of time? How so?"

"Well, if I had my office on the farm, I could do other things between clients. In town, it's more limited. I mean, I've been working on course material for Green Acres, but it's the middle of summer and I should be here weeding. We can write courses all winter."

The garden had over-grown a bit while Claire worked for Noel, that was for sure. Being pregnant seemed to suck a lot of energy out of Jo, but she'd tried to keep up. "We do need a mega cleanup soon, before Amber and Shawn's wedding."

Sierra nodded. "I'll close the office for a week and pitch in full time. It's a tough balance, isn't it?"

"Hmm?"

"Between making a living now and planning for our future."

Claire's breath huffed out. "That's kind of what I was saying all spring."

"I was worried there for a bit."

"About what?"

Sierra shrugged. "That you were going to get married and leave me, like Jo did. I mean, I know she's still next door..."

"You know better. I'm not going anywhere. Besides, Jo and Zach will be moving into the log cabin soon. They're here for half their meals anyway."

"It's not the same. We'd planned to build our own places eventually. I just didn't think it would happen this soon for Jo."

Sierra had dated more guys in college than she and Jo put together. Times ten. No wonder Sierra had assumed she'd be first. "You're stuck with me for the long haul. We'll be two old maids living here together, making cookies for Jo's kids."

"I'll leave the cookies up to you. I think I'll be the crafty auntie."

Claire chuckled. That sounded about right. Not that she wanted to be an old maid, though. *Dear God, please help Noel accept You.*

Was that a selfish prayer?

o0o

It couldn't all be Noel's imagination. Jess definitely bounced a little more and took more interest in the tarped-off mess area than she had in Galena Landing. If anything was going on, though, Simon seemed oblivious. He sat out at the tables sharing backslapping stories with Wade and James, guffaws ringing out across the camp.

Noel parked himself in a lawn chair under his trailer's awning and watched the bustling camp. He should be satisfied. Guys raised tents and backed campers onto rocks to find more level spots. Although everyone but Simon had been in Idaho, the pattern of the camp changed a little as crewmembers had become friends there and shifted their temporary homes to be nearer each other. It always took some time for a new season's crew to shake down and work together well. He had a good bunch this year.

"Hey, boss."

Noel glanced up as Jess plunked a lawn chair down nearby. He forced his face not to show amusement that her line of sight included the eating shelter. "What's up, Jess? Trouble in the ranks?"

Laughter rang out from the tents. Didn't sound much like problems.

She grinned. "No, not so much." Her gaze lingered on Simon.

Aha. Noel leaned forward to block her view. Her startled eyes met his. "I'll have no more of you mocking my love life— or lack thereof." So Jess wouldn't mistake his intent, he raised his eyebrows and jerked his head toward the mobile kitchen.

He'd never have guessed the girl had a blush in her. Jess raised her chin. "Oh?"

Noel grinned. "I've got two eyes. And I'm not stupid."

Jess fell back against her chair. "Well, nothing's going on, so it doesn't matter."

"You didn't believe me when I said that, so why should I believe you now?"

She glared at him. "Because it's true?"

"Uh huh." Noel looked over at the guys as they all clambered to their feet, slapping backs.

Simon grabbed a chair and trundled toward Noel's place as the other two headed to their campers.

"I'm going to enjoy this," Noel said softly.

Jess's nasty look didn't last long.

Simon set his chair down beside Noel's. "I've been wanting to talk to you, man." He glanced at Jess.

She started to her feet. "Should I leave?"

He shook his head. "Doesn't matter to me." Simon leaned forward on his elbows as his hands clenched and unclenched.

Interesting. "What's up?"

"My dad—well, I got some money from his estate. An inheritance. I got to thinking what I want to do with my life, you know? Here I am, pushing thirty-five, cooking for a forestry camp."

Noel sucked in a breath. No way did he want to lose Simon. He couldn't go through all that searching like he'd done in Galena Landing. It took time to find a good chef that loved to work in the backcountry. "I don't know how I'll replace you, man."

He didn't miss the glance between the other two, or Jess's eyes narrowing.

"I love it out here, boss. You know I do. I love smelling the pine trees and seeing the chipmunks skitter by. I like making good bucks over the summer and the freedom to ski in the winter. Well, you know. You do, too."

Noel nodded. So where was this going, then?

"I got no reason to think this, man, but I'll put it out there anyway, just in case. You thinking about selling Enterprising Reforestation? 'Cause I'm interested in buying. I got no doubt I could live this life forever. It's just how I'm meant to be, you know?"

"I, uh, the business isn't for sale."

Jess jumped to her feet. "And if it is, I get first dibs. Noel agreed. Right, boss?"

Noel rubbed his forehead. He had a vague memory of something like that. It'd been an ugly night.

"How would you have had this conversation if Noel's not considering selling?"

"He didn't say he hadn't considered it. Just said it's not for sale. That means now, today." Jess's hands had found her hips. "But that could change any time and, if it does, we've made an agreement."

"Wasn't trying to rile you up, Jess." Simon's voice remained easy. "How could I have known you had designs on the company?"

Jess slumped back into her chair. "You couldn't. Sorry for overreacting."

"Interesting this has come up recently." Simon stretched out his long legs as he settled deeper into his chair. "What happened in Idaho to make you think about it, Jess?" He gave her a pained look. "Did someone leave you some money, too?"

"No. I've been saving up." She sighed. "I'm sorry your dad died."

If Noel hadn't been watching Jess for the last couple of hours he'd never have guessed she was interested in the chef. At the moment she seemed more inclined to rip him to shreds. But hadn't Claire overreacted a time or two?

Not him, of course. He never overreacted. He let out a deep sigh.

"Yeah, thanks." Simon rubbed his head. "It's been a rough few months. Well, it was only an idea. I need to make some solid decisions for my future, and I like what you've done with ER, Noel. From what I can see, you started a solid business from scratch and keep it in the black."

"Wasn't always easy." Noel poked his chin in the direction of the mobile kitchen. "That bus took a couple of years of payments, but I couldn't run this outfit without it." He took a deep breath. "I don't know when you'd have time to cook and do all my paperwork. I'll be honest. Without a good chef, you won't have a reliable crew, and without an established team, you won't be able to bid on the best contracts."

Jess crossed her arms and cast a smug glance at Simon.

"I had a crew in mutiny in Galena Landing when my first cook there didn't work out. Seriously, it was bad. I can't afford that kind of problem, especially way out here in the boonies where the crew has no other options."

Simon frowned. "The kitchen looks in great shape, though. Clean. Well stocked in the basics."

"Claire Halford came on part way through the season." Jess glanced at Noel. "She's a trained chef there in Idaho. You might find the crew a little spoiled, Simon. We're used to strawberry shortcakes made the old-fashioned way. You know, with real whipped cream and berries ripened on the vine."

"Food service trucks don't carry those." Simon wiped his hands down his khaki shorts.

"She grew them in her own garden. Claire has a pretty sweet garden, doesn't she, Noel?"

Noel closed his eyes for a second to pray for patience. "She sure does." Had his voice been noncommittal enough? "I've got a few things to set up inside yet. See you guys in the morning." He stood up, folded his chair, and tucked it under the trailer in case of rain or wind.

Inside, he pulled the blinds shut on Simon and Jess, who seemed in no hurry to leave.

"Anything I ought to know about the boss?" he heard Simon ask.

Noel pressed the button on his mp3 player. He didn't need to hear Jess's answer to that one.

Chapter 27 --

Claire wiped her bangs off her forehead with the back of a garden-gloved hand and squinted at the sky. Unrelenting heat, unseasonable for the second week of July. A faint haze of smoke had settled over the valley since that day she and Noel had been on the mountain. A few more thunderstorms had blown through bringing very little rain and several more small forest fires. None near the farm, though.

If they hadn't been pouring spring water onto the garden beds, nothing would be growing, not even the weeds. Of course, the weeds were happy with plentiful moisture, and so were the raspberries. She'd picked enough for a big batch of jam.

The coolness inside the straw bale house welcomed her. She set the mounded baskets on the counter and rinsed her face with tap water. After pouring a tall glass of iced mint tea from the fridge, she crossed to the computer desk and brought up her email program.

Four emails from Noel? She blinked, and her heartbeat sped. The paper clip symbol showed attachments. What could he be sending her?

Photos. She bit her lip at the beauty of the first to download. Exactly the mood she'd hoped to convey on the website. Several more followed. His words were cryptic. "Here are the photos I promised you. Sorry I'm so late."

The last email contained several images with the Green Acres gang in them. Zach and Jo on the swing with Domino at their feet. Claire and Sierra and Amber bent over drawings. Claire in the kitchen.

She stared at the photo then glanced back at the body of the email. Nothing. Just 4/4. No message, nothing personal, but she could tell he'd photoshopped the picture to accent the lighting. He'd spent time on it. After their walk.

Had to be. He wasn't as impervious to her as he'd been pretending. Well, no, she'd known he wasn't immune. If he had been, it would have been no big deal to eat her food along with his crew. Being around her wouldn't have bothered him.

Her hands shook as she clicked the button to download the last batch of images. Was there still hope?

He'd taken a dozen photos of her in the kitchen that day, food for a catered party around her on the peninsula counter. The idea had been to show the personal side, to say, "This is the kind of food and attention you'll get when you sign for an event on Green Acres farm."

The expression on her face was radiant, but then she'd been looking at Noel. Maybe it was too over-the-top, too revealing for a public website. But possibly the casual searcher would think she loved catering so much that she'd do it all for them with the same smile. And that was true, wasn't it?

Noel always had the ability to capture her soul in his pictures. What must it have cost him to tweak the highlights and saturation on this one after he'd rejected her so brusquely?

He'd done all she asked for with photos for the website. After finishing the raspberry jam, she'd take the time to update the site. If this didn't help draw in more quality clients, nothing would. The man was a genius behind the lens.

oOo

A little creek danced down the mountainside near the tree-planting camp. Noel tossed a handful of pebbles in, but the evidence was gone in less than a blink. A few larger stones had no more effect. He heaved in a boulder.

Finally. It didn't stop the flowing water, but at least he could see a change. The rock looked like it belonged there. Water streamed over it, around it, bent on finding a downward path to the river below, then on to the ocean. There wasn't anything conscious about it, yet nothing would stop the flow.

Noel leaped from rock to rock, following the cascade down, his sport sandals providing firm footing. Around a bend, the little creek widened into a small pool. Noel stepped into a patch of weeds, the ground soft beneath his feet.

A sweet smell engulfed him.

Mint.

In an instant he stood beside Claire in the wet woods above Green Acres the day she'd found the mint patch. Her crazy pink boots. Her hesitant smile and the way she'd pulled back from him even then. He'd pursued her like crazy but, right when he was winning, he'd dropped everything and run.

What was he afraid of? Commitment? Claire herself?

That was dumb.

Emptiness engulfed him as he crouched down and crushed the saw-toothed leaves between his fingers. Mint grew like a weed in these mountains, anywhere a little moisture gave it encouragement. It was tough. Persistent. A guy stepped on it, and it only smelled sweeter than before.

Why had he left her?

Because she wouldn't leave the farm.

Why hadn't he stayed?

His business took him elsewhere. Like here, up a hillside that had seen a little more rain than Idaho's slopes had this summer. That day had been about the end of rain for the season...and the beginning of his infatuation with Claire.

Or was it love? Could it last? He hadn't thought so. Hadn't thought he had it in him, but maybe he'd been wrong. Maybe Claire was the one worth opening his heart to fully.

He'd known for a long time he couldn't miss Amber's wedding. It wasn't only for his sister's sake, though that had come to matter, too. He needed to see Claire. See if she felt it, that tenacity of love—if that's what it was—as persistent as mint roots.

He'd do it. He'd go. And meanwhile, he'd brew himself some wild mint tea and think about changes in his life.

o0o

"I can't believe the nerve of the man!" Eileen stormed into the straw bale house the Thursday before the wedding. Amber dragged their luggage behind her, head hanging low.

"Oh?" Claire, her heart sinking, rushed over to give Amber a hand. Had something happened with Shawn again? Wasn't it kind of late to cancel a wedding? After all, in forty-eight hours the whole thing would be over.

"My good-for-nothing ex showed up on my doorstep yesterday. Somewhere he heard Amber was getting married, so he assumed—*assumed*, mind you—that she'd want him at the wedding. Can you believe it? She's never set eyes on him in her life. Some kind of father he's been."

Amber met Claire's gaze and shook her head. "I didn't meet him now, either. I was at work."

Noel had hinted his dad was a mess. More than hinted. He'd cited the man as the reason he couldn't commit to a marriage. Because his dad had been an idiot. Sounded like he hadn't overstated that part, at least.

"And I didn't call her." Eileen thrust her handbag at the loveseat. "Bill has no right to see Amber. To pretend he's done anything for her in her entire life. She'd be crazy to want him at her wedding. And to walk her down the aisle?"

"Mom, relax. You told him I'd asked Noel."

Claire's heart skipped a beat. Noel was coming? He hadn't responded to her Paypal transfer other than to say thanks. He'd given no indication that he was returning to Green Acres.

Eileen swung to face Amber. "And your brother hasn't confirmed. He's up some mountain somewhere. That's fine. I'm perfectly capable of walking you down the aisle myself. And that Shawn had better prove he's cut from different cloth than the Kenzie men. My goodness gracious, Claire. Bill hasn't grown up a bit in twenty-five years. You should have seen him. Unkempt and looking at me with those big brown puppy dog eyes. As though he could bat those eyelashes and I'd let him back in my house."

Claire couldn't help being interested. "If you didn't let him in, what did you do with him?"

"Called my pastor. He came by and picked Bill up off my front step. Oh, don't look so shocked. I poured us each a coffee and sat outside with him. I wanted to know if, by any chance, he'd learned anything in all these years."

"Had he?"

"Not a bit, from what I could tell. My pastor took him down to the rescue mission for food and a bed. He could preach at Bill some, too. It would do him good to come face to face with God's call on his life."

"I'm sure it would."

Amber cast a desperate look at Claire. If she'd been listening to this kind of tirade all the way from Missoula, no wonder she looked a little frazzled.

"That sounds like a good place for him," Claire said.

Eileen planted her hands on her hips. "Do you think a person can change, Claire? Really honestly?"

How had she gotten pulled into this family quarrel? "Without God, few can. But with God, all things are possible." If only Noel leaned on God. Then he'd overcome the chains he felt from his dad's attitude through his life.

"I'd given up praying for Bill, I must say. I can't think why I once loved him. He hoodwinked me into thinking he was a proper sort of man."

"Oh, Eileen, don't give up. I notice you've never remarried, so you must still hold some affection in your heart for him."

Eileen harrumphed. "Just had my eyes opened. There's not a man out there that's dependable."

Poor Shawn. How had he ever been deemed acceptable as a son-in-law?

"I need to be near Amber to protect her. Shawn seems like a nice enough young man. Dedicated, hardworking. Amber told me she'd shown you her list. But, just in case, a mother has to be ready to support her daughter."

"That's why you're moving to Flagstaff, then?" Claire couldn't believe her ears. "Not for a job or change of pace, but to catch Amber if Shawn fails?"

"Yes." Eileen peered closer at Claire. "You don't think that's a good idea? You're not a mother. You can't possibly understand."

Oh, my. "Pray for them, Eileen. Let God do what He wants in their lives. You ever heard of a helicopter parent?"

"No, what's that?"

"It's when a parent hovers over her kids, ready to protect them. Kids don't learn anything from that. Amber is a well-adjusted young lady, so it couldn't be that you treated her that way when she was growing up. But…" Claire took a deep breath. Was she interfering too much? But Eileen had asked. She softened her tone. "You're sure sounding like one right now."

Eileen's face fell. "I don't mean to."

"You're probably trying to make up for her missing a father."

"And for the fact that her brother is never around, either."

"So you think Noel takes after his dad?"

The woman's gaze sprang to meet Claire's. "Oh, I'd never say that. Sure, he likes to travel, but he works for it. For Bill, it's always a handout. He figured the world owed him a living, if you remember that old song. He whined when someone got a promotion he thought he should get. It was always somebody else's fault if he didn't get a raise. They overlooked him. In reality, he was just plain lazy. There's not a slothful bone in Noel's body, I can tell you that. He's as responsible as the day is long. You know. You worked for him. He built that company from the ground up and he keeps it operating in the black. How is that like Bill? It's not."

A wave of relief flowed over Claire. "Noel did seem to be a good boss. His crew sure likes him."

"And what of you? You're not getting any younger living out here on this farm. I thought you were going to latch onto my boy and make him happy. Instead you look grumpier than ever."

Ouch. Eileen certainly told it like she saw it. Claire spread her hands wide. "Green Acres means everything to me, and his world is Enterprising Reforestation."

"So somebody needs to give a little. You can't pick when love will show up. Why, once I was rid of Bill I thought I'd meet some other man, somebody more deserving of a wife and family, but he never showed up." She rolled her eyes. "Now

Bill's back, thinking, as always, that he's God's gift to women. I wonder how many women he's gifted in the last twenty-five years? And he thinks to stroll back into my life? Heaven forbid."

The gap in Eileen's tirade came so suddenly that Claire didn't know what to say.

"So if my boy shows up here this weekend, you make sure he knows he's in the right place, you hear me? Somebody needs to talk some sense into him."

"I-I'll keep that in mind. Now, can I get you anything to drink? There's iced mint tea in the fridge, and a sample tray of petit fours in the pantry."

Eileen stared at Claire for a moment, then all the air seemed to flatten out of her sails. "That sounds lovely, thanks."

o0o

Noel drove west toward the forest fires raging in the Idaho panhandle. Nobody had mentioned any threat to Galena Landing or the plot of trees his crew had put in mere weeks before. Green Acres wasn't likely in a danger zone.

He was used to thinking of forests before people, but that's not what this trip was about. This was for Amber. Too bad he couldn't convince himself the wedding was the only reason his heart felt lighter. Jess had laughed her fool head off when he'd announced he left her in charge for a few days.

"Or forever, boss," she'd said with a huge grin. "I'll be plotting my takeover while you're gone."

If things worked out with Claire, he'd leave his business in the best possible hands. Possibly two sets of them, which seemed likely with the amount he'd seen Jess and Simon together lately.

"So long as it's not hostile," he'd replied.

"Nah. You'll make a great fishing guide."

"Don't you think you're getting ahead of yourself?"

"Doubt it." And she'd strolled away, singing something about Dreamboat.

Whatever. Let her think what she wanted. He owed it to Mom and Amber and Shawn to be a responsible family member. If Dad turned up from Denver, the least Noel could do was be there for the women in the family. Prove he was more stable than his dad. Shouldn't be that hard.

But yeah, the thought of seeing Claire put the whistle under his breath, even though he recalled their parting with a pang. He didn't dare let his own hopes get up there, but it was nigh impossible.

Would she think being a guide was sustainable enough to fit in with her farm? He wouldn't be opposed to doing a bit of digging and weeding, he supposed. Not if he could wake up every morning beside Claire.

Now who was getting ahead of himself?

A sign for a knife fair in Kalispell came into view. Noel slammed on the brakes, and the holiday trailer wobbled a little behind the truck. Knives. He'd used Claire's. They'd once been decent, but honed almost to the edges. She deserved better, for sure. He could afford an hour or two checking out this fair.

He rounded a corner of the booths and saw what he'd been hoping to find—a whole set of handmade kitchen knives. He hefted a blade. Solid. The wooden grip contoured to his hand. Would it fit Claire's?

"Good Damascus steel there. You won't find a better knife. Holds its edge."

Noel ran his thumb carefully across the blade. Felt sharp all right. Smooth and solid. A glance over the display revealed knives of nearly every description. He laid a large chef's blade next to the filleting knife he'd picked up first. Then a midsize paring knife and two smaller ones. He slid the group together.

The vendor rubbed his hands. He should be pleased. This represented a chunk of change.

Noel glanced up. "Got package pricing in place?"

The man scanned the selection. "Ten percent off."

"Fifteen."

He bit his lip. "Twelve."

Noel did the math silently and shook his head. "Fifteen."

"Twelve and I throw in a bonus." Suiting action to his words, the vendor added a peeler.

Noel cocked his head and looked over the group. "Done." He stretched out his hand and shook the vendor's in a strong grip. Then he pulled out his wallet and ran his card through the electronic slot. "Gift wrap?"

The guy pulled a brown box from under the table. "This okay?"

Noel sighed. "Sure." Would the vendor be any better prepared if it were close to Christmas, or did he always consider plain cardboard acceptable? Whatever. It kept the set hidden and protected while he decided what to do with it. Back in the parking lot, Noel stowed the package in a cupboard in the trailer before sliding back into the driver's seat and heading west again.

Knowing Claire, she'd value knives more than diamonds. Of course, she wouldn't be able to wear them on her finger. If she accepted the knives, he'd do something about a ring. He'd take her shopping with him. The picture pleased him.

No guarantee she'd let him stroll back into her life. He'd been the one to sever the ties.

If only she'd forgive him.

Seemed his heart made up its mind before his brain had decided. He could use a good set of blades himself if he chickened out with Claire.

Was he ready? What happened to his plans to have fun, live

the free and easy single life, and not get too serious about religion in his youth?

Maybe that attitude wasn't all it was cracked up to be. Yeah, he was ready for change.

o0o

Thursday night thunderclouds loomed over the valley. Claire shaded her eyes and watched the dark clouds roll in. Maybe this time it would actually rain.

Of course, it would be better if it waited until after Amber and Shawn's big day, but there weren't too many guests. They could easily fit under the pole barn if needed, and the reception could take place inside the house.

Amber's hand rested on her arm. "Claire? What if my dad shows up? What if he's drunk or something?"

Lightning flashed on the west side of the valley and a low rumble followed after a few seconds.

Claire tore her gaze from the storm and glanced at Amber. "Do you think it's likely?"

"I don't know. Mom said he came all this way because he heard about the wedding from some relative back east. He made it as far as Missoula. Why wouldn't he come the rest of the way?"

"Do you want to see him?"

"Well, yeah. In a way. Mom should've called me yesterday and let me make my own decision. She keeps trying to shelter me."

Truer words had never been spoken. "But—" Thunder crashed over the house.

"It's not like it would make any difference to the outcome. But I don't know what he looks like. What if he's there and I don't know it? What if he's there and he makes a big scene? I don't know what to expect."

Claire pulled Amber to her side. "I don't know, either. But I won't let anyone interfere. I promise."

A flash of flame shot into the air as a tree exploded in the distance.

Claire sucked in a sharp breath. Could she direct the wedding? Amber's dad? The weather was definitely beyond her control. Fiery. Scary.

Amber clutched Claire's arm. "That's a long way from here, right?"

"Yes." Not too far from the fire that burned a month ago. It'd taken weeks to get it contained, helicopters dragging huge buckets through the lake only to dump the water on the fire. Still, thousands of acres of farmland, much of it irrigated, stood between that flare and Green Acres. The odds of it burning across the valley were extremely low.

It would be easier not to worry if they'd get some rain with the lightning.

More bolts flashed.

Claire let out a shuddering breath. "It's in God's hands. What's in mine should be a lot of chicken rollups that need to be frozen for Saturday." She turned for the house.

"I can give you a hand with those."

The bride had become one of her dearest friends. "Sure, that would be great." She was going to miss Amber, and it wasn't just because of Noel. They entered the house to spot Eileen seated at the peninsula counter visiting with Sierra. "Hey, Eileen, did you sell your house yet?"

The older woman shook her head. "Not a nibble in sight. There haven't even been any showings."

"Oh, dear," Sierra put in. "I hope you haven't given notice on your job yet. Unless you plan to rent the house out if it doesn't sell?"

Eileen cast a pained glance at Claire. "I don't know if you girls' Christianity thinks this is a good idea or not, but I've put out a fleece on the subject."

Claire frowned. "Fleece? I don't know what you mean."

"Oh, some Bible guy—was it Gideon, Mom?" Amber asked.

This sounded vaguely familiar.

When Eileen nodded, Amber went on. "He didn't know what decision to make so he laid a piece of sheepskin—a fleece—outside overnight. He told God that if the fleece was dry when the ground around it was wet with dew in the morning, he'd know God wanted him to do what he suspected. And in the morning, that's just what happened."

Eileen twisted on the stool. "Gideon didn't much believe Him, of course. Didn't want to believe God's will, as it wasn't what he wanted to do. So he said, 'oh, that was too easy.' The next night he asked for the opposite—the ground to be completely dry and the fleece to be wet. God managed that, too. There was so much moisture in the fleece that Gideon could wring the whole thing out."

"Yeah," added Amber. "He got like a bucket full of water from it."

Claire needed to reread the Old Testament. "Wow."

Sierra planted her elbows on the counter. "So what kind of fleece did you put out, Eileen?"

The older woman slid a sidelong glance at Claire. "Well, I wondered if I just assumed I should move to Flagstaff if Amber did, or whether I'd actually asked God for His will."

Claire held her breath.

"So I asked Him to sell my house by the end of August. That's still a month from now. He could do it, you know."

"Sure He could." Claire moved in closer. "So you're saying you'd take a sale as God's will that you move to Arizona."

Eileen nodded, her mouth twisted to the side. "I realize it's not best to force God to do things the way I want Him to. But I do want to know what His will is."

"Makes sense." Sierra straightened and picked up the vegetable peeler with one hand and a carrot with the other.

Nice somebody else was on supper duty tonight. Claire had enough to do with the remainder of the prep for the reception.

A thunderous crash rolled over the house. If they'd still been in the trailer, the whole thing would have shaken like an earthquake hit it. Claire met Sierra's gaze an instant as the electricity flickered and the living room lights went out.

Chapter 28 --

Noel maneuvered the last few hairpin curves coming down over the pass as a thunderstorm crashed around him. Only a few raindrops spattered his windshield, but the wind rocked the trailer behind him. He turned into a full-on cloud of smoke as the road opened up over the Galena Valley. Whoa. That had been mere haze moments before. Where had it all come from? He'd had his tunes cranked and not the radio. He flipped the switch and sought a local station. Wynnton.

"Dozens of farms northeast of Galena Landing are on pre-evacuation notice as the wildfires, sparked by last night's thunderstorms, burn out of control. Crews are gathering to fight the epic blaze, but it's moving so quickly the chief says it's hard to know where to begin."

Northeast of town? *Dear God, no!* Noel stomped on his accelerator. Not after all the hard work the women had put into that farm. Green Acres must be one of the closest to the blaze. He had to get there and do what he could.

Gearing down to meet the speed limit within the town's boundaries was sheer torture. The town's single traffic light stopped him. No one waited at the cross streets. Maybe he should just run the light? Noel glanced around, fingers drumming the steering wheel. The light turned green, and he gunned the engine. The trailer wobbled behind him.

It'd be dumb to take it into the evacuation zone. Where could he leave it? Where did that Ed guy live, anyway? No idea. Noel glanced down a side street and saw the sign for Nature's Pantry. Wasn't that where Sierra had her office? He swerved right without signaling and yanked the wheel into the gravel parking lot. The open sign in the store's window wasn't lit.

Noel jumped out of the truck and jogged for the door. Acrid smoke filled the air. Maybe that dude in Wynnton hadn't realized the town of Galena Landing itself might be in danger. Noel's heart constricted as he tested the door. It swung open.

"Hello?" he hollered, not waiting for someone to appear behind the counter. "Anyone here?" He glanced frantically around the old storefront, wooden floors worn from thousands of feet over decades. In here the smell of herbs mingled with the smoke that had forced its way in with him.

"Be right there!" a woman's voice called. Feet jogged down wooden stairs somewhere out of sight then Sierra skidded into the room from the back.

He'd never seen her look anything but perfect in all his visits to the farm. Now her hair was mussed and her eye shadow smudged.

"Noel? What are you doing here?"

He motioned out the door. "What's going on?"

"Claire just called me. The wind shifted after I came to work. She said the fire is headed toward the farm. They're saying—" Her voice cracked. "They're saying we could lose everything."

And Claire already afraid of fire before this even happened. "What can I do?"

Sierra shook her head as though to dislodge buzzing insects. "You didn't answer my question."

"My sister is getting married." Or was she? Would the

wedding be postponed? Moved? What happened in situations like this? "I came for the wedding."

Sierra's eyes narrowed.

Oh, man. What was he supposed to say? Surely she wasn't dumb enough to think his sister meant nothing to him. A voice at the back of his mind taunted him that he'd avoided promising to come, so what else could Sierra think?

"Not for Claire?"

A sick feeling plummeted through his gut. "Her, too. For sure."

Sirens screamed past the health food store.

"Look, can I leave my trailer parked here? I'm headed out to the farm to see how I can help. I'll be able to get around much faster without it dragging behind."

Sierra's gaze flicked to the front door and back to Noel. "Sure."

He surged toward the door but spun back on his heel with his hand on the knob. "I didn't see your car in the lot."

Her jaw clenched. "We only have one running vehicle, Noel. I couldn't very well leave her with a fire on the mountain and no wheels, could I?"

"No. No, of course not." He stared at her. "Then how—why?"

"I biked. I helped pack as much as I could before I left, just in case, but we really didn't think it would come to this or I'd have stayed."

Noel made a snap decision. "Are you done here? Want to come with me?"

She started. "Give me five minutes?"

"You have until I get the trailer unhooked. Five minutes tops, then I'm leaving."

"You got it." She sprinted for the stairs.

Noel jogged back to his unit and backed it in at the rear of the lot. By the time he had the trailer jacked up and disconnected, Sierra had locked up the door to Nature's Pantry. He pulled beside her and she clambered in.

He couldn't think what more to say to Claire's roommate, so he didn't bother. He navigated the few blocks to rejoin the highway then noticed the flashing lights of a squad car at a roadblock up ahead. He groaned.

Three vehicles in front of him were waved back toward Galena Landing. The driver of the fourth stuck his head out the window and yelled at the state patrol officer standing beside his car. The cop shook his head and pointed south.

Noel drummed his fingers on the wheel.

Sierra clutched his arm. "They're not going to let us through, are they?" Her voice shook.

The car in front changed direction and flew back toward town, tires squealing.

"Is there a back way to get through?" Noel asked as he pulled the truck closer to the cop. Surely he'd know if there was.

Sierra shook her head. "It's a dead end road. No access other than this highway."

"Yeah." Noel pressed the button to roll down the window. "Good morning, officer."

The cop harrumphed. "Road's closed due to fire danger. No admittance."

Noel turned his hand to indicate Sierra. "She lives at Green Acres Farm at the end of Thompson Road and needs to get back to help her friends and family off the place."

"No can do."

"Look, officer, with all due respect, that's an unacceptable answer. I'm Noel Kenzie of Enterprising Reforestation. I know my way around the woods up there, and the fire crew on the mountain needs me as much as Ms. Riehl's people need her." He revved the powerful engine slightly. "We're going through."

The officer didn't budge, though his eyes narrowed. "Show me some paperwork. Prove to me you can be an asset."

Noel shifted to his left hip to pull his wallet out of his pocket. He flipped it open and pointed out a card proving his credentials.

The officer scrutinized it for a moment, glancing back and forth between Noel and the paper. Likely determining if he was the same guy. Then he leaned in and took a closer look at Sierra. "We're about to move Thompson Road to a full evacuation order. The fire isn't far."

"More reason for me to help get irreplaceable items and people off the farm." She laid a hand on Noel's arm. "I need this truck to do that."

Panic slithered across Noel's skin. She was asking to borrow his wheels? But if he were commandeered to fight the fire, he wouldn't need it. Anything to get Claire to safety. Mom. Amber. All of them must be at the farm.

The officer's radio crackled and he stepped aside to speak into it. Try as he might, Noel couldn't overhear. Maybe he should gun the engine and blast through the wooden barrier. It wouldn't damage the truck. Much. He'd be really tempted if he hadn't handed his wallet to the guy.

When the cop returned, he jotted down Noel's drivers license number. "This truck had better be back in town within the hour." He looked at Noel. "And you better not be. Report to the fire crew on Lindsay Road, then she gets the truck, grabs her stuff, and drives straight back to town." He squinted northeast. "Don't know if even Galena Landing is going to be far enough, but it'll do for now."

Noel nodded and plucked his wallet out of the guy's hand.

The cop stepped back and waved them through, then held up his hand to the vehicle behind them. As Noel pulled away, he saw the officer lean into the driver's window of the next car.

"Whew." He glanced at Sierra. "You sure you're up for this?"

She leaned forward. "Step on it."

o0o

Claire shoved the last of the wedding food into the trunk of Eileen's car. "I called Pastor Ron, and we can store all this in the fridge at the church. You'd better get going."

Eileen glanced up the crackling mountain as she headed for the driver's door, but Amber hung back.

"Get in the car, Amber." Claire pushed her shoulder. "This is your ride out. Everything you brought here is in that vehicle."

Amber parked her hands on her hips. "Everything except my friends. Like you."

Panic swelled. "I don't have time for this. Get going. I won't be far behind."

"You don't have room for that pile in the great room. Not in that little hatchback."

"I'll do the best I can, okay? I'm not allowing your wedding to be ruined any more than it already will be. But go. We're nearly out of time."

"Where's Zach? Jo took their truck without him."

Claire shook her head. "He's out on a farm call somewhere, maybe helping get some animals to safety. He's got his vet truck. I can't count on him getting back here in time to help."

Amber's jaw firmed. "The farm should come first to him. I mean, after Jo."

Claire pushed Amber. "Can we not argue about this? We're wasting time. Just go, *please*, and let me deal with what I can." At least Domino was safe. He'd been in Jo's truck when she pulled out.

Tears poured down Amber's face. She hugged Claire, but

Claire pushed her away.

"I'm going, I'm going. See you at the church?"

"I'll be there."

Claire gave herself a few seconds to wave as Eileen's car disappeared down Thompson Road. Then she strode back into the house, not allowing herself to look up at the mountain. Flames were visible—she knew that. The smoke had thickened, threatening to hurl her back to that night in Seattle. She'd loved Graham's little house.

How could God do this to her? She stood to lose everything all over again—her beautiful new home they'd only been in for a few months. Zach and Jo's cabin. The garden, the pole barn, the business they were trying to build. That would suffer with no place to host events. *Everything.*

A still small voice spoke into her rattled mind. Not everything. Not God. She still had Him, her faith, her friends. But not Noel. He was gone.

Now why had he come into her mind? A familiar rumble from outside caused her to run to the door.

Noel! He was here. His truck peeled down the driveway and skidded to a stop right by the deck railing.

Claire flung the door open and ran down the steps. "Noel!"

But why did Sierra jump down out of the cab?

Claire lurched to a stop. "Sierra? Isn't this Noel's truck? Where is he? How'd you get it?"

"I ran into him in town. Come on. Help me load up. We've got lots more room in this than just the car." Sierra charged past Claire, the screen door banging in her wake. "What's the top of the list? Got everything out for the wedding?"

Claire jogged into the house. "Didn't you pass Eileen and Amber? They left just a few minutes ago."

"No. I came in from the north and cut through Elmer's field. Thank God for four-wheel drive. We can take a bunch of the kitchen stuff. It's more valuable than anything else that's portable. Is the computer packed up?"

"It's in the car already." Claire snagged Sierra's arm. "Talk to me. Where's Noel? Why did you come in that way?"

Sierra shrugged off Claire's hand and ran into the kitchen. "You know they're not letting any traffic north on 95, right? So Noel had some trouble convincing the officer we had the right to come through. I dropped him off at the fire fighting marshaling point on Lindsay Road. He told me to get you out of the danger zone. Now move it!" She wrenched a drawer out of the kitchen cabinets and stacked pots and pans inside it.

And Claire had been stymied by the lack of boxes. Drawers were a great idea. She followed her roommate's lead, loading drawers and running them out to Noel's truck.

He'd come back. Even in the midst of her terror—she could hear the flames crackling outside—her heart lightened just a bit. A fire had separated her and Graham. Could one bring Noel back to her?

Of course he'd come for Amber and Shawn's wedding. But he'd known she'd be here. If he were really trying to avoid her, he wouldn't have come, right? Especially not the day before. He could've just come for the ceremony itself and disappeared again right after, but he hadn't. He'd come early. Only—

"How did you find Noel?"

"What?" Sierra looked up from her crouch on the floor. "He was looking for a place to park his RV and pulled in at Nature's Pantry."

"He brought his trailer?"

"Isn't that what I just said?"

Claire gave her head a quick shake and ran another load out. A loud crack from up the mountain riveted her attention upward. A tree exploded, sending a shower of sparks around it. Claire screamed.

"What happened?" Sierra appeared at her side.

"We're out of time."

"But the truck is half empty!"

"The car is loaded with bedding and clothes and the computer. We've got half the kitchen in the back of the truck."

"But our canning! The freeze—"

"Sierra! *Look.*"

Her friend turned and peered up the mountain into smoke that blocked out all memories of sunshine. A siren shrilled from the southwest.

Claire sucked in a deep breath and choked on the smoke. "It's time."

The wail of emergency vehicles came nearer.

"I guess you're right. But how can we leave everything else?"

Tears burned Claire's eyes, whether from grief or from smoke was hard to say. "Zach turned the sprinklers on the cabin roof and the house roof. It's all we can do."

A squad car peeled in the driveway with an officer yelling into a loudspeaker. "Everyone out! Evacuation order is now in effect."

Claire glanced back at the straw bale house and closed her eyes for a second as Sierra latched the door. The night in Seattle blurred with today. Fire. Her worst enemy. She ran down the steps to the old VW hatchback, turned the ignition with trembling hands, and headed down the driveway. A glance in the rearview mirror showed Noel's truck looming right behind her.

With Sierra driving.

"Oh, God, I don't want to lose everything we've worked for all these years. Please keep our home safe. Please, please, please." She blinked back tears.

It's only stuff. It's only a place. It's all just temporary.

Claire knew that. The words of the old hymn slid into her mind and she belted them out with gusto. "This world is not my home." Maybe the sound of her voice would drown out the sirens and the flames behind her.

Maybe all that was truly important was up ahead.

Chapter 29

If only Noel knew for sure Claire was safe. He couldn't jump into danger without that knowledge. The crew boss in front of him barked directions at the motley band of guys, but Noel hung back. What had he done? He wasn't prepared, wasn't dressed for this. He'd come for a wedding, not a fire.

"You there! Name? Experience?"

"Noel Kenzie. Owner of Enterprising Reforestation. My crew planted half that mountainside this past spring." They'd probably have to redo it, too. Along with the rest of the hillside if the fire was as big as it looked. That could put him in Galena Landing for a good long time.

Funny how wonderful that sounded.

"Ever fought fire?" The guy's voice sounded desperate.

Noel nodded. "Ran a crew in Colorado a couple of seasons, a few years back."

"And you know this hillside?"

"Like the back of my hand."

"The county is hauling out some heavy equipment. Any advice as to where we could use a D6 to cut a fire break?"

They had a Cat bulldozer in already? "Maybe. Depends on how far down the flames have moved. It's impossible to tell from here."

A helicopter thrummed in the distance, and the crew boss tilted his head to listen to it. "That's your ride coming in. I pray to God you know what you're talking about, Mr. Kenzie, because if you're wrong, we lose all these farms." He shoved a business card into Noel's hand. "Call me."

Noel gulped and nodded. The chopper hovered and came in for a landing in a nearby field, beyond the power lines. Noel ran toward it, ducking from the draft of the rotor. He'd always loved flying in one of these birds.

He clambered into the cockpit. "You're here to show me the extent of the fire?"

"Yes, sir."

The ground dropped and Noel thrilled to the sensation. A few seconds later all thought of the joy of flying shattered as he focused on the flaming forest beneath him. "Wow. When did this start?"

"Last night."

"Spreading fast." Noel bit his lip. "Ground's too dry."

"Not much snow pack last winter up high, nor a lot of rain this spring."

Noel nodded. "Yeah, my crew put in a block of trees on the south side of this mountain. I don't imagine they'll make it."

The helicopter swung around the mountain. "We can have a look."

Down below, Thompson Road drew a straight line from the mountain to just past Elmer's before twisting south toward Galena Landing. A small hatchback and a big pickup—his—barreled down the road. Noel's gaze lingered. Claire and Sierra were headed for safety. Good.

When he glanced back at the mountain, his gut clenched. The flames were way too close to Green Acres. "They're going to have to create a back fire right there, above that log cabin. See the fence? It surrounds a spring. Best to get above it if possible." The cabin had a sprinkler rotating on the metal roof. Not likely enough, but it couldn't hurt. "Never mind a back fire. Dig a trench right down to mineral earth. No point in trying farther up the mountain. There isn't time."

The pilot glanced at him. "Tell the chief."

Noel blanked for a moment. "I don't have his number."

"Didn't he give you his card?"

"Right." Noel punched the code into his cell as the chopper skimmed over the blocks of newly planted trees. Though the flames hadn't reached them, the small firs already drooped in the heat.

He gave crisp orders into his cell and was gratified when the voice at the other end replied, "Yes, sir. Good place to make a stand." The chief shouted orders as he ended the call.

"Which way's the wind blowing?" Noel asked the pilot.

"Out of the west, but it's still pushing down the mountain instead of up and over."

Noel shook his head. "There are quite a few farms tucked in against the length of the hillside. Probably should get crews down all the roads to try and protect those properties."

"Looks closest at the end of Thompson, though." The pilot circled around.

"Yeah. It does." Noel took a deep breath and let it out slowly. How would Claire manage if the home and farm she loved so much went up in smoke? Even if a stucco straw bale house couldn't exactly burn, the structural integrity would surely be compromised. Did the girls have good insurance? Could they rebuild?

Would losing everything make Claire remember this was only a place?

But Claire hadn't closed the doors to a relationship. He had.

o0o

Amber huddled, trembling, in a corner of the church's library, face buried in her drawn-up knees.

Claire didn't have time for this. She dug for linens through a jumbled heap in a garbage bag. Everything would need ironing. But wait. What was really the most important? A salvaged wedding, made to look like it'd always been meant to be held at the church rather than at the farm, or a radiant bride?

So much easier to block the thought of a burning house if she could keep busy. Focused. But Amber needed her. Claire dumped the mound of tablecloths on one of the tables strung out the length of the library. "Can someone get these ironed? And no, I don't know where an ironing board might be."

"On it, Claire!" someone hollered from the other end of the room.

"Thanks." She glanced over at Amber. The young woman had become like a sister to her over the months they'd planned her big day.

Now *that* was a dangerous line of thinking.

Claire prayed for wisdom, patience, and love as she grabbed two glasses of water and headed across the room. She plopped down on the floor beside the bride and bumped her lightly with a shoulder. "Hey, girl. How are you holding up?" As though she couldn't tell.

Sniffle. "Okay."

"I brought you a glass of water. If you want a coffee, I think someone's making a pot."

"Thanks." Amber swiped her face with her arm and reached for the glass. "Why does this kind of drama always have to happen to me?"

"Um, sweetie? It's not your house that's in the path of a forest fire. I don't think you can claim this as a personal disaster."

Red-rimmed eyes met Claire's. "I'm sorry. I can't even think straight. It must be ten times worse for you."

You think? But it wasn't Claire's wedding. She could give a little. "I don't think there's any need to figure out who got the worst end of this stick. It's pointy no matter which way we look at it."

"Everything is ruined." Amber sniffled.

Claire prayed for patience and tried a lighter tone. "You came to us for a wedding to remember. I think we're giving you that. How much more memorable can it get?"

"Very funny."

Okay, well, she'd tried. "Amber? What is the purpose of a wedding day?"

Amber stared at her blankly. "To get married."

"Right. So are you going to get married tomorrow?"

Amber bit her lip and nodded.

"I think the basics of a real wedding are a bride and groom, some witnesses, and an authorized person to perform a ceremony. In fact, I think you once told me you'd be happy to get married in front of a judge."

"Your point is?" At least Amber's chin had come up a little.

"Everything else is just trappings. The gorgeous dress—and yours is stunning, by the way, and it's safely hanging up in the other room. Your mom has borrowed a steamer from the pastor's wife."

"Oh."

Yeah, girl. Others are doing things for you while you sit and mope. "The flower-adorned chapel, the cake, the reception—even the friends—are not actually the wedding. Don't get me wrong. They're awesome. They show how important a milestone this is in your life. They give your family and friends a chance to get together and have a memorable party. But they're not vital to a good marriage."

Oh, right. Claire, the counselor. She'd broken her own engagement. She'd been afraid to trust God enough to even see what pull poverty in third world countries had on Graham. He'd had one conversation with her about practicing dentistry overseas, and she'd yanked his ring off her finger and blocked him from her mind. Just like that.

Could he have convinced her to join him if she'd been a bit more open? How would her life be different? Claire shook her head. Too much had happened in the three years since they'd parted ways. Graham had married someone else, for starters. The end.

"I always wanted everything perfect, you know? I've been dreaming of my wedding since I was a kid. I guess all little girls do."

"I didn't. Not really." Claire had always figured she'd keep standing on her own two feet. She'd lived the trauma of parents who argued every day and finally parted ways. Of course, Amber didn't even know her dad.

Amber shifted to stare straight in Claire's face. "Honestly?"

Claire shrugged. "My parents fought all the time. For years. Marriage didn't seem all that romantic to me."

"But I always thought it would be different. Because even though my parents didn't love each other—obviously—the guy I'd marry would be so smitten with me that everything would be perfect."

"Shawn does love you. All of this—"Claire waved her hand to take in the church basement, the town, the valley, and the forest fire "—isn't a result of his lack of love." A sudden thought struck her. "It's not a lack of God's love toward you or me, either."

"I guess." Amber's mouth twisted to the side as she thought. "I mean, I know it's not Shawn's fault. I wanted everything to be perfect for us as we started our new life together."

"You had your lists." Claire couldn't help but tease.

"Yeah, I do. Not just ones of how perfect Shawn is for me. Lists for everything. Have you seen my list of things to do before we move to Flagstaff?"

"You mean besides go on a honeymoon?"

"Yeah, besides that."

Claire counted the grin on Amber's face as a particular and personal victory. "You may know I've written more lists since meeting you than I ever had before, and not all of it has to do with creating a new business venture." She let out a sardonic laugh. "Not sure we can brag this one up in the books, though."

"Did you ever make one for your perfect guy?"

Heat spread across Claire's face as she clambered to her feet. "I should give Mrs. Graysen a hand with those tablecloths."

"Oh, no, you don't." Amber grabbed Claire's hand and yanked her back to the floor. "You did write a list, didn't you?"

Claire sagged against the wall. "Okay, so what if I did? It's not like it will get me anywhere."

Amber's brown eyes looked deep into Claire's. "It's my brother, isn't it," she said quietly.

"Don't worry, I'll get over it." She had before, with Graham. Somehow this was different. Though she'd once accepted Graham's ring, he hadn't filled her mind every waking moment as Noel did. To say nothing of her sleeping moments.

"Why would you want to?"

Claire stared at Amber blankly. "Why would I want to what?"

A grin twitched around Amber's mouth. "Get over him."

"Oh." Claire took a sip of her water. Maybe it would cool her face.

"My brother isn't perfect. I know that. But I'm willing to

bet he fits the checklist you've made to a tee. Doesn't he?"

"Not quite."

Amber tipped her head.

"What's number one on *your* list?"

Comprehension dawned on Amber's face. "That the guy love God with all his heart."

"Exactly."

Claire's thoughts drifted back to that day on the mountain when Noel had said God only wanted them to be happy. Had she been so busy feeling sorry for herself since then that she'd forgotten to pray for his spiritual wellbeing? Or maybe she'd felt guilty—selfish—for asking that of God. For sure selfish. Did she only want him right with God so she could marry him?

Involuntarily she shook her head. No. His soul was more important than her happiness.

Still, couldn't she have both?

"Shawn!" Amber let out a squeal as she jolted to her feet and dashed for the door. "You found us!"

Claire rubbed her ears to get Amber's high-pitched scream out of them and pushed to her feet more sedately.

Amber's soon-to-be-husband twirled her around and kissed her soundly. "Of course I found you. You texted me and told me." His glance took in Claire. "Heard anything about the farm since you left?"

She shook her head. "We had a lot of smoke, but the fire was a little ways up the mountain still."

A cell phone rang in the sudden quiet, and Jo tugged hers out of her shorts' pocket. "Hey, Zach." She bit her lip as she listened.

Everyone turned to eavesdrop on her end of the conversation, but there was nothing to hear. A few seconds later she swiped it off. Jo's gaze swept the room. "Zach's okay. He and Gary Waterman hauled some cattle across the river.

He's headed to our place to plow a wide berth along the edge of Green Acres."

"But they've ordered evacuations!" Sierra said. "He's not allowed to be there."

"They can't force anyone to leave." Claire grabbed the back of a chair. "Just prevent them from returning."

Jo met her eyes. "Noel's working with the fire crew. He's doing everything he can to save our farm."

Chapter 30 ---

Trucks hauling excavators and dozers on low-beds churned through the smoke to the end of Thompson Road. Noel made out Zach's pickup in the midst of the pack, and his opinion of the vet climbed higher. The guy had guts coming into the thick of it, untrained and all.

But Zach didn't join the crew at the base of the logging road. Instead, his truck veered off into his own driveway. Noel narrowed his eyes. What was Zach up to? Once he had this crew working, he'd go over there and find out. Maybe he came back for his dog or something and would be gone in a moment. How could Noel face those women if something happened to Zach?

Noel focused on the equipment operators crowding around him. "Our number one goal is to save that log cabin and this farm if possible. Whoever's driving the D6, push the trees down on the uphill side of the fence above the spring. Shove them out into the middle of that pasture. Once the duff is gone we'll have that fire break we need."

It was mighty close to the field of wheat Claire had shown him months ago, now yellowing with maturity. No matter. It had to be sacrificed or the whole place would be lost. Might be anyway.

He could hear minor explosions as boiling pitch blew tree trunks apart, and the ever-present crackles of dry needles burning.

Men ran to their equipment and engines rumbled to life. These guys were well trained and knew their lives were on the line to protect the farms. They'd do the best they could.

Another engine rumbled in the distance.

Noel turned and stared through the orchard between Green Acres and the Nemesek farmyard. That wasn't Zach's pickup he heard. More like an old diesel engine. A tractor.

Noel jumped into the nearest truck and roared down the driveway to the one next door. He peeled in beside Zach on the old John Deere and slammed on the brakes.

Zach glanced at him then continued to back the tractor a few more feet before hopping off.

"What are you doing?"

"Getting ready to plow as many furrows as I can along the edge of the pasture."

"You're crazy, man. I've got a D6 pushing trees out into that. Don't get in their way. Let them do their thing." Among other things, those guys knew what they were doing. Did Zach?

"I can help make a fire break. I promise I'll be careful and watch the fire."

"But what you're doing won't save your cabin. Only the crew can do that."

Zach peered at the hillside. Noel followed his gaze. Not a pretty picture. Already several trees waved in the air and toppled in front of the D6 bulldozer, while the hillside burned not far above.

If the wind picked up, they'd be in danger in no time.

Noel gripped Zach's arm. "I can't let you do this. It's too dangerous."

"It's my farm, my parents' farm. I can't rely on strangers to protect it when I'm not willing to."

"That hurts." Noel tried a grin. "I'm no stranger."

They stared at each other a few seconds longer. Zach had as much right to be here as Noel did. Maybe more. Sure, he might not be trained to fight fire, but neither of them were officially on the crew.

Noel clasped Zach's arm. "There's no time for this. If you're going to do it, get rolling, but stay out of the way of the dozer. Make sure I don't have to report an injury—or worse—to Jo." And Claire.

Zach saluted and bent to hook the plow to the tractor's three-point hitch. "On my way." He climbed back to the open tractor seat before bellowing down at Noel. "And besides, man, it's all in God's hands. Thanks for what you're doing, but God will determine the outcome. Pray for safety."

Pray for anything? When was the last time he'd done that? Since he'd met Claire, much more often than anytime in his life prior. He hadn't wanted to remember not everyone lived to a ripe old age, but the sight of that fire threatening the valley brought it home. Any one of those guys trying to create a firebreak could die.

Zach could die.

Noel could, too.

He jumped into the truck and ripped back down the road. "Please, God. Please keep everyone safe. Especially Zach." He took a deep breath. "And me. Not quite ready to meet You face to face, but I'll get right on that when there isn't a fire breathing down my neck. Please keep me in one piece that long."

He spared a thought for Claire. She'd be safe enough in town, at least for now. Whether she'd ever forgive his stupidity, or not, was still up in the air. But he'd be in a lot better shape if he kept her home from burning.

o0o

Claire looked around the small group in the church basement. "Okay, it's time for the wedding rehearsal. Anyone have any questions before we go upstairs?"

Amber shook her head and took Shawn's hand. They headed toward the stairwell, Eileen right behind them. A door clanged shut in the foyer.

Claire grabbed the stack of programs and followed along. Footsteps halted above her and Eileen's voice quavered, "Bill?"

Some guy said, "Is this my little girl?"

Claire broke into a run and jogged up the stairs to see Shawn's arm protecting Amber, who stared at the strange man.

Eileen advanced on him, hands on her hips. "Nobody invited you to this wedding. Get out."

"Are you my father?" Amber pushed away from Shawn slightly.

The man looked like Noel might when he turned ninety. Tall, but bent. Paunchy. Balding head with blotchy skin. And yet, in there somewhere, the resemblance showed. Claire couldn't tear her gaze from Noel's father. She grabbed for the stair railing to keep steady as she climbed the last two steps.

But he had eyes only for Amber. And Eileen. His gaze flicked back and forth between them as he licked his chapped lips. The guy did not look healthy by anyone's standards.

Amber clutched Shawn's hand and dragged him closer. "Dad?"

"Get out, Bill." Eileen edged between father and daughter.

"Nah, she wants me here. See?" He peered around his ex-wife. "I heard you was getting hitched and figured you'd want your old man to give you away."

Claire's fingers tightened around the railing. The nerve of him. But still....he was her father. Apparently.

Amber laughed, the sound brittle and false. "Good to meet you, Dad. But you can't exactly give me away."

Eileen grabbed Bill's arm and towed him toward the door. She hissed something in his ear that Claire couldn't quite make out.

He pulled loose and turned to Amber. "That's a father's job."

Amber shook her head. "A father's job is to be there for his kids. To take them sledding and fishing and to church on Sunday. A real dad tucks his kids in bed at night and reads them stories and drives them to school when they miss the bus." Her voice rose incrementally with each sentence as she advanced on him. "All my life I've needed a real dad, and where were you?" She stabbed a finger into his chest. "Where. Were. You?"

Bill's gaze flicked from Amber to Eileen and back again. "I, uh…"

Shawn slid his arm around Amber's waist, tugging her close. "I'm Shawn Jackson, soon to be your son-in-law. What my bride is trying to tell you is that the wedding is tomorrow at two-thirty, and you're welcome to be our guest. However, Amber's brother will be giving her away."

"But—"

Claire remembered she was in charge of this wedding. "Excuse us, Mr. Kenzie. We're running on a tight schedule here. Like Mr. Jackson says, the wedding is at two-thirty, and the doors will open promptly at two. We hope to see you then. Now, if you don't mind…" She let her voice trail away as she took Eileen's arm and steered her toward the sanctuary. With any luck Amber and Shawn would be right on their heels. And where was the rest of the bridal party? Still hanging out in the basement?

Ah, no. They'd gathered at the top of the steps and listened to every word of the interchange. Too bad. Yet they were friends of the couple and wouldn't think the worse of either of them because of Bill's intrusion.

Shawn's sister, the maid-of-honor, crowded close to Amber as the exterior door swung shut behind Bill. "Is your brother really going to walk you down the aisle? So cool."

Amber opened her mouth to speak as her gaze fastened on Claire's, but Eileen beat her to words. "If not, I am. You're my little girl, and I can do the honors as well as anyone."

"For tonight, we'll need you to stand in for sure." Claire smiled at Amber's mom. "Everything else depends on the fire, I suppose." She looked around the little group. "It's good that you were able to notify everyone of the change of venue."

"I did not tell Bill." Eileen glowered.

Claire shrugged. "But he found out, so it stands to reason word got out to the people you wanted to send the information to. At any rate, let's get this rehearsal started. Pastor Ron is in his study whenever we're ready."

Flowers banked the platform and Amber squealed in delight. "Oh, it's almost as beautiful as the pole barn at the farm. Where did these all come from?"

Claire let out a breath she'd forgotten she was holding. Mrs. Graysen had come through at Sierra's request. She'd promised to scrounge her flowerbeds and those of all her friends to create a magical garden for Amber. "After all," she'd said, "all this smoke can't be good for the blossoms, so they may as well be put to good use."

Roses, daisies, and masses of sweet peas framed the dais. The women of the church had done a wonderful job under Mrs. Graysen's direction.

Maybe one day it would be for Claire. Her mind slid to Noel, out there in danger while she played dress-up in town with his sister. It didn't seem right. Would he even get a break overnight or would he keep working right through? When would he sleep? Ah, she might not know when, but she did know where. His trailer was parked just a few blocks away outside Nature's Pantry.

She turned back to the group, who awaited her instructions. When this rehearsal was over, she'd slip over to the trailer and see Noel with her own eyes. Make sure he was all right.

o0o

Noel staggered up to his trailer in the dark. He couldn't remember ever having been this exhausted in his life. He'd fought fire before, but never with this personal investment.

He only hoped the wind wouldn't pick up overnight. He'd only allow himself four hours in bed—and if he hadn't been worried about being caught in the flames, he'd have slept on the deck right there at Green Acres after sending Zach back to town.

Something fluttered on the trailer's door, and Noel tried to focus enough to peel it off. He unlocked the door and managed to get inside before shrugging out of his smoke-soaked clothes. Yeah, that meant the stench followed him in, but what else could he do? He cranked the vents open to max and started the exhaust fan then tripped his way into the bathroom and turned on the shower.

He'd parked in such a hurry he'd forgotten to light the hot water tank. Cold water sluiced over him, turning black as the drain pulled it out of sight. He wrapped a towel around himself and went back into the main room to pour a glass of water. His gaze fell on the paper he'd removed from the door.

Dear Noel.

His skin shivered, and not just from the cold water.

I'm so thankful you came back for your sister's wedding. Zach told us how tirelessly you've been working to save Green Acres. I owe you a huge debt of gratitude for your efforts. Rest assured, though, I won't blame you if the farm burns. God has been showing me that some things are far more important than where I live. I'm praying for you. Claire.

If she was saying what he thought she was saying, he could work with that. But not tonight. Not while the farm lay in danger.

Chapter 31 --

Against her better judgment—but according to Eileen's wishes—Claire met the family for breakfast Saturday morning at The Sizzling Skillet. She was so tempted to skip. They didn't really need her for anything. But what if Noel showed up? She couldn't bear not to see him if he could spare the time. He hadn't acknowledged her note, which was perhaps not too shocking. Though would it have taken too long to send a text?

She'd peered out the window of Sierra's office above Nature's Pantry when she heard his truck arrive after midnight. It'd been gone when she woke up. Of course he had more important things to think about than her. The fire, for one. His sister's wedding, for another.

Claire straightened her lacy top over her capris and eyeballed the front door of The Skillet. She hadn't set foot in there for more than ten weeks. Alrighty then, she could do this. She strode across the parking lot and pulled open the heavy wooden door. A blast of country music nearly slammed her back outside.

"Claire! Good to see you!" The hostess beamed at her. "Are you here to see Nevin about the job posting?"

Claire stared at the girl. "Are you serious? He's still looking for a chef?"

The girl's smile faltered. "But of course. We had so many complaints about the quality of food going down since you left."

"I'm sorry to hear that." Claire tried to see past the hostess. "I'm here to join the Kenzie table. Are they here?"

"Kenzie?" The girl's eyes blanked for a moment. "Um, yes. The big booth in the back corner. Let me show you."

"I've got it, thanks." Claire edged past her and more than a dozen tables.

Locals greeted her, asking if she was working here again, inquiring about the fire. Claire kept her answers brief as she made her way to the back.

"There she is!" Eileen scooted over to make room.

Claire set her purse on the seat as she greeted Amber and the other women at the table.

Eileen leaned closer. "I was just holding my news until you got here."

The woman couldn't possibly be getting back with her deadbeat husband. Claire raised her eyebrows. "Oh? What's up?"

"I've decided to stay in Missoula, at least for now. I really like my job, you know? And my house may not be large, but it's paid for. Why move now?"

Whoa. Not what she'd expected to hear at all.

Claire glanced at Amber, who parked her elbows on the table around its curve. "You're serious, Mom? There are plenty of reasons to move to Flagstaff. Like me."

"Oh, sweetheart, it's not that I wouldn't love to be nearby. But I think you and Shawn need a bit of time to adjust before he has to deal with an interfering busybody of a mother-in-law, don't you think?"

Shawn's mother reached across and patted Eileen's hand.

"I'm sure the kids will be just fine without us."

Eileen dabbed her eyes with a cloth napkin. "You're probably right. Claire is so wise. Not only can she plan and cater the most gorgeous weddings, she's simply a person who sees through the fluff and focuses on what's important."

Claire stared at Noel's mom, aware her mouth hung open. Eileen actually heard her words. Who knew?

"May I take your orders?" A young waitress Claire didn't remember stood with pen poised over her notepad.

"I'd like a coffee," Claire said. Everyone else's hands already nursed a mug. "And brown toast and a poached egg."

"Oh, do have a real breakfast." Eileen leaned closer. "I'm picking up the tab, and who knows if we'll get a chance for any lunch? It's a long time until the reception."

"It's enough for me, thanks." If only her gut weren't gnawed into holes, worrying about Noel's safety. Funny how she barely thought of the house, the farm. It was all about the man.

The others ordered then Amber focused back on Eileen. "Are you serious, Mom? I was so happy you were coming, too."

"Oh, sweetie, that does my heart good. We'll see how things go in time but for now, my place is in Missoula. We'll talk often."

Amber's eyes narrowed. "Is it because of my father?"

"Don't be silly." Eileen took a sip of coffee. "We were done many years ago."

Hmm. Could Amber be right?

Eileen glanced around the table, apparently aware that she had to say more about the situation. "I don't see any reason to think we'd ever get back together. On the other hand, this is the first time in twenty-five years he's tried to make amends. My pastor in Missoula says Bill sounded quite contrite. Only God knows his heart."

"Good to see you, Claire." Nevin's heavy hand clamped over her shoulder. "When can you start back?"

Claire tried to pull away but the booth was too tight. She stared up at her former boss. "I'm not coming back to work here, Nevin. Thanks anyway."

"But where else can you make such a good wage doing what you love?" He winked at Shawn's mother. "And such tips, too! I know you love to cook. Where could you possibly find a better place to work than right here?"

"I'm catering weddings and special events now and having a great time with it. In fact, Nevin, please excuse us. I'm busy with a bridal party at the moment, so you're kind of interrupting." She added a smile at the end to soften the sting.

"But—"

The twangy country music fell abruptly silent. A siren sounded through the speakers then a radio announcer spoke.

"Voluntary Evacuation Alert. Residents of Galena Landing should be prepared to evacuate. The fire on Galena Mountain is growing and has leaped one of the barriers the fire crew dug over night. A firefighter has been injured. Several properties are in the direct path of the flames, and heavy smoke is pushing into Galena Landing. All residents are advised to gather needed supplies and prepare to head south in the event the evacuation orders ramp up. Volunteers are going from door to door advising residents."

Claire should worry about the farm, worry about her catering career, but what about Noel? Surely if he were the injured fighter, someone would have called Eileen by now. No one would call Claire. She didn't have the right to know.

oOo

Noel's radio crackled. "Fire jumped Dobson Road."

His dulled senses crashed. They'd banked so much on all the trenches and firebreaks the equipment had been digging up for the past 24 hours.

"Two miles north, almost at the Canadian border." Zach looked as exhausted as Noel felt. Dirt and soot streaked his face, and there was no telling what color the guy's shirt had once been. "River should stop it, though."

"River?" Noel stared at Zach dully.

"Yeah, Watermans are up that way, just over the bridge. There's a feedlot between the river and the mountain."

"So the feedlot is probably in trouble." Noel pushed himself to standing. He and Zach had stopped for a break, but time had run out.

"There's nothing you can do, Noel. There's a crew working there, too. Our job is here. Protecting this stretch of land."

Zach was right. The state and county crews had finally arrived and taken over, relegating Noel back to civilian status. The chief had agreed he and Zach could stay and help defend Green Acres as long as the fire didn't jump the guard. They'd proven themselves.

Noel sagged against the pole barn where his sister's wedding should have been taking place in a couple of hours. He sure hadn't expected the weekend to go like this. He'd begun to daydream a new start with Claire.

Both guys stared up the mountain and the jagged line where the Cat had bulldozed a firebreak beyond the cabin.

"It's a curious mix," Zach mused.

"Hmm?"

"Remember that Sunday a while back when Pastor Ron spoke about how temporary our life on this Earth is?"

Noel nodded. No way could he forget that sermon.

"Here we are, protecting a little patch of dirt to the best of our ability. What we're doing matters, sure. But not in the eternal scheme of things. You know?"

The wind picked up and immediately the roar from the fire grew. As a kid, this conundrum fascinated Noel. Blow on a fire and it should go out, like birthday cake candles. Forest fires didn't work that way. Even campfires didn't.

"Kyle got trapped up there. Young guy probably thrilled to be facing danger for the first time in his life. He's lucky they pulled him out. He'll be even luckier if he isn't scarred from the burn."

The kid's clothes had caught ablaze from a shower of embers off a crashing tree. "Yeah." Noel's eyes weren't seeing the fire any more. "The preacher was right that day. This stuff isn't that important."

Zach cocked a quizzical eyebrow at Noel.

"I always thought I'd get right with God when I was too old to have fun any more." Noel huffed a laugh. "You know, like forty."

Zach grinned.

"But there's nothing certain, is there." He wasn't really asking for an answer. "You never know when it might be too late."

"There's that." Zach leaned closer. "There's also a positive way to look at it."

"Oh?"

"God gave everything for us. Absolutely everything. We get a lot of joy in living for Him, too."

Noel chuckled, but not from disbelief. "Not just for ducking the nasty stuff?"

"Yeah, not only. It's worth living for Christ from an eternal viewpoint. But it's worth living for Him today, too. Right now."

A shout sounded above the inferno.

Noel jerked around to see what happened now.

A helicopter dumped a load of water above the log cabin.

Zach stared. "If the cabin burns, we'll build again. It doesn't matter, Noel. It really doesn't matter."

If only Noel could have the same faith. But he had more than yesterday.

o0o

Organ music flowed through the Galena Gospel Church and wafted into the library just off the foyer. Claire surveyed the women waiting in the room. Only minutes to go.

Amber, dressed in a floor-length gown with a layered hem, smiled back. If the bride's bouquet of pastel garden flowers hadn't been trembling, Claire might not have picked up on her nerves.

Rebekah, Shawn's sister and the maid of honor, wore a similar dress in bold pink. Every time a whisper came from outside, she glanced toward the door. Several times she opened her mouth to say something, then bit her lip and turned away.

Eileen narrowed her gaze at the clock. Her pastel pink short-sleeved suit rocked her slightly graying hair. "I'm sorry, sweetie. I don't think he's coming."

Chin up and eyes glistening, Amber nodded.

Claire didn't have to wonder who Eileen meant. At least she knew it wasn't because Noel didn't care for his sister. Or that he was trying to avoid Claire. But still, she'd really counted on him being here. For Amber's sake. Not hers.

If only he were safe, but she had no way to know. Zach would have told her, wouldn't he? He'd arrived minutes ago, freshly showered, and slid into the pew beside Jo.

A huge sigh huffed out of Rebekah. "Your brother is so hot. I wanted to see him again."

The girl could use a swat, but it wasn't Claire's place to provide it. Maybe she could get away with it as the wedding coordinator? No one would believe her motives. Better not chance it.

The clock ticked over to two-thirty. Claire slightly shifted the lace panel on the library's window to the sanctuary. The music changed as Pastor Ron led Shawn and his best man from the pastor's study, all three men in black tuxes. When they turned to face the well-wishers, the tails of Shawn's jacket swung a tad.

The organist glanced over.

Claire raised her hand then let the curtain fall. "Time to go." She led the way to the door.

One last chance. She glanced toward the big double doors leading to the parking lot. The foyer was empty.

At the back of the sanctuary, Rebekah stepped forward as the organ music switched once again. Shawn's sister minced down the aisle, bestowing wide grins to folks on both sides of the church.

Amber took Eileen's arm and stepped into position.

A door clanged behind her, and Claire whirled.

Noel! Long hair, soaking wet but combed, suit jacket slightly askew with his white shirt untucked, but here.

"Noel!" Amber stage-whispered and flung herself at her brother as the wedding march began. The shuffle, as the gathered friends stood, covered her voice.

"Oh, there you are, son." Eileen's face contorted between joy to see him and something else Claire couldn't name in that instant. "I'll just get an usher to take me to my seat." She turned to wave one of the young men over.

"No!" Claire hissed at her. "The march is already playing."

"But it's Noel's job now."

Amber straightened her brother's jacket as he tucked in his shirt.

Claire rushed over with the box from the florist. One last

boutonniere to pin on.

Behind her, the music mounted. No doubt the organist and everyone else wondered what the hold up was. They'd understand in a minute.

She grasped Noel's lapel to pin the flowers in place, and he caught her hand as she finished. "Claire."

For a second like an eternity he held her eyes. Then she licked her lips, and his gaze dropped to them. "Show's on," she whispered.

Noel nodded, and held his arm for Amber. "Shall we?"

Amber looked around. "Where's Mom?"

Oh, Eileen. Where'd she go? Claire whirled around.

Eileen stood in the last row, blinking back tears but smiling. Beyond her, Bill edged closer. This was so not going to work.

"Stop for her, please," she whispered to Noel.

He nodded and brushed his fingers against her cheek.

Claire all but wilted at his touch.

Amber stepped through the doorway on her brother's arm and a collective sigh rose from the audience. A few steps in, the siblings paused, and Noel held out his other arm to his mother.

Eileen shot a questioning glance back at Claire, who nodded enthusiastically. Eileen tucked her trembling hand into the crook of Noel's elbow and allowed him to guide them both down the aisle.

Claire shook her head. Eileen should've stepped to Amber's other side. But then how would Amber have held her bouquet? The family was halfway to the front by now. It didn't matter.

Noel's broad back filled out the charcoal jacket he wore, his dark hair hiding the collar. His black pants could have used a pressing but, under the circumstances, that was quite forgivable.

Claire released a breath.

He was here. In the flesh.

She hadn't seen him in over a month. How she'd cried in

her pillow, longing for his touch. Still, the same things that had driven them apart in June remained.

Today she'd feast her eyes upon him, because this time when he walked out of her life, it would be for good.

"Who gives this woman to be married to this man?"

Claire turned for the basement stairs. As much as she'd love to stare at Noel, she had to make sure everything was ready for the reception. She couldn't leave Tony to manage on his own.

o0o

The pastor's words stumped Noel for an instant. He should've come to the rehearsal. Then he'd have known how to answer the all-important question.

Mom squeezed his arm. "Her brother and I do."

Shawn stepped closer, his eyes filled with Amber. She beamed at him for an instant before turning to hug Mom, then Noel. "Thank you," she whispered.

"Go get 'em," he whispered back, steadying her. She turned to face the front of the church and Pastor Ron, who waited to carry out the ceremony.

Mom slipped into the front pew and looked at him expectantly. Yeah, he really should have been to rehearsal. That spot was usually for both parents, wasn't it? Not brothers. He strode down the center aisle to the back then turned to survey the gathering as they took their seats.

Where was Claire? At least he could sit beside her.

"Son!"

Whoa, what was Dad doing here? He was even halfway cleaned up. A quick glance around didn't reveal Claire's whereabouts. He'd have to catch her after. Noel slid into the pew next to his father.

"She's beautiful," Dad whispered.

"Yeah, she cleaned up pretty well, considering what a tomboy she was," Noel whispered back.

His dad frowned. "I meant your mother."

Oh. Okay. Too much information. Noel smiled at his dad, not having a clue what to say, and hunkered down in the seat, crossing ankles and arms in the process. He'd love to shed the jacket—even though the ceiling fans worked overtime—but no. He was determined to do this wedding by the books from here on in.

Pastor Ron started in on the joys of a Christian marriage. That caught Noel's attention.

Dad tugged at Noel's sleeve, but Noel shushed him. A Christian marriage? He could do this, given half a chance. If only he knew what it looked like. Amber and Shawn would soon be living too far away to observe. But he'd seen Zach and Jo. He pulled his thoughts back to the message.

"Your mother and I—we had a beautiful wedding, too. I ruined everything."

He certainly had. And now he needed to talk about it in the middle of his daughter's ceremony?

"I'm really sorry, Noel. Can you ever forgive me?"

Noel shot him a glance, hoping to quell the speech. Oh, man, his dad had tears streaming down his face.

"I know I owe you money. I'll find a way to repay you."

This was a new line. "We'll talk about it, Dad. Later. Okay?"

The grip on Noel's arm tightened for a second as his dad peered into his eyes. The man nodded, and Noel turned back to learn all about loving one's wife.

oOo

Just get through it. Just get through it. Claire managed to keep her fingers busy, but her mind would not release the look in Noel's eyes as his finger ran down her cheek. Even now she couldn't stop the tremor that ran through her entire body.

She didn't dare read too much into it. She was hired help. The families depended on her to create the perfect atmosphere for the reception, even in a venue they'd never once considered. A local greenhouse had come through, offering potted trees and garden latticework to decorate the area behind the tables. Sierra had taken charge after midnight, winding twinkle lights and lace throughout the plants, making the church basement look better than Claire would have dreamed possible.

Still, the sandwiches needed to be set on trays, ice added to the punch, and petit fours arranged on Eileen's crystal platters. Claire could find stuff to do in the kitchen for a long time yet. She could ignore the ceremony through the sound system, but at least it alerted her when Pastor Ron prayed over the luncheon and invited everyone downstairs.

Jo ran into the kitchen. "Everything under control in here?"

Claire glanced up. "Yes, we have it all covered. You go enjoy yourself."

Jo lingered. "Zach says the fire burned right up to the firebreak, but the farm is okay. Even the cabin's okay."

Claire crushed Jo to her. "Oh, I'm so glad. So thankful." But to have Noel? He would be worth giving up the farm for. She knew it now.

Just a bit longer. Every time the double doors to the kitchen swung open, she glanced up, but it wasn't Noel. He'd been messing with her mind again. That touch should have been illegal.

"Claire!" Tony called out. "There's no knife by the cake."

She stared blankly. She'd put one there. She knew she had. Eileen had brought the thing with a satin-wrapped handle. "Check with Eileen?"

"She hasn't seen it."

Amber's mother must be frantic something had gone wrong. Strange she hadn't come in here herself.

But there was no time to go hunting. Claire yanked open the knife drawer. "I guess one of these will have to do." Was there even one long enough and sharp enough to get through the hard frosting? Every church kitchen she'd been in had the dullest blades imaginable.

"Need a good knife?" Noel's voice swept right to her core. "I happen to have a solution for you right here."

He stood framed in the doorway, minus his suit jacket and tie. His white shirt was open by several buttons and partially untucked. On some guys it would look messy. On Noel, it was perfect. The way she remembered him. His hair, now dry, begged to be smoothed.

"It needs to be a long blade," she managed to say, gripping the edge of the countertop.

"I think I have one long enough." He grinned, and his dark eyes glimmered. "Come see if it will do."

"J-just show me here. I'm not going out there. There's too much to do. Or show Tony. He knows what's needed."

Noel glanced at the teen. "Good to see you again, Tony. I'm glad you're keeping up with Claire. Still planning on going to culinary school?"

Tony's gaze flicked to Claire then back at Noel. "Yes, sir. That's the plan."

Noel nodded and held out his hand. "Come, Claire. The knife is out here."

"Speech! Speech!" someone called from the reception hall.

A comical expression crossed Noel's face. He closed the few steps between them and pulled Claire into his arms.

She stared up at him. He met everything on her checklist. Every item but one, and he knew it.

His lips brushed hers and for an instant she clung to him.

"Come," he whispered. "I have to toast the bride." He grabbed Claire's hand and towed her out of the kitchen.

Claire's free hand swept her face. Was her hair in place? Did she have any crumbs on her outfit? It didn't matter. He wasn't letting go, and he wasn't slowing down.

Noel strode to the microphone set up between the cake table and the punch. He lifted a goblet with his left hand, his right still firmly gripped around Claire's.

"Thank you all for coming to share in Amber and Shawn's special day. I could give you some stories about Amber growing up..." He paused until a few people began to snicker. "But I don't want to embarrass her too much today. Get back to me next week."

Laughter, while someone—Sierra?—pressed punch into Claire's free hand.

"Seriously, though. Amber is an awesome young woman and I'm honored to be her brother. To the bride!"

He raised the goblet, and the guests echoed him. "To the bride!"

Claire tipped her glass along with the others, trying to tug free of Noel's grasp. What must people be thinking? Eileen eyed her speculatively, and Rebekah's eyebrows had pulled together. Amber winked.

Winked?

Noel didn't let go. "I have another toast to propose."

Uh oh. She pulled harder, but he had her hand in an iron grip.

"I'd like to honor my mother today. She was a single mom for most of my life."

Claire peered up to notice Bill staring at his son, his face wet. Tears? Could it be?

"She juggled two little kids to get her degree and start a successful career. She sacrificed so much for Amber and me. I think she's proud of the woman Amber has become." His voice lowered. "I just hope she isn't too embarrassed of me."

"Never!" Eileen called out.

"I'd like to present the mother of the bride, Eileen Kenzie. To Mom!"

"To Eileen!" people murmured, lifting their goblets.

Noel paused so long Claire was certain he was done, though he hadn't moved away from the microphone. "I just need a knife for the cake," she whispered fiercely.

He looked at her and grinned, that goofy dimple making her heart ache. She couldn't handle much more.

"Ready?" he whispered. "Don't worry. I ran this past Amber."

Ran what past Amber? He wouldn't... He hadn't... The look in his eyes was what she'd dreamed of seeing. Was this for real?

Noel set his goblet down and secured Claire with his arm tight around her waist. "One more thing!" he called out.

The soft murmur of the assembly ebbed again as folks turned back.

Claire held her breath.

"I've been ignoring God for most of my life. It didn't seem like it was any fun to be a Christian. I figured when I got old I'd take God up on salvation. But I've learned a couple of things."

Claire didn't know where to look, but it didn't seem right to stare at her shoes. Off to the side, Jo waved and Claire met her gaze. Zach stood behind his wife with both arms wrapped around her, holding her tight. He grinned and winked. Amber, beaming and nestled in Shawn's arms, gave Claire a thumbs-up.

A flush stole up Claire's cheeks.

"I prided myself on not being afraid of anything. I've jumped out of planes with nothing but a parachute. I've jumped off bridges, sometimes with a bungee cord. I've climbed cliffs without so much as a harness. But underneath it all, there was one thing I was afraid of."

She could sense him looking down at her, but there was no way she could meet his eyes. Not like this. Not here in front of everyone.

"I was afraid of commitment."

The room was dead silent. Did that mean everyone could hear Claire's heart pounding?

"I'd never found anything worth committing to. In the past few months, I've found two reasons to change my mind. God has loved me with unfailing love, as a father has for his child."

Claire wouldn't look at Bill. Not now.

Noel's arm around her tightened almost imperceptively. "And I've found a woman who will make every minute of my life worth being committed to." In an instant he was on one knee in front of Claire, a long box in his hands.

Where had it come from? All that talk, but this wasn't an engagement ring. She'd never seen one in a box this big. Claire wrapped both arms around her middle, suddenly chilled without Noel's touch.

Sierra rescued Claire's goblet before she dropped it.

Noel set the box down and tugged her hands free.

"Claire, will you marry me? My life isn't complete without you. I love you, and I need you."

The vision of her list swirled through her mind. Mentally she took a felt pen—one with permanent ink and a broad black tip—and made a big check mark beside the top entry.

"Yes." She met his gaze through vision swimming with tears. Tears of joy.

He picked up the box and laughed. "The romantic thing would be a diamond ring." He grinned at her, eyes twinkling. "I'll get there, I promise. But here, for now—this is for you." He tilted the lid of the box.

The fragrance of mint wafted out.

Five gleaming knives lay nestled on a bed of her favorite herb. The workmanship of the blades and their hand-carved wooden handles took her breath away. "Oh, they're gorgeous." He'd planned this, even without the ring. And where had he found the mint?

He swept her into his arms and twirled her around. "Mint will always make me think of you. The patch below the spring survived the fire just fine."

Her arms wound around his neck—someone rescued the box—and pulled his lips to hers. Oh, yes. Sweeter than mint. By far.

"To Claire and Noel!" Amber shouted.

Glasses clinked.

Oh, yes.

The End

Recipes for Wild Mint Tea

Spearmint leaves make the best tea. Peppermint or other mint varieties may be used if spearmint is unavailable.

For Iced Mint Tea:

2 quarts water
6 cups packed fresh mint leaves

Place in a large saucepan and bring to a boil. Turn off the heat and allow to cool. Put 3/4 cup (or to taste) of honey or sugar into a one-gallon jar and pour the strained mint tea over it. Stir to dissolve. Fill with water.

Serve over ice.

For Hot Mint Tea:

Bring 1 quart water (or more) to a boil in your kettle. Use a bit of the hot water to rinse out your teapot. Fill teapot with boiling water. In a spice caddy or cheesecloth, place a handful of fresh mint leaves or 2 tablespoons of dry leaves and drop into teapot. Steep to desired flavor and remove the leaves. Sweeten each teacup to taste with local honey. Add cream if desired.

Alternatively, you can use a French press to make loose-leaf tea, or put the leaves into your teapot unbound and strain as you serve it.

Noel's Recipe for Taco Stew

© 2013 by Linda Sprinkle

This bold stew is very versatile. If you prefer, you can cook it in a 300° F oven for an extra hour on so. If you want taco subs, cook it about a half hour longer, until the beef can be shredded easily. Let it cool a bit before shredding. You can use regular rolls or do a burrito wrap with flour tortillas. A pork shoulder roast would also be excellent in this stew.

Ingredients:

2 pounds chuck roast
Peanut oil
¼ cup chopped cilantro
Salt and pepper
2 tablespoons lime juice
1 tablespoon olive oil
1 large onion, chopped
2 poblano peppers, chopped
5 cloves garlic, minced
1 teaspoon ground cumin
1 teaspoon ground coriander
1-2 canned chipotles, minced
1 teaspoon adobo sauce
2 tablespoons tomato paste
4 cups beef stock
2 cups cooked black beans
1 tbsp chopped fresh oregano
Juice of ½ lime

Garnishes:

4-6 corn tortillas
Shredded cheddar, jack, or
    pepper jack
Chopped cilantro
Diced jalapeño peppers
Diced fresh tomato
Lime wedges
Mexican crema or sour cream
1-2 diced avocados

Mise en Place:

1. Chop, mince, or shred all the veggies and herbs, as noted in the ingredient list. Measure out the remaining ingredients, except the avocados.
2. Remove the silver skin from the chuck roast. Cut beef into 1-1/2" cubes, discarding the large chunks of fat.
3. Puree ½ cup of the beans with 1 cup of the beef stock.
4. Cut the corn tortillas into strips or wedges. Fry in the peanut oil until crisp. Drain on paper towels.

Preparation:

1. Season the beef cubes with salt and pepper. Heat the olive oil in a Dutch oven until it shimmers. Add half the beef cubes and brown them on all sides. Put on a platter. Repeat with the rest of the beef, adding another tablespoon of oil if your pan is dry.
2. Reduce the heat to medium. Add the onion and poblano peppers. Sauté until the onion is translucent and starting to soften. Add the garlic, cumin and coriander and sauté for a minute to release the oils.
3. Add the chipotles and tomato paste. Cook until the tomato paste turns a dark brick red.
4. Add a half-cup of the beef stock. Bring to a boil and scrape up the browned bits from the bottom of the pan. Add the rest of the beef stock, the browned chuck, the pureed beans and the cooked beans. Bring to a boil, reduce the heat, partly cover the pan and simmer 1-1/2-2 hours, stirring occasionally, until the beef is easily pierced with a fork, but not falling apart.
5. Add the oregano, cilantro, and lime juice. Add salt and pepper to your taste.

6. Dice the avocado at the list minute, tossing it with lime juice to retard oxidation.
7. Serve in bowls with the desired garnishes.

Substitutions:

1. 1 teaspoon dried oregano can be used if fresh is not available.
2. Cilantro can be omitted, if you're one of those to whom it tastes soapy.
3. I prefer dried, freshly cooked beans, but 1 can, drained and rinsed well may be used.
4. If you can't find poblanos or pasillas, omit the chipotle and use up to a tablespoon of chili powder and 1/8 teaspoon of cayenne pepper.

Dear Reader

Do you share my passion for locally grown real food? No, I'm not as fanatical as Jo or as fixated as Claire, but farming, gardening, and food processing comprise a large part of my non-writing life.

Whether you're new to the concept or a long-time advocate, I invite you to my website and blog at www.valeriecomer.com to explore God's thoughts on the junction of food and faith.

Please sign up for my monthly newsletter while you're there! It's the best way to keep tabs on my food/farm life as well as contests, cover reveals, deals, and information about upcoming books. I welcome you.

Enjoy this Book?

Please leave a review at any online retailer or reader site. Letting other readers know what you think about *Wild Mint Tea: A Farm Fresh Romance* helps them make a decision and means a lot to me. Thank you!

If you haven't read *Raspberries and Vinegar*, the first book in the series, with the story of Jo and Zach's romance, I hope you will.

Keep reading for the first chapter of Sierra's story, the third book (of six), *Sweetened with Honey: A Farm Fresh Romance*. Following that is the first chapter of *More Than a Tiara*, my novella in a Christmas duo entitled *Snowflake Tiara*. Both will be available from most online retailers in ebook and print in the fall of 2014.

Sweetened with Honey

A Farm Fresh Romance

Book 3

Valerie Comer

GreenWords Media

Chapter 1 --

"Are you sure you want to do this?" Sierra Riehl set the jar containing two honeybees onto the table in her office.

"I think so." Her friend eyed the bees crawling up the side of the glass. "I've read a lot of reports that say a sting really helps. My rheumatoid arthritis seems worse every day."

Sierra had to agree. Doreen Klimpton had been vibrant and active not that long ago. Now she'd lost weight and seemed shrunken in on herself, moving more slowly and grimacing often in pain.

"Where are you going to apply it?" Doreen kept her eyes on the jar as she settled in the reclining chair in Sierra's naturopathy office. "Are you going to sting me twice?"

"Maybe." Sierra slipped a lab coat over her orchid-toned dress. "I plan to start with one as a test. If things go well, we can do a second one. Or not, as you wish."

Doreen nodded. "I can't believe I'm doing this. Getting stung on purpose."

Sierra couldn't, either. She'd done a lot of strange things studying natural medicine, but this seemed right up there with applying leeches to let blood. Straight out of medieval times. Yet, since she'd taken up apiculture, she kept hearing old beekeepers say they never had arthritis. The venom from the many stings they inevitably incurred in the line of duty kept their joints at ease.

Unprovable at the moment, but she'd be glad of the side benefit. She'd never expected her landlady to test the theory.

Doreen closed her eyes. "Do it already. The anticipation is worse than the sting will be."

"You're sure you don't have allergies?" Sierra had asked before, but man, all she needed was to see Doreen go into anaphylactic shock.

"I was tested. It should be fine."

Sierra took a deep breath. Should she swab Doreen's hand as though she were giving a needle of some other kind? Probably. She reached for a cotton pad and a bottle of alcohol and wiped the area at the base of Doreen's thumb.

Needles normally went into tissue-laden areas like biceps, not bony parts. But it wasn't a needle. A bee's stinger wasn't nearly as long.

Just do it.

She unscrewed the lid, grabbed a bee with a pair of tweezers, and put the lid back on. Did she have the bee in a decent grip? It looked like it. "Last chance to refuse treatment."

Doreen turned her face away. "I'm ready."

Sierra held the bee's rear against Doreen's hand. A sharp intake of breath revealed the insect had reacted as predicted, releasing its venom.

A man's voice came from the doorway. "What is going on in here?"

Sierra whirled, dropping the tweezers and the bee.

"Oh, Gabe!" Doreen struggled out of the deep chair. "It's so good to see you. I wasn't sure you were ever coming home."

She flung herself in Gabe's arms.

Wow, that Romanian orphanage had treated Gabriel Rubachuk right. He looked leaner—better—than Sierra remembered.

Gabe's piercing blue eyes met hers over Doreen's head. "You didn't answer my question."

Sierra thrust her chin up. "Applying bee-venom therapy for her rheumatoid arthritis." Speaking of bees, what had happened to the one she'd used? Not that it mattered much, since bees could only dispense venom once before dying.

His laugh echoed harshly in the small room. "Are you some kind of quack?" He looked down at the older woman in his arms. "Didn't the doctor prescribe medicine for you, Doreen? Isn't it working anymore?"

"I don't like how it makes me feel." Doreen sniffled against his chest, clutching him close. "And it doesn't work as well as it did at first. Don't be angry with Sierra. I asked her to do this. I researched it online."

Gabe shook his head. "You can't believe everything you find on the Internet. Anyone can make stuff up and act like an expert." He eyed Sierra. "I thought better of you. Anything for a buck?"

That stung. No pun intended. "I'll have you know there's plenty of evidence to support the articles Doreen found. Even when I was in school, venom was noted as relief for several types of arthritis and multiple sclerosis. Besides, people get stung all the time. It's less invasive than the pinprick of a needle."

What Sierra didn't know was how the toxin affected Doreen. She touched the older woman's shoulder. "Can I ask you to sit back down, please? I'd like to have a look at the site."

Doreen released Gabe, who patted her back awkwardly, then resumed her seat. She held out her hand.

Sierra scrutinized the area. A fiery mound the size of a nickel surrounded the white prick mark. That didn't look good. "I'm afraid you'll need to stay with me a while longer, until the swelling stops spreading."

"If she's allergic to the sting, get her to a real doctor." Gabe loomed closer. "They can give her an antihistamine shot. What's it called, an Epi pen?"

The scent of his aftershave filled the air. Who knew those commercials for Old Spice would make it hip again for guys under fifty?

Sierra's nose twitched as she put a bit of space between them. Better hope she didn't sneeze. She parked her hands on her hips. "Would you get out of my office and let me do my job? I'm perfectly capable of monitoring Doreen and dispensing a countermeasure if needed. For now, it bears watching, but impeding the venom will also nullify the good it's doing against arthritis."

"I'm not going anywhere until Doreen comes with me." Gabe leaned against the wall, muscular arms crossed over his striped button-up. "Then it looks like I'm taking her to urgent care."

Lifting orphans must've provided a great workout. Sierra pulled her gaze back to his face. "Now who's overreacting? I've been keeping bees for two seasons. A lot of people have a quick reaction that subsides just as fast." Though most of Doreen's hand now looked puffy.

If only Gabe weren't in the room, blocking Sierra's ability to think. Of all the ways she'd dreamt they'd meet again, this wasn't one of them. He'd come into Nature's Pantry and commend her for the way she'd helped Doreen pull the business into the black while he'd been off in Europe. Or he'd stroll in at Green Acres Farm to see his buddy, who was married to Sierra's best friend.

In either case, his eyes would light up at the sight of her.

Yeah, she'd been dreaming. He'd never see her that way. He'd never see anything but the woman whose father's semi-truck had rolled right over his wife's car, killing her and their unborn child instantly. Such a shame Bethany had swerved from the deer that jumped in front of her car and hit the semi instead. She'd probably have survived the deer.

Sierra had hoped three years away would be long enough for Gabe to heal up and move on. Just her luck he'd now see her as a quack…or worse, a con.

o0o

Dread of returning to Galena Landing, Idaho, had dogged Gabriel Rubachuk for three years.

Staring down Sierra Riehl while she fussed over Doreen came as a welcome distraction. Something to focus on besides the apartment that had once been his home.

"It's so good to see you, Gabe." His former mother-in-law's sad eyes found his. "When did you land in Spokane? I thought you'd let me know when you were coming home."

How could he explain? Bethany had been close to her mom, but what linked him to her now? Just the health-food store. He and Bethany had bought it from her as newlyweds, but she'd taken over running it when he bolted for Romania after Bethany's death.

"I wasn't sure." It sounded lame. He'd had a pretty good idea when he bought the tickets, after all.

"Looks like the swelling has stopped spreading," Sierra said. "How are you feeling, Doreen?"

Doreen looked down at her hand.

Looked inflamed to Gabe. A twinge of regret crossed his mind. He'd known her RA had flared, but it hadn't brought him back to the US. He'd just ditched her with all his other responsibilities.

"It's kind of hot and itchy," she ventured.

Sierra nodded. "That's to be expected. I know we'd talked about doing both hands today, but I'd rather wait and see how this one fares."

Sting her again? No way. Gabe pushed off from the wall, mouth open in protest.

Sierra pinned him with a glare as she tucked a strand of long blond hair behind her ear. A curl sprang loose immediately. "This is none of your business, Gabe. You are interfering with my ability to provide quality care to a patient who came to me voluntarily."

"But Doreen—" What? Wasn't capable of making decisions about her own health care? Ouch.

"Furthermore, you're trespassing."

Gabe shook his head. He knew the answer to this one. "You are. This is my building. My store downstairs. My apar—" He choked on the word. "My apartment up here." He forced his gaze to rove the area. This would have been the baby's room. He tugged at his shirt collar. Breath nearly failed him.

"You left Doreen in charge, and she leased this space to me." Sierra's gaze softened. "I'm happy to let you have it back, Gabe. We just didn't know when you were coming. Last we heard, you were thinking of staying overseas until the New Year."

He'd returned to sell the business. What he'd do then, he didn't know. Sticking around in the small town that held all his memories of a happy marriage seemed a bad idea. Maybe he'd go back to school. Get a degree in something useful. Who knew what?

"It's okay. I-I'm not sure I can handle living up here anyway." He took a deep breath and let it out slowly. "It looks nice. Thanks for helping Doreen."

"Gabe's right," Doreen said. "He doesn't need to stay here for now. He can live with me."

His head was shaking before she'd even finished. "No, that's okay. No need to put you out." The only thing worse than this apartment was Bethany's former bedroom in her mom's house and the kitchen where he'd taught her to bake chocolate chip cookies when they were thirteen.

"But—"

"Steve and Rosemary are expecting me. I'll bunk out at the farm with them for a few days until I figure out what I'm doing." Besides running again. "No need to put anyone out."

Doreen pushed out of the chair. "You're staying with Nemeseks? They knew you were coming, and I didn't?"

He liked Doreen fine. Respected her. Hated to see her in pain. How could he gently remind her she didn't have a claim on him anymore? "We've stayed in touch since they came home from Romania. Being out at the farm will do me good."

Their son, Zach, had been the other integral part of his growing up years. He and Zach and Beth hung out lots as a threesome, but Gabe had plenty of memories of his buddy that weren't dependent on Bethany. Yes, staying with Zach's parents was the best idea.

"I needed to see the store before I drove out there. Looks good. Well stocked." He backed toward the door. "Thanks, Doreen."

Tears glistened in her eyes.

He'd bet they had nothing to do with her arthritis or the bee sting.

"That was Sierra." Doreen's voice trembled. "I haven't been up to much lately."

Gabe managed to get the words out. "Thanks, Sierra." Just his luck he was beholden to her, of all people. Yeah, he knew he'd left Doreen in a bind with the business. He'd lost a wife, but she'd lost her only daughter. Why had it seemed okay for him to run, forcing her to take on his responsibilities on top of her own grief? He'd been blind.

Still was. It helped.

"You're welcome." Sierra's jaw tightened, and she looked ready to say more. She shook her head and turned away.

He couldn't stand it. "What?"

"Nothing."

With women it was never "nothing." He hadn't been married for five years without learning a thing or two. But did he really want to push it? No. Not with her.

He stared hard into her blue eyes. She needed to keep her distance. Not be so sweet to Doreen when he wasn't. Not to take care of the business he'd abandoned. Not to be happy and carefree in this place filled with his painful memories.

She took a step backward, her eyes widening as her lips pulled into a straight line.

Good, maybe she was getting the message.

"I don't feel so well."

Gabe took a step closer as Doreen's head lolled against the back of the deep chair, but Sierra got there first. "Doreen? Are you okay?"

"She's passed out. That's it. I'm taking her to urgent care."

Sierra glared up at him. "There's no need. Give her a moment."

"Get out of my way." Gabe gathered Doreen into his arms. She hardly weighed a thing. "You've done enough."

Snowflake Tiara

Angela Breidenbach Valerie Comer

1889

2014

Snowflake Tiara

September 2014

A Christmas Romance Novella Duo
Angela Breidenbach
Valerie Comer

What if someone sees you doing good?

The Debutante Queen by Angela Breidenbach

Helena, MT, 1889: Calista Blythe enters the first Miss Snowflake Pageant celebrating Montana statehood to expose the plight of street urchins. But if her hidden indentured orphan is discovered, Calista's reputation and her budding romance with pageant organizer, Albert Shanahan, could both unravel. Will love or law prevail?

More Than a Tiara by Valerie Comer

Helena, MT, 2014: Marisa Hiller's interest in competing in Miss Snowflake Pageant for the city of Helena's 150th anniversary is at zip zero zilch when she discovers the official photographer is Jase Mackie. Can Jase make amends for past mistakes and offer her, not only a tiara, but a partner in her crusade to help needy children and families?

Chapter 1 --

Just ahead of her, a group of at least a dozen people drifted into The Parrot Confectionery, talking and laughing. Marisa Hiller growled in frustration. First a large delivery truck blocked the alley so she couldn't drop her box of fresh rosemary at the back door, and now the front of the candy shop was clogged with customers. So much for agreeing to Brian's late-afternoon request for the herb.

She shifted the large box to her other hip and peered in the wide glass windows. Yup. It would be a few minutes before she could edge her way through to the back of the business.

Her gaze caught on the wooden notice board sheltered beside the door with dozens of posters in various degrees of tatter. Homemade ads with photos offered puppies, while tear off strips provided the kennel's phone number. Pampered Chef parties, the Helena Symphony, a new daycare in town. A person could live their whole life off a board like this.

A larger poster in the top corner begged attention. Miss Snowflake Pageant? She narrowed her gaze and stepped closer to see the details. Back in the day, she'd have been the first in line to sign up for this kind of competition. Now? Not so much. Not after. . .

"Marisa? Marisa Hiller?"

For an instant she thought her imagination was simply too vivid if she could hear that voice so clearly, right when her memory of him had surfaced. She'd slipped back in time, maybe. But no. The voice had been real. She pivoted.

Jase Mackie.

Her gut lurched. What was he doing in Montana? She hadn't seen him since JFK airport. Since. . .

For a second he looked like the old Jase. The shock of red hair she'd once run her hands through. The blue-green eyes that once looked adoringly into her own. She'd kissed those freckles on his nose.

But then his eyebrows pulled together and his gaze grew wary. "It is you. I thought I must be imagining things."

"Real and in the flesh." Marisa did her best to tamp any feelings out of her voice. It'd been twenty-seven months and nine days since they'd flung hostile words at each other beside the luggage carousel. She'd grabbed her bags and run for a taxi, blocking out not only Jase's words but Terry's. Yeah, that had gotten her fired. She was supposed to keep personal matters out of her work.

She yanked her gaze free of Jase's and glanced through the confectionery door beside her. Maybe she could squeeze past the late-season tourists peering into the candy case if she lifted the box above her head. "Been nice seeing you." *Liar.*

"You look good."

In jeans with a ripped knee? A tank top with tomato stains? Not precisely the runway model apparel he'd last seen on her. Marisa's gaze locked back on his.

He looked surprised to have let the words out then his chin jerked toward the notice behind her. "Going to enter that pageant? It looks right up your alley."

"I just noticed the poster, so I don't exactly have any plans. Never heard of it before." Not in this century, anyway.

"Oh." His gaze slid away, then back.

She'd missed him. Missed everything she'd dreamed might happen in those heady days.

Before he'd ruined everything.

Marisa took a deep breath. He'd never come after her. Never apologized. Her conscience pricked. Not that she'd left a forwarding address with Terry. No, she'd left everything behind in one go. She'd returned to the apartment she'd shared with two Broadway actresses, packed up her stuff, rented a truck, and driven across the country. Mom needed her, she'd told herself. It'd been true. Still was. The farm wasn't huge, but it was theirs, and needed them both to make it work.

She shoved her hands into her jeans pockets. Cropped, unpolished fingernails wasn't how Jase remembered her.

"Marisa, I—"

She shook her head and backed up a step. "I've got to go."

He reached past her and tapped the poster.

Every fiber of her being stretched toward the heat from his arm. She shifted away. Wished she could shift nearer instead.

"You should consider entering. I can totally see you doing something like that."

She blew out a breath. The nerve. "You lost any chance to give me advice."

"It's not advice." A shadow crossed his face, and his lips tightened. "I'm a friend drawing attention to something you may not have noticed."

"You lost the right to call me your friend, too. What are you doing here, anyway? Go back to New York. Just get out of my life and stay there."

"This is home."

"Since when?" East coast city boy, born and bred. Helena, Montana, might not be the Wild West anymore, but it wasn't big enough to hold the likes of Jase Mackie.

"My folks bought a resort west of town last year, planning to semi-retire, and I moved my studio here a few months ago." He pointed up the walking mall that'd been created along historic Last Chance Gulch.

She could make a snide comment about following mommy and daddy, but who was she to call the kettle black? She slept in her old bed, with Mom's room down the hall.

"How about you?"

Marisa lifted a shoulder. "This is where I grew up. On a farm."

His face brightened. "I'd love to do a piece on a local farm. Could I—?"

Their eyes collided for an instant, then the light went out of his and his shoulders slumped. "Never mind."

"I'd rather not." It would never do to be seen as eager. She wasn't. Not really. She'd been doing her best to forget him. Seeing him again created a pothole in her road, but she'd get back up to speed in a minute. But—what if he still cared? What if he was so awkward here, right now, for the same reasons she was? Attracted but burned. Oh man. Had she just admitted her infatuation, even to herself? Was there any hope?

She took a step back. "If you want to do a farmer story, get in touch with the Tomah CSA. There are more than a dozen member farms. Maybe someone will be happy to work with you."

"CSA?"

"Community supported agriculture. People in the Helena area can pay a monthly subscription fee and get a box of produce delivered every week."

"Oh. I've heard of that sort of thing."

Well good for him. It was her life. Her chosen life, she reminded herself. A worthy calling providing real food to people. She'd been trying to do that in Kenya, too.

Stay clear of Jase Mackie. He's a dream smasher.

She pivoted and yanked the door to The Parrot open. She'd edge her way to the back one way or another.

"Marisa!"

She'd walked away in JFK, and she could do it again.

~*~

Jase pulled into the parking lot at Grizzly Gulch Inn. He rested his forehead against the Jetta's steering wheel. Man, he'd bungled that. For over two years he dreamed of what he'd say, how he'd apologize — if he ever found her again. How she'd throw herself in his arms and forgive him for being an idiot.

Um, right. Hadn't happened. But still, he'd seen her. She looked as good as always, even with minimal makeup and her long brown hair pulled back into a lopsided ponytail. The casual look of someone who worked for a living and got her hands dirty, like that day in Kenya.

He'd tried to convince himself he was over Marisa. After all, he'd been seeing Avalon for several months. Did she even have a down-to-earth side?

She definitely couldn't hold a candle to Marisa.

He groaned and thumped his head on the wheel a couple more times for good measure. Maybe he'd knock some sense into himself.

A tap sounded on the car window. "Jase?"

He glanced up at his sister's concerned face. With a sigh he pulled the handle and opened the car door.

Kristen stepped out of the way as he exited. "You okay, little brother? You look like you just had a nightmare."

"I'm fine."

"You don't look it."

"Thanks. I think." He glanced around the parking lot and

spotted her rental car. "I didn't know you were coming up this weekend. Did you bring the kids?"

"Yes, they're around back in the playground with Dad. Todd had to work, and you know how much the kids love it here. So much more room to go wild than the apartment."

Jase fell into step beside her as they headed toward the side door that led to their parents' penthouse suite. "Why did you come?"

She turned laughing eyes and pouting lips his way. "At least pretend you're happy to see me." Her elbow caught his side.

"Why wouldn't I be? You're my favorite sister."

"The only one." Kristen sighed dramatically. "Good thing I gave you a niece and nephew, or you wouldn't even notice my existence."

"Not so." He grinned down at her. "But it does help."

"You need to get married and have a family, Jase. Seriously. The kids adore you. And besides, they need cousins. You wait too much longer and Charlotte will be old enough to babysit instead of play with them."

Images of Marisa flooded his mind. She wore a strappy gown and crazy tall heels, shorts and beachwear as she had in Kenya, jeans—

"Earth to Jase?" Kristen's voice mocked his thoughts. "Your brain headed over to—what's her name—Avalon, isn't it? When do I get to meet her and see if she's worthy of my little brother?"

He gave his head a quick shake. "Oh, she won't be." In his mind, Avalon frowned, her lips pulling into a pout as though tempting him to kiss her displeasure away. But it was true. Kristen would see through Avalon in a heartbeat. Why hadn't he? Why had it taken a chance encounter with—?

"Right." Kristen studied him as he reached past her to

open the door to their parents' penthouse suite. "Well, I can solve your problem."

"My problem?" A wave of irritation sloshed over him. "It's none of your business. Sweet sister."

Kristen went on as if he hadn't interrupted. "The pageant is drawing in all these beautiful, poised women. You might meet somebody new."

Or someone from his past.

"Hi, you two." Mom floated over. "Dinner's ready, so you're just in time. Grandpa will be up in a minute with Charlotte and Liam."

"Sounds good." Kristen dropped her briefcase on the marble kitchen island. "Guess what I found out." She opened the latches and pulled out her laptop.

Jase leaned his elbows on the counter and faked a bright, interested smile. "The sun sets in the west?"

"Oh, you." She swatted at him, and he shied away with years of practice. "No, really. Mom and I were talking last weekend about how registrations for the pageant have been kind of slow."

He'd been in Wyoming, shooting a fall wedding on a leaf-studded ranch. "There's still lots of time."

"Yes and no. The businessmen are loath to sink their money into it if we don't get a big name or two on the list. Somebody who will pull in some attention for the pageant among all the other events going on for Helena's 150th birthday. We may not need a full docket for another month, but we do need the right woman or two to make sure people take the event seriously."

Jase angled his head and nodded. "Makes sense."

"And I found someone. I mean, not that I've asked her yet, but it's why I'm here this weekend." Kristen's green eyes glowed with excitement.

The door flung open and a four-year-old locomotive slammed into Jase's leg. "Uncle Jase! Uncle Jase! I comed to see you!"

Jase squatted and pulled his nephew into a hug. "Hey, Liam. Good to see you, buddy." He reached out his other hand, and Charlotte placed hers in it with a little curtsy. "Princess Charlotte." He pressed a kiss on her palm. He knew how mere subjects presented themselves to royalty.

"Sir Uncle Jase, I am pleased to see you." Then the princess dissolved into little-girl giggles and snuggled against him.

"See? Jase needs kids of his own."

He looked up at his sister, whose hands waved as she talked to their parents. Sure, he wanted a family, but at the right time. With the right woman. He blocked Marisa's image and plunked on the floor to tickle the stuffing out of these two.

"It wasn't as difficult as I thought," Kristen went on. "There weren't many descendants along the way, but you'll never guess what I found."

All tickling aside for the moment, Jase leaned against the base of the leather love seat. "What are you talking about, Kris? I'm completely lost."

"Oh. Mom and I talked about how cool it would be if we could find a descendant of Calista, the first pageant winner in 1889, the year Montana became a state. If there happened to be a woman of suitable age, etcetera, and she could be persuaded to run, we'd easily get all the backers we need for the whole pageant."

"Sounds like a long shot."

Liam tackled him again, stubby fingers inflicting more pain than pleasure.

"It seemed like it." Kristen nodded. "But it turned out to

be a fabulous idea. There is one person who has the perfect credentials, more than we'd dreamed of."

"Tell us already." Mom apparently felt like Jase did. Kristen always dragged everything out for the most dramatic effect.

"Okay. So you know Calista married Albert, who'd been the owner of the original Tomah House. The family sold it in the 30s and bought a small farm on the other side of Helena. And they still live on that farm."

"It would help if Miss Snowflake is a local girl." Mom sounded excited, especially for someone who wasn't so local herself.

"Right. But it's even better than that."

The laptop creaked open, but Jase couldn't see the screen from his spot on the floor.

"She's actually modeled in New York. She's drop-dead gorgeous. See? She's done a bunch of work for Juicy Couture. Tory Burch. Michael Kors." Kristen glanced over at Jase. "You might even know her. You've shot sessions for some of those designers, haven't you?"

Jase's jaw clenched and the room tilted a little. Good thing he was already on the floor. He held Liam off at arm's length. "What's her name?" But he knew.

Author Biography

Valerie Comer lives where food meets faith in her real life, her fiction, and on her blog and website. She and her husband of over 30 years farm, garden, and keep bees on a small farm in Western Canada, where they grow and preserve much of their own food. Valerie has always been interested in real food from scratch, but her conviction has increased dramatically since God blessed her with three delightful granddaughters. In this world of rampant disease and pollution, she is compelled to do what she can to make these little girls' lives the best she can. She helps supply healthy food—local food, organic food, seasonal food—to grow strong bodies and minds.

Her experience has planted seeds for many stories rooted in the local-food movement. *Raspberries and Vinegar* and *Wild Mint Tea* will be followed by more books in the Farm Fresh Romance series including *Sweetened with Honey* (November 2014) and three additional tales set on Green Acres Farm in 2015-2016.

To find out more, visit her website at www.valeriecomer.com, where you can read her blog, explore her many links, and sign up for her email newsletter. You can also use this QR code to access the newsletter sign-up.

Made in the USA
Las Vegas, NV
16 January 2021

16007956R00198